SECRETS SHE KEPT

MARTINA MONROE BOOK 5

H.K. CHRISTIE

KEEKSTAR MEDIA

Copyright © 2022 by H.K. Christie

Cover design by Odile Stamanne

If you would like to use material from this book, prior written permission must be obtained by contacting the publisher at:

www.authorhkchristie.com

First edition: June 2022

ISBN: 978-1-953268-11-2

ALSO BY H.K. CHRISTIE

The Martina Monroe Series is a nail-biting crime thriller series starring PI Martina Monroe and her unofficial partner Detective August Hirsch of the Cold Case Squad. If you like high-stakes games, jaw-dropping twists, and suspense that will keep you on the edge of your seat, then you'll love the Martina Monroe crime thriller series.

The Neighbor Two Doors Down is a a dark and witty psychological thriller. If you like unpredictable twists, page-turning suspense, and unreliable narrators, then you'll love *The Neighbor Two Doors Down.*

The Selena Bailey Series (1 - 5) is a suspenseful series featuring a young Selena Bailey and her turbulent path to becoming a top notch kick-ass private investigator as led by her mentor, Martina Monroe.

A Permanent Mark A heartless killer. Weeks without answers. Can she move on when a murderer walks free? If you like riveting suspense and gripping mysteries then you'll love *A Permanent Mark -* starring a grown up Selena Bailey.

For a full catalog, or to purchase signed paperbacks and audiobooks direct from H.K. Christie go to: **www.authorhkchristie.com**

At **www.authorhkchristie.com** you can also sign up for the H.K. Christie reader club where you'll be the first to hear about upcoming novels, new releases, giveaways, promotions, and a **free e-copy of the prequel to the Martina Monroe Thriller Series, *Crashing Down*!**

1
TINSLEY

WITH MY REMAINING STRENGTH, I CRAWLED MY FINGERS over to Emmy's hand. Upon contact, a shiver ran through my body. Her soft hand was ice cold. No doubt, that was my fate as well. I could no longer move, which I didn't mind. It would all be over soon enough, that much I knew. At least I wasn't alone. I had Emmy. *Oh, Emmy.* This was my fault. She didn't deserve what they'd done to her. My thoughts were interrupted by those vile creatures. Unable to open my eyes, I could only hear, and that was worse. The retching. The crying. The sniffling. What did they have to be upset about? They'd done this.

I wondered if there was a heaven and if that's where I would go when they were done with me. Would Emmy be there? Of course she would be. She was good. My fate was less certain. *Oh, jeez.* Mom. Dad. How would they cope after I was gone?

The vomiting stopped and footsteps drew near. A shaking voice said, "She's still breathing. We have to call for help."

A cooler, detached voice said, "It's too late for that. We have to finish what we started."

The shaking voice grew louder. "No. This is insane. We can

still save her. This has gone too far — a million miles too far. It needs to stop."

"The other one is already dead. We can't let her live."

"Why?"

"Are you stupid? If anyone finds out we did this, all of our lives are over. Done. We might as well be dead, too. Don't you get that? We're in this together."

Farther away, more sobbing. The shaking voice stepped away, probably horrified by the scene they had created. How could they do this? How could anyone? Were they possessed by demons? By Satan himself?

A meek voice said, "I don't agree. If we get her help and she lives, it's better. We can tell the cops it was an accident and that we just tried to scare them and it went too far. If we save Tinsley, it will help our case. Maybe we'll only get probation or something."

"Are you an idiot? Emmy is dead! We will go to jail. No college, and no future. We have to finish this and fast. We need to get out of here."

The quiet one cried, "She doesn't deserve this!"

The cold voice said, "What the hell do you know about what she deserves? She deserves what I say she does. If you want to stop me, I dare you."

The quiet voice mumbled, "You're evil."

A devilish laugh erupted. "You don't know what evil looks like. I do. Now, stop your whining and help me, or I'll finish you off too and add you to the pile."

The pile? Emmy and I had been reduced to a pile. In time, a pile of corpses.

The quiet voice sounded closer. "I won't help you. You're beyond help. You're freaking crazy." With that, footsteps pattered away.

Had my only hope of surviving run off?

The evil voice said, "Damn it. Give me the knife. I need to do this quick and get out of here."

Nobody approached. The devil sighed before walking off and then returning.

Not that I could move or speak or plead with them to stop and convince them I wouldn't tell anyone. If only they'd spare my life, I would keep their secret forever. It was wishful thinking. They had clearly decided they were going to finish what they had started. Why didn't they just leave me to die? Surely, death wasn't far. What else were they going to do? And why? What had I done that was so awful to end up like this? I felt pressure on my chest, as if there was someone straddling me.

A sharp prick on my neck. A searing pain. The knife. The shaking voice from afar said, "It's not too late. You don't have to do this."

The devil said, "Yes, I do."

The pain intensified, and with it came a chill, and then it was colder and colder until I finally drifted away.

2

MARTINA

THE BUZZING OF A CIRCULAR SAW CUTTING THROUGH THE front of the skull was unnerving. Worse yet, when she removed the cranial cap to reveal the human brain contained within, I thought I'd had just about enough. A few weeks earlier, when Dr. Scribner had offered, and even suggested, that I sit in on a full autopsy, I thought it was a great idea and felt lucky to have the experience. Considering I wasn't one to be squeamish. I'd seen war, but this was different. I didn't think it would affect me like it had. Even when Dr. Scribner sliced open the man's chest, leaving a Y-shaped incision, and pulled out the organs, it hadn't fazed me. But something about her gloved hands removing the human brain from its cavity and gingerly placing it on the scale, leaving the corpse without a central processing unit, seemed wrong. It wasn't so much that it was gruesome, more like eerie. Although Dr. Scribner had conducted the autopsy with great care, the process of dissecting the body made it seem like it was no longer human — like it wasn't real, even though it had once been a living, breathing person with a family and maybe even children. Whatever the man had been before his death, he was no longer.

Detective Hirsch had explained that, in his job as a homicide detective, he had witnessed quite a few autopsies, and it was important to do so, which was why I had signed up for the viewing. He'd been on the job ten years longer than I had been an investigator. My work as a private investigator and security consultant rarely involved medical examiners. Well, not until I had contracted with the CoCo County Sheriff's Department's Cold Case Squad. In that role, I was exposed to all kinds of different aspects of law enforcement — most of which were truly unpleasant. Despite the darker side of the job, like watching a human become something else or being stalked and attacked, it was rewarding.

Hirsch, who had arrived in the autopsy suite a few minutes earlier, nudged me. "How is it going?"

He had smartly opted out of today's show, claiming he didn't need to view any more autopsies than absolutely necessary. I said, "It's going."

He smirked playfully. "Don't worry. The brain is basically the grand finale. After she weighs and examines it, she'll put him back together again."

The story of Humpty Dumpty came to mind. "That's good." *I guess.* I supposed it would be better if all of his parts were together as opposed to not. Overall, I was glad I'd watched Dr. Scribner take internal and external pictures, clip fingernails, scrape evidence off the body before washing him and removing the fluids and tissues. I could see how the experience would be helpful as I continued to review autopsy reports for the cold cases we worked. But yeah, *I'm done for the day.*

With the brain still on the scale, Scribner raised her hand and waved at Hirsch before stepping closer to us. "Martina, how are you doing? Is it all that you dreamed it would be?"

More like I hoped it *wouldn't* haunt my dreams. "It was definitely interesting. I appreciate you letting me sit in. I think I have a greater appreciation for the types of things to look out for when we arrive at crime scenes or review cold cases."

"Most detectives find that it's pretty useful. Right, Detective Hirsch?"

Hirsch nodded. "I sure do."

"All I have left is to finish up some weights and measurements and then return his insides and sew him up. So, if you're ready for a break, this is probably a good time."

"Thank you, Dr. Scribner. I appreciate it. Hirsch and I have some work to finish up."

Hirsch said, "Always."

"Well, you two have a good day, and I'll be seeing you around."

We waved, removed our protective gear, and found our way to the hallway. Hirsch said, "Any thoughts on changing careers and becoming a medical examiner?"

"Not a chance."

Hirsch chuckled. "Do you need a coffee or sustenance before heading back to the Cold Case Squad Room?"

"I need coffee and a protein bar. You want to join me?"

"As tempting as a protein bar sounds, I'm good and fully caffeinated, but I'll meet you back in the Squad Room."

I said, "It's a plan. See ya," and watched Hirsch as he headed down the corridor toward our building where our team, the Cold Case Squad, gathered and worked.

I couldn't believe Hirsch and I had worked together for nearly two years, and honestly, I couldn't imagine my life any differently. Considering my professional life at the CoCo County Sheriff's Department and my personal life were so intertwined within the Cold Case Squad, I couldn't get away if I tried. Hirsch and I were practically best friends, and I was becoming good friends with his girlfriend, Kim, too. The two made a great couple, and I was happy he'd found someone who made him smile.

Kim and I had gone shopping on several occasions, with and without my daughter, Zoey. We had even gone out for a girls' night with another friend of hers. We went to dinner and then to see a romantic comedy in the theater. It had been ages since I had a carefree night amongst girlfriends. And Kim adored Zoey. It was hard not to. *And that is my completely unbiased opinion.* Zoey looked up to her like she was the greatest thing ever. Sometimes, I was a little jealous, but I got over it. Kim was a lot of things I wasn't. She was sparkly and liked to wear makeup and fingernail polish — some of Zoey's favorite things. In contrast, I wore a uniform of all black, sensible shoes, and no makeup. It was nice for Zoey to have an auntie figure like Kim.

Our family's connection to the squad didn't end there. Much to my surprise, after a BBQ at Hirsch's last year, my mother started dating Sarge — the Cold Case Squad's boss, only second to the sheriff. Since my mother, Betty, lived with us, we'd seen a lot more of Sarge. There was no escape from the CoCo County Sheriff's Department. I didn't mind. My time with the department had been an interesting and exciting experience — and it had expanded my family in the best way.

The squad had solved many cold cases, bringing justice to a lot of families, and it was almost like a regular job where I could spend more time with Zoey. Since joining the squad, I didn't miss her school plays or Girl Scout meetings anymore. Sure, I still worked late sometimes and occasionally on weekends. But overall, I spent a lot more time being there for my daughter. She had Grandma at home with her, but I was her only living parent, and I needed to spend as much time with her as possible. She would start fifth grade in the fall, and after that, she would be in middle school. *Ugh.* My daughter would be in middle school in a year. Time went by too fast. I tried to capture each moment that brought me joy in my memory. And I tried to be grateful for my blessings every day.

Like the fact my mother and I had reconnected around the same time I met Detective Hirsch. She lived with us and helped take care of Zoey. She cooked every meal and was an amazing cook. We had to fend for ourselves a few more nights a week since she started dating Sarge, or Ted, as she called him. But it was nice to have a little more alone time with Zoey, too. We always had Friday night movie nights, but now we had extra time on the weekends together since Mom was out hiking with Ted or checking out a museum. Things had become peaceful. I mean, I hadn't been in the hospital in over a year. Nobody had attacked me or followed me in at least six months.

Had life turned boring?

Hardly.

This job was never boring. The adrenaline rush of finding clues and solving the case kept us engaged 100% of the time. Yet, most of the time, it was almost like I had a 9-to-5 job. Who would have ever thought that would be my life? Not me. And I thanked the Lord every day for such a blessed existence. It wasn't always like this. Just over two years ago, my world was filled with storm clouds and thunder at each turn. No sunshine or birds chirping.

I reached the kitchen and grabbed a mug from the cupboard, slid it under the machine, fed it a pod, and pressed go. Comfortable, that's what this life felt like. Life was comfortable and filled with joy and purpose. As the coffee dripped into my mug, a stirring in my gut gave me pause. Could this really last forever? Or was it just the calm before the storm? Cup filled, I headed to the Cold Case Squad Room.

I stepped inside and saw Hirsch chatting with Vincent and Detectives Leslie and Ross. They stopped when they saw me.

Leslie said, "Hey, Martina. I heard you got to watch your first autopsy."

"I sure did."

"How was it?" Vincent asked.

"It was an experience. You ought to watch one."

"Maybe later, but now..." Vincent smiled widely as if he knew something I didn't.

Hirsch said, "The team has an interesting new development in Georgia's case."

Georgia had been six years old when she went missing from her front yard twenty years ago. Her body was found several days later. Based on Vincent's smile, it had to be big. "What did you find?"

"Our forensics team found DNA on Georgia's dress."

"Any matches?"

"Yep. Turns out it was a neighbor still living in the Bay Area. Wolf and Jayda are executing the arrest warrant as we speak."

That was fantastic news. I said, "That goes to show that we should examine every piece of forensic evidence again when we reopen a case."

Hirsch nodded. "Yep."

The door opened, and I glanced over my shoulder as Sarge entered. He didn't come into the Squad Room often. He pretty much left us alone to do our jobs, and we gave him updates. What was up?

He approached our huddle. "Hey, team. Hirsch, Martina. The sheriff wants a meeting with the two of you."

I looked over at Hirsch. He shrugged as if he didn't know what it was about.

"When?" I asked.

"First thing tomorrow morning."

"What does he want to meet with us about?" Hirsch asked.

Sarge let out a breath and said, "Word is he's picked your next case."

"What's the case?"

"He won't say, but rumor has it, it's a big one. A tough one. In the meeting tomorrow morning, the families of the victims will be there."

"Don't you think it would be better if he prepped us before meeting the families?" I asked, confused.

Sarge nodded. "I think that too, but it's the sheriff's call."

"Any idea what the case is?" Hirsch asked.

"Nope. But it's an election year, so it must be one that's big enough that if you solve it, it will help his reelection campaign. So, hold on to your hats. I have a feeling it's gonna be a doozie."

Sarge provided us with the details for the meeting the next morning. My intuition had been correct. This was the calm before the storm. Would we make it through, or would it be the one that took us out? It was no secret to the team that the funding for the Cold Case Squad was always up in the air, considering fresh cases had priority. The current sheriff was a fan of the squad and had confirmed our funding for the entire year. But if there was a new sheriff, that could all change. My gut said the sheriff would use that leverage to push us hard. Fingers crossed it wouldn't break us.

3

HIRSCH

COMMOTION SOUNDED AS MARTINA AND I ENTERED Sheriff Lafontaine's massive office. Two grieving mothers and two grieving fathers pushed out of their chairs and stood up. Something in their faces sparked a memory in my mind. I thought, *No*. Sheriff Lafontaine walked around the conference table and extended his hand to me. "Detective Hirsch. It's good to see you."

After a firm shake, the sheriff turned to Martina. "Ms. Monroe. I don't believe we've had the pleasure. I'm Sheriff Lafontaine. It's very nice to meet you."

"It's nice to meet you too, Sheriff. I'm glad we're finally getting to meet one another in person."

The sheriff grinned, showing off a pearly smile. "Agreed. I would also like to introduce you to four very important people. I know the two of you will get justice for them and their families. Here, we have Mr. and Mrs. Olson, the parents of Emmy Olson, and this is Mr. And Mrs. Reed, Tinsley's parents. Their two daughters were murdered ten years ago."

Martina said, "I'm so sorry for your loss."

I added, "I'm sorry for your loss."

My mind sparked. I knew exactly who these people were and why they looked familiar. Their tear-stained cheeks and desperate pleas had been all over the news ten years ago when their daughters were murdered in what appeared to be a satanic ritual. *The Twin Satan Murders*. The girls were not twins, but they looked very similar and were best friends. The case had made national news, so I knew the original investigative team had named suspects because those boys were paraded on the news as well. The suspects were three local boys from wealthy families who were known to be into devil worship and the occult, but law enforcement didn't have enough evidence to prosecute any of them.

Sheriff Lafontaine said, "Why don't we all take a seat so we can get started?"

I nodded. Martina and I headed over to the conference table, and everyone took their seats.

Sheriff Lafontaine said, "Detective Hirsch, Ms. Monroe, the Olsons and Reeds — I wanted all of us to meet so that we could get set with a plan for bringing justice to your families. I have no doubt that our Cold Case Squad will solve Tinsley and Emmy's murders. Detective Hirsch has nearly twenty years on the force, previously as a homicide detective, and is now our Cold Case Squad leader. In addition, Ms. Monroe is a contracted private investigator who works alongside Detective Hirsch to investigate and, more importantly, close cold cases. You may recognize them from the news. They've solved quite a few cases — tough cases — since the inception of the Cold Case Squad just under two years ago. If anybody can solve the murder of Tinsley and Emmy, these two can."

Mrs. Olson nodded. "Thank you, Sheriff. We've been trying to find out who hurt our girls for ten years. And just so you know, Detective and Ms. Monroe, we have hired our own private investigators in the past, and they could not come up with anything usable to prosecute those responsible. We haven't given up hope, but we are a little disheartened."

Martina spoke. "I can appreciate that. As somebody who has worked for one of the top private investigation firms in California, I've taken on cases like this in the past before I was contracted here at the CoCo County Sheriff's Department. What I think will be most helpful is if you can tell us about your girls. Tell us what their life was like, their personalities, and the types of activities they partook in. All of which could be a possible connection to who did this to them."

I said, "Yes, as Martina said, anything you can tell us about the lives of your two daughters will be most helpful. We will, obviously, review the existing case files, previous witness statements, and the forensic evidence. We will do our best to find the truth."

The sheriff interrupted. "I have Vincent, a member of our Cold Case Squad and our top researcher, pulling all the files related to Tinsley and Emmy as we speak."

He brought in Vincent before us?

"That's much appreciated, Sheriff." For such a huge public case, it would've been helpful for the sheriff to have let us know ahead of time before meeting the families. Why had he chosen to blindside us? I glanced to my right at Martina and wondered if she was feeling the same way. Or if she'd heard of the murders or if she just thought this was another case of two murdered girls.

Thinking back to all those years ago, the parents looked almost exactly the same — like grieving parents. But older, more tired. Both mothers resembled their daughters, with their blonde hair, blue eyes, and fair skin. The fathers wore the same dark power suits, but one had balded, and the other sported salt-and-pepper hair that once was a mousy brown. The years had taken a toll on them. For a moment, the room was silent. Martina said, "Mr. and Mrs. Reed."

The woman said, "Please call me Mary, and this is Jeffrey."

"Mary. Jeffrey. Why don't you get us started and tell us about Tinsley? What was she like as a little girl? What were her favorite classes and extracurricular activities? Who were her friends and boyfriends?"

Mary Reed nodded. "Tinsley was one of the most caring, loving girls. Even when she was little. When she was three years old, she began taking ballet lessons and fell in love with dancing. She was an honor student and did little outside of ballet because she had to practice several hours a day. She had a few boyfriends. Nothing serious, though. Her boyfriend at the time she died was Jesse Maddox."

"Jesse was one of the original suspects?" Martina asked.

That answered my question of whether Martina knew the case. Although it would be difficult not to. It had been huge news. Two blonde haired, blue-eyed girls from a wealthy neighborhood in the Bay Area had been killed in a satanic ritual. We would be hard-pressed to find somebody who hadn't heard of the case.

Mary said, "That's correct, although we never believed it."

"Why is that?" I asked.

"We've known Jesse since he was a little boy. The families all belonged to the same club, and his parents were at the same benefits, and our kids were in the same schools. He just wasn't the kind of person to hurt anyone like that."

I passed a box of tissues over to Mary, and she thanked me. She sniffled, and I gave my best reassuring smile. "And Emmy and Tinsley were best friends, right?" I asked.

Mary said, "Yes. Since they could walk and talk."

The families of the two girls must have been terribly close. "Mr. and Mrs. Olson, what can you tell us about Emmy?"

"I'm Jane and this is Bob. Emmy was shy. She loved to read and wanted to grow up to be a novelist. Like Mary said, Emmy and Tinsley have been best friends since they were toddlers. Our two families have lived in the same neighborhood for the last twenty-five years. Although the girls were best friends, they didn't always run in the same circles."

"What do you mean?" I asked.

Jane said, "Well, Tinsley hung out with a group that Emmy wasn't a big fan of."

"Who were these people in the group that Emmy didn't particularly care for?" Martina asked.

Mary said, "Odie, or Odessa, Skye, Haisley, and Lorelei. They were one of the most popular cliques at the high school, and they were a year older than Emmy and Tinsley. We live next door to Odie's family. She and Tinsley have been friends since they were little, so Tinsley often hung out with the entire group. Emmy tagged along just to be with Tinsley, but it wasn't like Emmy would ever hang out with any of them by herself."

"Did that ever cause problems between Tinsley and Emmy?" Martina asked.

Both sets of parents turned to each other and shook their heads. Mary said, "No, they were like sisters. And even though Emmy didn't care for the group, they included her in activities like prom weekend when they all took the same limo and stayed in a hotel in San Francisco together after the dance."

Kids staying in a hotel by themselves?

"Did Emmy have a boyfriend?" I asked.

Jane shook her head. "No, she was pretty shy with boys. She liked ballet and took part in sports like lacrosse and softball. Emmy had nearly every hour booked. She had good grades and wanted to go to Yale. She wasn't interested in boys and cars and shiny things like those other girls were."

"Did Emmy have friends besides Tinsley?" I asked.

Jane said, "She had some friends from lacrosse. She'd go out after the games with everybody else, but she mostly socialized with Tinsley and the group, outside of something related to school or sports."

Martina glanced over at me, and I nodded. "I'm going to be very forthcoming with both families. I know you've been through a lot, and although we haven't seen the case files yet, Martina and I both have heard of your daughters' case. As I'm sure you would expect. But what might be helpful right now, since you have been living this for the last ten years, is if you can give us some insight based on what you have found — you said you hired a private investigator, and I know there's a website for anonymous tips. Is there anything you've uncovered that maybe won't be in our case file that could help guide us in the right direction?"

I sat back and waited.

Jane turned to Mary. "Why don't you go ahead?"

Mary Reed was clearly the ringleader.

"Okay." Mary turned toward us. "The private investigator couldn't find anything of use. All they found were things that we already knew. We shared the information with the original investigators ten years ago, and they compared notes but found nothing significant."

Trying to think what else to say to them, I was still a little miffed the sheriff hadn't briefed us on the case before meeting the parents. If we'd had the opportunity to review the case ahead of time, it would've been a lot more useful, and we could have asked the right questions.

We didn't know what they had already investigated, what forensic evidence there was, who the witnesses were, or their backgrounds. The sheriff and I had gotten along fine in the past, but I wasn't exactly a fan since he seemed too interested in politics and stats — that wasn't my game. This ambush had me pretty ticked off.

Martina said, "Detective Hirsch and I will give you our business cards. You can contact us anytime during the investigation. Before we conclude today, is there anything else you'd like to tell us about the case before we get started?"

"Will you get started right away?" Mary asked.

I said, "Yes, we will." *We would have gotten started earlier had we known.*

Mary Reed let out a breath. "Thank you for not giving up on our girls. We know the truth is out there, and somebody knows something. Our community isn't large enough to have this big of a secret without somebody knowing what really happened."

"That's good to know."

The sheriff said, "Mr. And Mrs. Olson and Mr. and Mrs. Reed, thank you for coming down. We will find out what happened to your girls. You have my word."

Is that so? I wasn't sure Lafontaine had my vote come election time.

"Thank you, Sheriff."

We all shook hands and provided business cards to the family. As they walked out, I held in my anger at the sheriff for promising two families we would solve their daughters' murder case when an entire team of detectives before couldn't do it. And without consulting Martina or me.

Once the families left, the sheriff shut the door and turned back around. The winning smile was absent from his face. "Okay, here's the deal. You need to solve that case, and we need it done ASAP."

With as much composure as I could muster, I said, "With all due respect, sir, the case went cold for a reason. I'm not sure it's going to be a slam-dunk case."

"The two of you need to work your magic. I need it done by the end of summer."

Martina furrowed her brow and looked at me. "Why by then?" she asked the sheriff.

"It's when my reelection campaign starts, and I need the Reeds and the Olsons supporting me. This will benefit you, too. If I remain in office, the Cold Case Squad will remain intact. A new sheriff may not agree with spending so much on cold cases when we have so many fresh ones. Do you understand?"

I understood perfectly. The sheriff was a snake, and all he cared about was getting reelected. "Perfectly, sir."

"Yes, sir," Martina said, as if she were still in the Army.

We exited the sheriff's office, and when we were for sure out of earshot, I said, "What do you make of that?"

"Well, I know who I'm not voting for this year."

Cracking a smile, I said, "No kidding."

"Do you know much about the case?" she asked.

"Just what was on the news."

She said, "Same here. But I think if we have to solve this by the end of summer, we're going to need some help. I don't think we'll be able to make it happen on our own."

"I agree. We could use the entire Cold Case Squad to help us."

"Aren't Ross and Leslie about finished up on the last case? We could use them. And try to free up the others."

"That's true. Let's go talk to Sarge and let him know what the sheriff just did."

As we marched down the hall, I wondered how we were going to solve a ten-year-old cold case that several groups of people had already investigated. It felt like it was a test, and I wasn't sure we were going to pass.

4

MARTINA

WITH SHOCK AND AWE, I WATCHED AS VINCENT WHEELED in the dolly stacked high with banker's boxes filled with the case files on the girl's murders. This wasn't like our other cold cases. It had been thoroughly investigated by law enforcement and private investigators before. I needed to stop thinking each case would be our toughest case — because each time I did, we landed one more difficult than the last. Not only that, but I should have known better than to even *wonder* if things would remain in a state of sunshine and daisies. *Silly me.* "Is that everything?" I hoped so.

Vincent said, "This is it for the case files. Evidence is another story."

I glanced up at Hirsch, who stood with his back against the wall, studying the boxes. "Have you been in the evidence locker room to determine how much physical evidence was collected?"

Hirsch said, "Not yet, but with these types of cases, I'm sure there's quite a bit or, at least, I hope there is. I'll give CSI Brown a call and see if he can have a member of his team come down and go through the forensics with us."

Hirsch and I had decided to take a preliminary look at the

case before involving the other investigators, but seeing the sheer volume of paperwork that had been produced from the investigation, I thought it might be a good idea to bring them in earlier to get extra eyes on the pages. Something was telling me my 9-to-5 job was over, and this was going to be a morning till night kind of gig until we found out who killed Tinsley and Emmy — and why.

From what their parents had said, they were normal teenage girls living a privileged life surrounded by other privileged people. There was no reason for their murder. Not that I could tell. I walked over to the dolly and helped Vincent put the boxes on top of the conference table. They were labeled one through four.

We'd start with number one. I lifted the top of the box and looked inside. It contained three large binders. I peered over at Hirsch, who had his phone to his ear, presumably calling CSI Brown to get a look at the forensic evidence. I wondered how long it would take to get through all these binders. The idea that I'd be falling asleep reading the latest John Grisham just drifted out the window. Case files would be my bedtime reading for the foreseeable future.

Vincent and I removed all the binders from the boxes and set them neatly in order. "Anything else I can get you two?" he asked.

"Yeah, could you give us a hand with reviewing the reports?"

"I need to finish up some research for homicide. Detective Daniels asked me to look into an old case for them that may be connected to a fresh case, but this is top priority, right?"

It was a valid question. In most cold cases, the victims had been long dead and time wasn't as critical as if it were a fresh investigation. Not that anybody wants to go slow or act like we had a leisurely pace, but when a higher priority came up, it was necessary to switch gears and put all the effort into the top priority. "Okay, let's wait until Hirsch gets off the phone and see how he wants to tackle this. Fresh cases are typically higher priority."

"All right."

Impatiently, I opened the first binder and read the intake report. A man walking his dog had found the bodies of the two girls. The dog pulled on the leash, trying to go toward the bodies. The man said he knew right away the two girls were dead because of the amount of blood at the scene and the gray of their skin. The officer's notes showed that the witness who found the bodies seemed pretty shaken up. We definitely would have to re-question the man who found the girls. It wouldn't be the first time the person who supposedly found the bodies was, in fact, the one responsible. I kept reading and reading and reading.

Hirsch stepped over. "Is that everything?"

"Yep. What did CSI Brown say?"

"The head forensic scientist can meet with us next week after she reviews the evidence collected and tested. She'll do a full presentation on that and give her recommendation for additional testing."

"Next week?"

"Brown says they're pretty slammed, and he wants to make sure they can give it the attention it needs."

"Understood. I asked Vincent to stick around and help us with the case files, but he needs to finish up some research for homicide."

"Great idea, but Vincent, you should finish up the work for homicide and then come back. That way, you can help us come up with a plan for the legwork. You're still interested in field work, right?"

"Yes. Definitely. I'll try to be quick."

Hirsch said, "Don't rush. I think this will take us several days."

"Cool. I'll be back," Vincent said, before rushing out.

I knew Hirsch had a conversation with Vincent about expanding his responsibilities beyond electronic and physical research. Usually, Vincent was behind a desk or rifling through case files, not out in the field, pounding the pavement and asking questions. But he had good instincts, and Hirsch wanted to give him a development opportunity to work alongside us.

I said, "Why don't we read through the files and flag things to put up on the murder board? When Vincent comes back, the three of us can continue flagging and then build the board together. Vincent can read as you and I build it out."

"I like it. When we're done with the board, we'll bring in the other investigators."

TWO DAYS LATER, THE THREE OF US HAD READ THROUGH the case files. It was the most gruesome case I had ever worked, and I had to practice calming techniques as we started building the murder board. In our last session, Hirsch and I recorded as Vincent sat propped up on the conference table prompting us with details of the murders.

Tinsley Reed, sixteen-year-old junior at Redwood High School, extracurricular — ballet. Boyfriend Jesse Maddox.

Emmy Olson, sixteen-year-old junior at Redwood High School, extracurriculars — ballet, lacrosse, and softball.

Both found murdered inside an abandoned home in a regional park in Orinda.

Description of injuries:

Emmy, cause of death blunt force trauma to the head. Her clothing was cut down the middle, and her body was slashed post-mortem.

Tinsley, cause of death exsanguination — after her carotid artery was cut, she bled out. Prior to death, she'd been bludgeoned and sexually assaulted. Her clothing was cut down the middle, and her body was slashed post-mortem.

My body shuddered at the description Vincent read aloud.

Who would do that to two innocent girls? Vincent set the binder down on the table and looked up at us. "You want to see the crime scene photos again?"

"Do I?" I asked. *No.*

Hirsch said, "We don't want to see them again, but we need to double and maybe even triple check everything."

He was right. I set down the marker and made my way over to the binder with the crime scene photos. I swallowed and tried to contain my horror.

The two girls lay side-by-side with their hands touching. Emmy's face was smeared with dried blood. Her dress had been ripped down the middle, and she had slashes on her bare chest.

Next to her lay Tinsley. Her head tilted to the right as if looking at Emmy. Her right hand rested atop Emmy's. Her neck had a bloody gash, and under her head and neck was a pool of blood. Her dress had also been cut off, with several angry slashes along with an inverted pentagram on her chest. There was blood on her inner thighs. There was blood every-where. There was no way the killer had not left a trace of their DNA or hair or fingerprints or some other kind of evidence.

How had the perpetrator been able to subdue both girls and commit this evil? On the stone walls of the room they lay in was an inverted pentagram painted in blood along with the text, 'Satan Lives'.

I turned away from the binder and took a moment to catch my breath. The girls were so young — babies, really. Like Zoey. What kind of evil would do that to them? Who had they crossed paths with that had led to this ending? I knew the world could be a very dark place, but this was unfathomable. We were definitely going to need additional help because I didn't know how I could continue to look at these crime scene photos. Every time I saw Emmy Olson's blue eyes staring blankly up at the heavens, I saw Zoey's. My stomach gurgled, and I rushed over to the garbage can and spewed the contents of my breakfast. Was it something I'd eaten, or was it more than I could handle? Admittedly, the first time I'd seen the photos, I flipped through them pretty quick. After wiping my mouth, I stood up and turned around. Hirsch and Vincent stared at me. "Are you all right?" Hirsch asked.

Embarrassed that I'd lost my composure, I said, "I'll be all right."

Hirsch said, "It's one of the worst I've seen."

Vincent met my gaze. "We will find who killed Tinsley and Emmy."

I nodded. "Yes, we will."

5

HIRSCH

Looking out at the Cold Case Squad, I was filled with pride. There were smiles and laughter and camaraderie. The group was tight. There wasn't anything they wouldn't do for each other. Yet, it would be the first time the team would work on one case together. I turned on the projector, and the room quieted down. "Good morning, Cold Case Squad."

Multiple renditions of "good morning" and hoots and hollers followed. It was a high energy team who loved their job and gave everything to it. "Today, I've got a special announcement. The sheriff gave us our next case. And when I say us, I mean every single person sitting in this room."

Detective Leslie raised her hand. "What about our current cases?"

I explained, "We'll get them to a good stopping point, and then you'll work on them as you have time. But the new case will be your number one priority."

"So, if we can't actively work on the new case, we can work on our other ones?" Ross asked.

"Correct."

"What's the case?" Detective Ross asked.

"I'll get to it." I advanced the slide, and I could hear gasps throughout the room. "Martina and I had a sit down with Sheriff Lafontaine last Tuesday morning, and he's tasked us with solving the Twin Satan Murders." I paused for dramatic effect. "That's not all. He says we have to have it solved by the end of the summer."

The group broke into exuberant reactions and side conversations. Raising my voice, I said, "Calm down. I need you to listen carefully."

The room silenced. "Martina, Vincent, and I have gone through all of the original case files, and we'll meet with the forensics team in a few days to go over the evidence and testing that was done ten years ago and provide guidance on next steps based on advancements in technology." I flipped to the next slide. "This is the murder board, based on what Vincent, Martina, and I gathered from the case files. We have two victims — sixteen-year-old best friends Tinsley and Emmy. At the time of the murders, there were three prime suspects, as you can see on the left: Arlo, Warren, and Jesse. All three boys were seniors at Redwood High School. All three were known to have an interest in the occult and dressed in black clothing and wore black eyeliner. They were Goths. Jesse, the supposed ringleader, was dating Tinsley. On the right side of the board, you can see a list of female names. Those are known friends and close acquaintances of the girls. Odessa, commonly referred to as Odie, Skye, Haisley, and Lorelei. They were the last four people to see Tinsley and Emmy alive. Besides the group of four, the second to last to see the two girls alive were Sarah Runion and Connor Deven, who saw them get into Odie's car with the others around nine o'clock. The original statements say that Odie, Skye, Haisley, and Lorelei dropped off the girls around midnight at the Nation's Burgers in downtown Orinda."

Detective Ross asked, "Were there any witness statements corroborating that the girls were dropped off at the burger restaurant?"

I said, "No."

"Was the area canvased to look for witnesses?" Ross asked.

"Not that we could find. All the restaurants and shops in the area were closed. In addition, you'll see the name Donald. He was the man who discovered the two bodies when he was walking his dog the next morning. He said he never touched the scene, as it was obvious they were dead."

"Are you going to show the crime scene photos next?" Leslie asked.

"I won't project them. They're in the binders. I have to warn all of you they're gruesome. Bad. Some of the worst I've ever seen. I know we've got a lot of experienced detectives in here, so it's nothing new. But some of us are researchers and haven't worked in the field. It can be upsetting — even for the seasoned detectives in this room. The binder with the crime scene photos is over there on the desk. The murders appear to have been some sort of ritual — likely a satanic ritual. The girls had inverted pentagrams carved on them, and they were cut up pretty badly. In addition, on the walls inside the house where they were killed, the phrase 'Satan lives' was written in Tinsley's blood."

The room went back into murmurs and discussions among the investigators. "If I can get your attention again, please."

Martina passed out a packet of papers to each of the team members.

"Martina is handing out the assignments and how we divvied up the work. We'll break after this meeting and get started. Are there questions?"

Martina said, "Review the preliminary assignments. If there's any reason we need to switch things around, this is the time to do so. We'll still hold the daily briefing, but we focus solely on this case. Anything outside of this case that you need to discuss with Hirsch or myself, we'll do on a one-on-one basis. Understood?"

Heads nodded.

"Based on everything we read in the original case files, Martina and I came up with an approach we think will be the most effective, albeit a bit laborious. We will treat this case as if it were fresh. Even so, it'll be a good idea for each investigator to read the original case files — every page. Fair warning, there are a lot of pages. But I want you all to look at this like it's day one. That means we will be re-interviewing every single witness. We will revisit the crime scene. We will look at every piece of forensic evidence and have our techs come up with an approach to either validate the original results or redo them if there're enough materials. We will come up with new theories, besides the previous ones. We will solve this case. Any questions?"

Vincent asked, "Did the sheriff say why he wanted the team to work on this case?"

I smirked. "It's an election year."

The team shrugged and acted as if it wasn't a surprise the desire to solve this decades-long double murder was politically motivated. I added, "But that doesn't mean these girls' families don't deserve closure and for us to find who did this horrific crime and bring them to justice. If there are no more questions, we'll get started."

Everyone nodded and flipped through the pages that Martina had handed out.

Martina added, "All right team, let's get it done."

Some enthusiastic calls sounded before the team broke up and discussed the investigation. I turned to Martina. "Are you ready to go to the scene?"

"As ready as I'll ever be."

Understood. I, for one, wished it wasn't part of my job. Standing at the scene of a homicide made it even more real and *disturbing*.

6

MARTINA

THE STUFFED ANIMALS, MIXTURES OF BOUQUETS OF DEAD and fresh flowers, cards, and signs in memoriam of Emmy and Tinsley made the spot where they died rather obvious. Ten years later, people still visited the site, bringing new mementos and flowers. It was pretty remarkable how the families had not given up and had fought tooth and nail to make sure nobody forgot their daughters. After reviewing the crime scene photos, I couldn't imagine what kind of monster would do what they had done to those two young women. The motive was unclear, as such savagery could only mean they were sick, sociopathic individuals who didn't see the two girls as human. Had it been Satan worshipers? Or those practicing the dark arts? If that were true, how had they chosen Emmy and Tinsley as their victims? As horrific as both murders were, Tinsley had been tortured while she was still alive, unlike Emmy. Tinsley had been a fighter, despite the brutality inflicted upon her. It had taken a lot to remove her life force. Why did Tinsley get it worse than Emmy?

Hirsch and I approached the stone building and the memorial to the two girls. "We should get detailed photographs of all of this. It's possible whoever did this returns and possibly even leaves items."

"Agreed."

"I can see why they chose this spot. It's secluded, yet not that far from the parking lot to the trailhead."

I said, "Yeah, the original notes mentioned the local high school kids used to come here to drink and party and God only knows what else."

Hirsch read the historical site signage. "Says here this home was originally built in the early 1800s but abandoned in 1849 during California's Gold Rush."

I pointed to the right side of the memorial. "You take pictures of this half, and I'll take the other."

Hirsch agreed, and we photographed the remaining memorial items. Some were old and faded — whatever had been written was gone from time and the elements. But there were definitely freshly written cards, signs, and cut flowers. I lifted a faded purple teddy bear that wore a tiara that once shimmered silver but had faded to white and gray. A once sparkly princess bear. It was something Zoey would have. Could this happen to my daughter if she trusted the wrong people? It was one thing to have a family member killed in the manner in which Tinsley and Emmy had been, but I didn't know how the parents went on. Trying to make the best use of time, I flipped open each card and snapped a photo without reading them. That could be done later. Plus, I wasn't sure my constitution could handle so much grief when I needed to keep a level head.

Setting down the last bouquet of flowers, I lifted myself up and stared out at the stone building. There was something about the air that I couldn't quite put my finger on. I wasn't sure I believed in spirits, but there was a thickness that told you something terrible happened here. A light breeze scraped the back of my neck, and goose bumps covered my skin.

I glanced over at Hirsch. "Shall we head inside?"

He nodded without a word.

We stepped inside the building made of stone. There was dirt and dust on the floor. There were no doors or windows, just openings where they once existed. The space couldn't be more than five-hundred square feet, and it was one large, open room. Bloodstains were no longer visible on the floor. Someone must've come and cleaned them up. But who? I certainly hoped the crime scene team had collected samples from the floor as part of the original investigation. Whoever carved up those girls had to have left something behind. The walls still hosted various graffiti, but the markings from Tinsley's blood had been removed. That was probably for the best. I couldn't imagine returning here to bring flowers and seeing my daughter's or my friend's or my sister's blood smeared on the walls proclaiming that we were surrounded by evil.

After photographing the inside, I took the back exit, trying to envision how many people could've contributed to the murders. How many witnesses hadn't come forward? It was a strong theory that it was more than one person who had committed the crimes. But the theory didn't include how many were involved. We still had to have our meeting with the forensics team to understand better. There had been advancements in technology that we hoped would help us solve the case. Maybe something hadn't been tested that the original team hadn't thought was important when, in fact, it might've been. Hirsch and I saw it all the time in cases that the Cold Case Squad had investigated. Some cases were opened and closed quickly because of the advancements in fingerprint and DNA technologies, but something in my gut was saying it wouldn't be quite that straightforward in this case.

Outside the building, I surveyed the area. There were clusters of large trees all around. Plenty of places to hide if you wanted to. Could there be a witness who had seen it all go down? I continued pacing around the area, snapping pictures as I went. I didn't recall the perimeter the CSI team took ten years ago, but looking at it now, I would think it would have been pretty large considering people could have been going in and out of the house into the trees and onto the trail. I hoped to goodness they hadn't just cordoned off around the house and left it at that. *Mental note — recheck the photos*. Staring at the house, I tried to envision how the murders could've taken place. Glancing up to the blue skies and green trees, I saw it was actually a lovely spot. How could something so horrific have happened amid such beauty?

Hirsch exited the building and said, "You find anything interesting?"

"No, I'm just hoping when the original CSI team came out here, they made a big enough perimeter."

"Me too. I was examining the stone walls closer, and I think when we meet with the forensics team, we should ask them to re-swab the walls to see if anything may have been stuck in the crevices that wasn't picked up before. From the looks of it, there could still be dried blood or hairs stuck in there that could've been missed the first time."

"True, but somebody already cleaned up the scene. There's no visible sign of Tinsley's blood on the walls or on the ground."

"It would be difficult to really clean these walls and the floor adequately. On the surface, yeah, but deep down, there could be more."

Nodding, I pulled off my latex gloves. "What do you think of this place?"

"I think it's got an eerie vibe."

Exactly. "I get that, too. It's as if there's a heaviness to it, like something once beautiful has been tarnished and made ugly."

Hirsch said, "Yep. Well, there's nothing more here to see. Shall we go meet Jesse?"

"We shall." Jesse and his two friends were the number one suspects ten years ago. He'd been dating Tinsley and apparently was the ringleader of the Goth group he hung around. The three boys had been suspected of performing a satanic ritual on the two girls, but there was no way to actually physically link them to the crime. As a result, they remained free and had gone on to live full lives, including college, careers, and some were married. All the things Tinsley and Emmy should have experienced but didn't get the chance.

7

MARTINA

Standing outside the hospital doors, Hirsch asked, "How many Satan-worshiping teenage murderers grow up to become doctors?"

"Is this a trick question?"

"Nope."

I said, "We're about to find out if there's at least one." Vincent's background check found that Jesse Maddox was now Dr. Jesse Maddox in his second year of residency at UCSF. After high school, he went to UCLA for undergraduate studies and then on to Stanford Medical School before becoming a resident at UCSF. Based on his background, you would think he was highly intelligent. Was he smart enough to get away with murder?

Considering he was a physician, and may have patients, we had called ahead, and Jesse agreed to meet us outside the hospital. I could understand him not wanting homicide investigators at his place of work.

The street was loud and busy with cars and pedestrians. I spotted a café on the corner and hoped Jesse wouldn't mind joining us for a cup of coffee.

A man in his late twenties with dark hair and wireframe spectacles wearing a white lab coat walked toward us. Based on his DMV photos, it was our guy. "Jesse Maddox?" Hirsch asked.

He nodded.

Hirsch said, "I'm Detective Hirsch. This is Martina Monroe. You have enough time to go to the café and grab a cup of coffee while we talk?"

"Sure. I could use a boost."

On the walk to the cafe, we made small talk to ease him into the interrogation. "What kind of medicine are you practicing?" I asked.

"Right now, I'm working in the psych ward."

"Interesting work?" I asked.

"It keeps me on my toes."

"How long have you been here?" Hirsch asked.

"This is my second year in a three-year residency. After that, I'm hoping for a staff position."

"They keep you pretty busy?" I asked.

"They do. Not a lot of sleep, which is why when someone offers coffee, I always say yes."

His casual demeanor didn't scream killer to me. But then again, how many of us were the same person we were at eighteen? I certainly wasn't. For one, I was on the other side of the law and had drank myself into a stupor on more occasions than I'd like to admit. Jesse didn't appear gregarious or full of bravado — like a narcissist who enjoyed killing.

We reached the café, and Hirsch held the door open for both Jesse and me. After we got our three black coffees, Hirsch went over to the counter and dumped a bunch of sugar and creamer in his before we took a seat at a small bistro table.

"So, you're reopening the case?" Jesse asked.

I said, "Yes, we have the entire Cold Case Squad on it."

"My guess is I'm the first to be re-interviewed?"

We hadn't told him we were starting with him. Maybe he was just perceptive. "That's right."

"Well, then you probably know back then the case almost ruined my life. As if it wasn't bad enough that my girlfriend was brutally murdered. But then I was portrayed on the news like I was some sort of satanic killer. I almost lost my spot at UCLA — it was a nightmare. Not that I don't still have nightmares," he added quietly before sipping his coffee.

"What type of nightmares do you have?" I asked.

He set down the coffee. "When they arrested me, along with Arlo and Warren, the detectives on the case threw down crime scene photos at us, telling us to explain why we did this and to confess. Over and over. The first time I saw the photos, I threw up right there in the interrogation room. What they did to her..." Jesse quieted as his voice quivered. "I really hope you find who did that to them. Emmy and Tinsley did not deserve that. Nobody deserves that."

Hirsch and I shared a glance. "Do you remember the last time you saw Tinsley and Emmy alive?"

"Yes. I'd been with Tinsley the night before she died. She came over to my parents' house. They were out at a fundraiser, so we had the house to ourselves."

"Were there any witnesses to corroborate that?" I asked.

"No. But we were together."

"What did you do when you were together that night?" I asked.

"We watched a movie, ordered pizza, and fooled around."

"Fooled around?" I asked.

Jesse lowered his voice. "We had sex that night."

And therefore it was conceivable we'd find his DNA in Tinsley's rape kit, and if we did, he had a reason for it to be there other than he was with her the night of the murder. Interesting.

"And then what happened?" I asked.

"She drove home around midnight."

"On Friday night?" I asked.

"Yes."

"Is that something she did often? Go over to your house and fool around?" Hirsch asked.

"Not that often. But both of our parents were at the same fundraiser, so we took advantage of the time we had."

"And you never saw her again after that?" I asked.

"No."

"How long had you and Tinsley been dating?" I asked.

"Maybe a month."

"Were you serious?" I asked.

Jesse shrugged. "She was sixteen, and I was about to turn eighteen and go off to college. I liked her a lot, but serious? Not really. It wasn't like we were going to get married."

"What was Tinsley like?" I wondered if his description of Tinsley would match the one her parents had given us.

"She was sweet, nice, really smart. Caring and kind. Not like the others."

"The others?" I asked.

"Yeah, I'm sure you have Odie, Skye, Haisley, and Lorelei on your list — mean girls if there ever were. But Tinsley was different. Well, she was at least nicer than the rest of them."

"What about Emmy?" I asked.

"Emmy, I didn't know as well. She hung out with Tinsley. They were best friends, but she wasn't really with the other group, you know what I mean? She was only there because Tinsley was there. I always got the vibe that she didn't care for the others. Or me, to be honest."

So, that checked out. "Were you near the woods that night?"

"No. I had an alibi. We all did. That was the crazy thing. I can't believe they arrested me and Arlo and Warren. All three of us were at a basketball game."

I looked over at Hirsch, who looked just as surprised as I was. "You were at a basketball game? Which one?"

"It was a college game in Davis. We told the cops, but they didn't listen. They said we were just covering for each other. Not true."

I pulled out my phone and made a note to verify the three boys' alibis for that night. If that were true, why had the cops focused in on them back then? Even I remembered their young faces on the news: three boys in a cult killed two happy, bright blondes from Orinda. "Why do you think the police focused on Arlo, Warren, and yourself?"

He shook his head. "Probably because of the way we dressed. And I was dating Tinsley. But they had absolutely no evidence we were there because we were at the basketball game."

"How did you dress?" Hirsch asked

"We were going through a phase. Rebelling from our white-bread neighborhood. I wore all black and even wore eyeliner. We were basically trying to look Goth. We weren't into the occult, or Satan, or anything like that. They just thought that because we wore all black. It was stupid." Jesse shook his head in disgust. "You know, the three of us wanted to rebel against our rich parents, but when you see those guys from *Paradise Lost* — a movie I watched a few months back — those guys were clearly not guilty, but the West Memphis Three were poor kids who couldn't afford good lawyers and sat in jail for a crime they most likely didn't commit. Now, I'm grateful for my parents and their money that bought us the best lawyers because I can only imagine what would have happened if they hadn't. We'd probably be in jail right now, just like those other guys. I'm telling you, we didn't do this. We were together that night. I would never have hurt Tinsley or anyone. I have no motive, and I wasn't into Satan."

He wasn't wrong. There were some theories that the reason they got off when they were guilty was because of their rich parents. But if what Jesse was saying was true, and he had a solid alibi and there was no forensic evidence, maybe they didn't do it? "Do you still talk to Arlo and Warren?"

"Yeah. I mean, we're practically brothers. We've been friends since we were five years old. Arlo is a lawyer now, and Warren's a high school teacher. Warren just got married last year. As much as it made me angry at the time that the investigation could have ruined my life, I think of Tinsley and Emmy and how their lives are gone forever. When I say I hope you find who did this, I mean it. Anything I can do to help, I will."

Hirsch said, "We appreciate that."

"Is there anything else I can help with?" Jesse asked.

He seemed sincere, but I wasn't buying it yet. Hirsch said, "Do you have any ideas about what happened to Tinsley and Emmy that night? Anybody who may have been harassing them? Anybody hanging around who seemed suspicious?"

"Not really. We lived in a relatively small community. Everyone kind of knows each other there."

"Do you think it was someone who knew them?" I asked.

"Honestly, I would think it would have to be. Tinsley wouldn't have gone off with just anybody."

"Any ideas of who may have hurt them?" Hirsch asked.

"It's hard to believe I know anybody who could be capable of doing what they did."

I peered into his eyes. "But you might."

Jesse looked away. "Maybe."

"Did Tinsley have any enemies? Did Emmy?" Hirsch asked.

"No enemies — but have you heard the term frenemies? Odie, Skye, Haisley, and Lorelei could be a tough bunch. I never saw them really fighting, but I used to date Odie, and she didn't take the breakup very well, especially after I started dating Tinsley. She acted like she was fine, but I didn't buy it."

"That's Odie — Odessa Johnson?" I asked.

"That's right."

"Do you still talk to her?" Hirsch asked.

"No, thank you. She was crazy. I can only imagine what she's like now. But I heard she's a lawyer."

"Crazy enough to want to hurt Tinsley for stealing her boyfriend?" I asked.

"Physically, no. If I remember correctly, Odie was more into psychological warfare."

"Anything else you can tell us?" Hirsch asked.

"Not that I can think of." He glanced at his wrist. "If there's nothing else, I need to get back."

"Would you be open to giving us a DNA sample?" I asked.

"Do you have a kit?" Jesse asked.

Hirsch said, "No, but we could come back, if you agree."

"I have nothing to hide. I'm willing to give my DNA. Just tell me when."

Interesting.

Hirsch and I nodded. "Thanks, Jesse. We'll be in touch."

We watched the young physician leave the coffee shop before I focused on Hirsch. "What do you make of that?"

"I don't know. Jury's still out. What I can tell you is that I'm really looking forward to speaking with the others, especially the mean girls."

"Amen." I was interested in speaking with them too, but something was telling me Jesse hadn't told us everything he knew about the double murder.

8

TINSLEY

EMMY THREW HER HEAD BACK, LAUGHING. I SAID, "OH, MY gosh, that is not even funny."

She continued to laugh and said, "It's so funny."

"You know, Emmy, you're one of the funniest people I know, but that was one of the worst jokes I've ever heard."

She sat up with a wide grin. "Oh, Tinsley..." Emmy paused, and her smile faded. "Look who's here," she said with slight annoyance in her tone.

I glanced up. "Hey, Skye. Haisley. Lorelei."

"Hi, Tinsley. Hi, Emmy. How's it going?" Lorelei asked.

"Pretty good. Where's Odie?" I asked.

Skye said, "Ugh, she's probably somewhere with Jesse. I swear, like, get a room already."

"Odie and Jesse are dating?" I asked.

Skye grimaced. "Yeah, I'm surprised you haven't heard. They hooked up at a party this weekend, and they've been sucking face ever since — it's totally gross."

With a sinking feeling in my chest, I pretended not to care. I'd had a secret crush on Jesse since the beginning of the school year, but I was too shy to make a move. He was cute and smart and athletic, and he would be going off to college in the fall. If he was dating Odie, I feared my chance with him was over. Not that there weren't other guys to choose from, but there was something special about Jesse. There was something about him that made him stand apart from the rest of the white hat wearing golf team members who made up most of our student body. Lorelei said, "Speaking of ..."

The three girls giggled.

Odie said, "Hey, ladies."

"Hey, Odie," they said in a singsong voice.

I watched Jesse rake his fingers through his floppy brown hair. His style of black shirt, black pants, and black eyeliner was new, but I kinda dug it. It made him seem more mysterious and interesting, like if we dated, we might be breaking the law or something.

"We ordered fries and soda if you want to join us," I offered.

Jesse said, "Sure, sounds great."

They all sat down at Emmy's and my table. Emmy wasn't a huge fan of the girls, but she tolerated them since she was my best friend. I didn't see why we couldn't all be friends and didn't really get why she didn't like them. Jesse met my eyes. "Hey, Tinsley, how's it going?"

"Pretty good. Have you finished the physics homework yet?"

"Not yet. It's a pretty big problem set."

I nodded. "Oh, I know. I've only finished half of them."

Jesse blasted a bright smile. His eyes met mine, and I turned away and said, "When will those fries get here? I'm starving."

I did a quick glance over at Odie, who was now glaring at me. Great. She was the last person I wanted to make mad. Odie wasn't always the nicest person or the most pleasant or the most kind or the most easy to be around, but we had lived next door to each other since we were little. At this point, it would be too hard not to be friends with her. She was kind of like that annoying cousin who was kind of mean, but she was still your cousin.

When the fries arrived, everyone dug in, except for Emmy. "What's wrong?" I asked.

"I'm not hungry."

"Okay." Maybe she was worried about our physics homework? We were supposed to stop at the mall just to grab a bite to eat before going back to my house to finish our homework. Emmy was also in my physics class with Jesse. It was typically reserved for seniors, but both Emmy and I had high enough grades that we could petition to get into the course. It was harder than I thought it was going to be, but it was kinda cool, too. I wanted to go to school to become a doctor, and I knew science was an important part of the curriculum. So, if it would give me an edge to get into a good college to take physics and calculus in high school, then that's what I would do. It meant a lot of homework, which meant meandering in the food court and talking about boys and clothes and makeup with the girls was limited.

When the fries were gone, Jesse and Odie walked away, hand in hand. Jesse turned and gave me the quintessential head tilt as a goodbye, and Odie kept giving me the evil eye. Dang it. I would have to try to smooth it out with her later.

Emmy said, "Hey, do you want to do a quick perusal at Wet Seal and see if there are any cute clothes?"

Emmy hadn't been concerned about homework after all.

"Let's do it. Girls, do you want to come?"

Skye said, "No, we're not really into Wet Seal anymore."

"Yeah, it's like so last year," Haisley said in a snotty tone.

I rolled my eyes.

"Well, then, we'll catch you later." The girls were seniors and liked to remind us at every turn. They were one year older, so what? They thought that somehow being seniors made them so much wiser, but it didn't. We waved and Emmy said, under her breath in a mocking voice, "Tinsley, that's so last year."

We giggled as we ran toward the shop.

THE NEXT DAY AT SCHOOL, I SAT IN THE CAFETERIA chatting with Emmy when Odie approached with a look of fury on her face.

"Hey, Odie, what's up?"

"Oh, I think you know what's up, Tinsley." With her hands planted on her hips, her face was turning beet red.

"No, Odie, I don't think I do."

"You were totally flirting with Jesse yesterday. Admit it."

Oh, jeez. "I was not flirting with Jesse. We have physics together. That's all." I hoped she bought it. I mean, that was all, from Jesse's perspective, I was sure. Of course, how could I not be into Jesse? What I didn't understand was why he was into Odie.

"You were totally flirting with him. Don't do it again, or you will be sorry." With that, she knocked over my soda before walking off in a huff.

I looked down at my brand-new jeans that were now covered in brown soda.

Emmy said, "Well, that was normal."

"Seriously. I wasn't even flirting with him."

"You weren't flirting, but the sparks between the two of you were pretty obvious."

My eyes lit up. "Really?" I asked, completely forgetting about the fact I was drenched in soda.

"Don't get too excited. I think Odie would end you before she let you take her boyfriend."

"I'm not afraid of Odie."

"Suit yourself. You should change out of those, or they'll stain."

Shaking my head, I grabbed napkins from the middle of the table and blotted up the soda before getting up and heading toward the gym to change into my spare clothes I had for after ballet practice. Odie was so overly dramatic. Jesse wasn't even into me. Was he?

9

HIRSCH

As we drove toward Arlo Jeffries' law firm, I said, "What did you think of Jesse?"

Martina said, "He didn't seem like a cold-blooded killer who tortured and maimed his victims, but I'm not sure he was telling us everything."

"Why do you say that? He was willing to give his DNA."

"He seemed cagey when we asked if he knew who killed Tinsley and Emmy."

Thinking back, I agreed with her assessment. "But you don't think he killed them?"

"People can change over the course of ten years, but I don't think it's likely he did it. And I think his willingness to give DNA says he wasn't at the scene of the murders. He's a doctor. I'm sure he understands DNA."

True. "You ready to go talk to Arlo?"

"Yes, sir."

It was lucky for us that Arlo also worked in San Francisco, so we could hit two birds on one trip. We parked in the garage beneath an ultra-tall building and took the elevator up to Arlo's law firm. We had called ahead, but although he told us he was too busy to chat with us, we showed up anyway. The elevator doors opened, and we made our way to reception. "How may I help you?" the receptionist asked.

"We're here to see Arlo Jeffries. My name is Detective Hirsch, and this is Martina Monroe."

"Do you have an appointment?"

"No, but he knows we're coming." *Sort of.*

"Okay," she said, hesitantly, while picking up the receiver on her phone and dialing. "Mr. Jeffries, there's a detective here to see you."

We waited.

"Okay, Mr. Jeffries, thank you." She set the receiver down. "He'll be out in a minute."

I said, "Thank you."

We stepped aside and waited for Arlo. The fact that he said he was too busy to meet with us today had me on high alert. Jesse made time to help with the investigation, yet Arlo tried to push us away. What did it mean?

A few moments later, a man with a dark, shiny suit, chiseled chin, and wavy brown hair emerged. "Detective Hirsch. Ms. Monroe."

We stepped toward him. I said, "That's us."

He extended his hand. "Arlo Jeffries. It's nice to meet you both."

"Glad you're able to speak with us," I said pointedly.

"Like I said on the phone, Detective, I only have a few minutes. I have a very busy schedule today."

"Is there somewhere we can talk?" Martina asked.

"Yes, follow me."

So far, I wasn't getting a friendly vibe, more like a chill in the middle of summer. We entered Arlo's office. He shut the door behind us. "Now, what can I help you with?" Arlo asked.

"Well, as I mentioned on the phone, we have reopened Tinsley and Emmy's murder investigation."

Arlo shook his head. "I don't think I'll be of any help."

Martina said, "Really? You were one of the prime suspects ten years ago, and you have nothing to say?"

He shook his head and pursed his lips. "It's ridiculous. They had no evidence then or now. All three of us had an alibi. We didn't hurt Tinsley and Emmy. There's really nothing more I can say. If you have nothing specific, I'm going to have to ask you to leave."

Martina stared him in the eyes. "Are you still into the dark arts?"

Arlo smirked. "Ridiculous. That was nothing more than satanic panic. We wore dark clothes and lit candles, pretending to be into the occult. It was Jesse's idea to annoy our parents. Everybody in Orinda is basically the same. The same clothes, the same fancy cars, and the same expectations for greatness. We wanted to rebel. So, every once in a while, we'd say we were into Satan to rile up our parents. We weren't Satan worshipers, and we didn't kill Emmy and Tinsley. They had no motive or evidence. Hence why we were never charged. Now, I'd like you to leave."

"So, you never saw Tinsley and Emmy that night?" I asked.

Arlo huffed. "I have nothing more to say."

"Would you be willing to give a DNA sample?"

His body stiffened. "Not without a warrant. Now, really, I must go. You can see your way out." With that, he opened the door of his office and walked down the hall, presumably to a meeting or to somewhere he wouldn't be questioned about a double homicide.

I looked at Martina. "Well, shall we leave?"

"Interesting that he's not willing to talk to us. Makes you wonder why, doesn't it?"

Before I could answer, a large man wearing a security guard uniform approached. "Sir, ma'am, now that your business with Mr. Jeffries has concluded, I will escort you out."

I said, "No problem, we were just leaving."

Back in the elevator, I turned to Martina. "Let's hope we have better luck with Warren."

Martina said, "Seriously. Jesse's change from high school seemed dramatic. I have a feeling Arlo, not so much."

It was exactly what I was thinking. Did that mean the original detectives were onto something all those years ago? What was Arlo hiding? He certainly didn't like that we asked for his DNA. What did he have to hide?

10

HIRSCH

In front of the high school, the dismissal bell rang, and a sea of teenagers swarmed out of classrooms and headed toward the parking lot. With the students on their way out, it was time for Martina and me to interview Warren Denver, the third prime suspect from ten years ago. According to the most recent information, Warren had graduated from Cal Poly and was a high school teacher in the Bay Area. Jesse had me thinking of the West Memphis Three — teenage boys who had been accused of murdering three boys in what looked like a satanic ritual. However, the West Memphis Three had a much different fate than Jesse, Arlo, and Warren. Instead of sitting in a prison cell for a crime they didn't commit like the former, the latter three had all attended college, postgraduate school, and had careers — surprisingly untarnished by public accusations of a heinous crime.

Without words, Martina and I strolled on to campus, and it made me wonder what Martina had really been like as a teenager. She told me she had been rebellious and wild. I couldn't even picture it. My high school years were relatively tame in comparison, with no trouble made or drugs taken.

Alcohol came later, in my college years. I was one of those kids who had been on the college track, and that's exactly what I did. It's interesting to think that if Martina and I had known each other in high school, we wouldn't have been friends, since I considered her my closest friend — the person I could always count on, no matter what.

I was so relieved she and Kim got along so well. Kim was truly like my other half, and I was grateful each day that I had met her. She was bright and bubbly, smart, and optimistic. I had never known a love as deep as my love for Kim. Despite being Martina's near polar opposite, which was why I was concerned at first, they hit it off right away. And Kim adored Zoey. Zoey had talked Kim and Martina into going shopping together, and it seemed to have solidified their friendship. It made me think of what Kim would be like as a mother. I thought she'd be fantastic.

Martina said, "I think it's right up here."

I followed her lead. We had set up a time to meet with Warren since we knew he was a schoolteacher and preferred to make sure we had his full attention and didn't want to disrupt his classes. We didn't want rumors floating around the school that could damage his reputation if he had been wrongly accused. Seeing all the kids with their backpacks hurrying down the hall and chatting with friends, I questioned if they were safe. Did they have someone in their lives who could hurt them like someone had hurt Tinsley and Emmy?

We reached room 17, and Martina did a quick rap on the door before opening it, not waiting for a response. It looked just like I had remembered school rooms looked like. A man stood at the desk at the front of the classroom. Martina said, "Are you Warren Denver?"

"I am. You must be Ms. Monroe and Detective Hirsch."

We shook hands.

"Thank you for taking the time to speak with us today."

"Sure. Anything to help."

Unlike Arlo.

He pulled two plastic chairs from the side of the room and set them next to his teacher's desk. "Please have a seat." He took the teacher's chair and rolled over to face Martina and me. The smell of chalk dust sent me back to a younger, simpler time in my life. I'd always loved school, especially learning new things and getting to see my friends. Not all kids were that lucky. Like so many of the survivors and victims we had come across. I had grown up privileged, with excellent parents. Tinsley and Emmy's case was the first set of victims, in a long time, who I could relate to. Not that my life didn't have dark spots, but all-in-all I was fortunate.

Martina said, "We've met with Arlo and Jesse but would like to ask you about what life was like ten years ago. Were you really into the occult?"

Warren shook his head. "No, not at all. Looking back, it was so stupid. I even see kids now in my classes dress how we used to dress with their dark eyeliner and trench coats. Like them, we were just rebellious teens, and that's pretty much where it ended."

I said, "You had no affiliation with the occult or Satan worship?"

"No. Well, not really."

I cocked my head. "What do you mean, not really?"

"Well, I don't know if the other guys told you this, but it started out with Jesse trying to rebel against his parents. Jesse came up with the idea, but once we morphed into these personas, we took it a little further. At first, it was to make our image seem more believable. We visited a shop in Oakland to get some occult books and candles to pretend to do spells — that kind of thing."

"Any sacrifices?" Martina asked in a stern voice.

"No, nothing like that."

"Nothing with animals or insects?" Martina asked.

"No, I'm telling you, there were no sacrifices. There weren't even any pretend sacrifices. These were more like rituals. Like, you know, drawing a circle with salt and lighting candles out in the old..."

"The old what?"

Warren deflated. "At the old house where Tinsley and Emmy were killed."

Martina raised her brows. "So, you had been there before their murders?"

"Yeah, we all had. Before we were Goth, too. We'd go there to drink and smoke pot and fool around with girls. Teenage stuff."

"And you did rituals there?" I asked.

"A few times, we went there with the girls and lit some candles to spook them. Nothing serious."

"Which girls are you referring to?" I asked.

"Odie, Haisley, Lorelei, Skye, and Tinsley. I don't think Emmy ever went out there with us. That was basically the girl group we hung around with most. I mean, Jesse made his way through the group. You know what I mean."

I glanced at Martina and then back at Warren. "No. What do you mean?"

"Jesse started off with Haisley and Skye. Both were a one-time hook up, if you believed Jesse. And then he dated Odie for a while before Tinsley."

Jesse was a ladies' man?

"How long did Jesse date Odie?" Martina asked.

"I don't know, maybe a month or two."

"Pretty serious for high school, right?" she asked.

"I don't think Jesse took it seriously. But Odie was pretty pissed off when he dumped her for Tinsley."

"Like, what did Odie do to make you think she was upset about the breakup?" Martina asked.

"She started being mean to Tinsley. I think they had a few screaming matches where Odie called Tinsley a back stabber and bad friend before the rumors started. It basically broke up the friend group. Tinsley was essentially exiled from their little clique."

"Tinsley and Odie were no longer friends?"

"They stopped hanging out for a while, but they made up a little while after — shortly before the murders."

"Everybody was happy again before Tinsley and Emmy were killed?" I asked.

"Yeah, I mean, Odie even seemed fine that Jesse and Tinsley were still dating. She even invited them over for dinner at her house. Odie liked to hold dinner parties when her parents were out of town — they went out of town a lot."

"And what about Emmy? Did she get along with Odie?"

"Emmy got along fine. She was quiet, but I got the vibe she didn't like the rest of us."

"Why's that?"

"Emmy was smart and nice. The rest of the girls were, well, a clique of mean girls. I swear sometimes I see the kids around here, and I see those same popular girls doing the same stuff the girls did back then."

"So, then, overall, everything was fine between the friend group when the girls were killed?" I asked.

"Yeah. We were all devastated after what happened to Tinsley and Emmy. It made us really think, like, wow, that could happen to us, you know?"

"And where were you the night of the murders?" I asked.

"At a basketball game in Davis with Arlo and Jesse."

"Was that something you had planned?" Martina asked.

"No, it was a last-minute thing. We ended up getting tickets from some guys on the street."

"Did anybody see the three of you at the game?" she asked.

"I mean, there was a whole stadium of people. But it was just the three of us who went from our school as far as I know."

"Would you be willing to submit a DNA sample?"

"Sure."

Also, unlike Arlo.

"Anything else you can tell us about what happened back then or that night that could help us with the investigation?"

Warren stared out the window and said, "I don't know what happened to Tinsley and Emmy." He returned his focus to us. "My mom still goes out and puts flowers at the site. I personally can't go back there. Just thinking about what happened to them makes me queasy. If there's anything else I can do to help, let me know. If those people are still out there, they could hurt somebody else. I work with teenagers every day, and most of the mean ones are not that bad. Most the time, they're just scared, awkward kids, but some... some are rotten to the core."

Interesting.

"Do you like being a teacher?" Martina asked.

"I do. It's a tough job and a thankless one at that, but I like to think I might make a difference in at least one of their lives. I'm not foolish enough to think I can help all of them, but if I get through to one or two a year, I consider that a job well done."

Martina said, "Thank you for speaking with us today. If you think of anything else, call us."

We handed him our business cards before seeing ourselves out. Within the confines of our vehicle, I said, "Well?"

"Between the original three suspects, we have two do-gooders, Warren and Jesse, and then we have the lawyer, Arlo."

"What's that gut of yours saying?"

"It's saying they didn't do it, but I also think they're all hiding something."

"I got that, too."

"Hopefully, forensics will help us steer the direction of this investigation because we have found nothing new."

"Maybe the rest of the team's interviews will give us something."

"Let's hope. We need someone who knows what happened to start talking."

11

MARTINA

STARING AT THE MURDER BOARD, I DIDN'T LIKE THE direction the investigation was going. Hirsch strolled up. "What are you thinking?"

"It feels like we've made no progress. We spoke to the first original suspects, Jesse, Warren, and Arlo. Of those three, only two will talk to us and give us their DNA. The rest of the team has followed up with the four women who were the last ones to have seen the girls alive. Only two will talk to us. Don't you think that's strange?"

"I do."

"You think we should press harder on Lorelei and Haisley? They were the last people to have seen Tinsley and Emmy alive — that we know of. They have to talk to us, right?"

"Not if they don't want to. We can go to a judge to make them, but it's a little early for that. We should try to convince them on our own."

"Like a surprise visit?"

"Exactly."

Studying the school photos of Tinsley and Emmy with their angelic looks and smiles that said the world was theirs, I hoped we would find the truth, but my gut was telling me those not talking were the ones with the most to say. We needed to get through to them, but how? If we were lucky, advancements in forensic technology would break the case wide open.

A knock on the Squad Room door drew my attention to Hirsch. "Is that Brown?"

He went over to the door and opened it up. Sure enough, CSI Brown stood there, wearing his typical Warriors jersey and baseball cap on backwards. The only time I'd seen him in something different was at a crime scene where he wore coveralls. With him was a woman in her late thirties or early forties with dark hair pulled back into a tight bun. I said, "Hey, Brown, how's it going?"

"I'm doing great. And yourself?"

"Not too bad."

"This here's my associate, Dr. Katerina Dobbs. She's the head of our forensic science team. She works with lab rats," he said with a chuckle.

Katerina Dobbs stepped forward, shaking Hirsch's hand, and when I got closer, she shook mine. "You can call me Kiki."

Brown set a large banker's box down on the table and said, "It's a heck of a case. Kiki will go through what we have for evidence and the crime scene photos, as well as what testing was done and what else we can do that they couldn't ten years ago."

They impressed me. "Sounds great."

Kiki removed her shoulder bag and pulled out a laptop. "Is there somewhere I can plug in so I can project?"

Hirsch said, "I can help you with that."

As they set up electronics, I moved closer to the evidence box. I'd seen the crime scene photos and could only imagine what the evidence looked like. Brown was laying it out on the table. The whirl of the projector diverted our attention. Kiki said, "We're all set."

Seated, Kiki advanced to the first slide, and a shiver went down my spine. It was the chilling photo taken from above the crime scene. It showed the two girls lying side-by-side, staring out with inverted pentagrams carved into their chests, a ghoulish gray color to their skin, and blood everywhere. The most striking thing about the photo, other than the gore, was that the two girls were holding hands. Or I should say it looked like Tinsley had reached out and held on to Emmy's. Averting my eyes, I focused on my breathing. A third look at the photos didn't make it easier.

Kiki said, "You both have seen the crime scene photos, right?"

I said, "We have — a few times."

Kiki nodded. "Okay, I've gone through and reviewed the autopsy report, and the evidence catalog, and all the testing that was done on the girls. Emmy, the one lying on the left, was killed first. Cause of death, blunt force trauma."

"Do you know what type of object she was struck with?" Hirsch asked.

"The original ME's notes indicate something long and metal, like a tire iron or a pipe."

"Was it retrieved at the scene?" I asked.

"No."

"What about the other marks?" I asked.

"The knife wounds in her upper thoracic region were inflicted postmortem, as was the carving of the symbol on the lower abdomen. It appears that her dress was slit down the front and just peeled open to inflict the postmortem wounds."

"Was she sexually assaulted?" Hirsch asked.

Kiki shook her head. "Emmy was not sexually assaulted. At least, there was no sign of it."

"Was the weapon that did the carvings and the stabbings recovered?" Hirsch asked.

"No, neither the blunt object nor the knife was retrieved."

They had never found the murder weapons. Maybe if we could find them, we could finally connect them to whoever did this horrific crime.

"Time of death?"

"Time of death was approximately sometime between 10 PM and 2 AM. Emmy died first, approximately thirty minutes before Tinsley."

Which gave the perpetrator plenty of time to torture Tinsley.

Kiki continued, "Tinsley's death wasn't quick. I know you read the reports, but let's just go through it."

All three of us nodded.

"Tinsley was also struck, likely with the same object. It didn't kill her, but it likely knocked her out or at the very least incapacitated her. That was when the killers really started in on her. She was still alive for the sexual assault."

"Any semen or hairs recovered?" Hirsch asked.

"They did swabs, but there was no semen present or any hairs that didn't belong to Tinsley."

It wouldn't be a slam dunk without semen, hair, or DNA.

"We believe that after the sexual assault, a knife severed Tinsley's carotid artery. It was the fatal wound. The report shows she wouldn't have survived much longer, but I assume the killer or killers wanted to finish her off before inflicting the chest wounds and the symbol. As you can see, Tinsley's dress was also slashed but all the way down the front. It's kinda hard to see in the photographs because they're drenched in blood, but it's framing her upper body."

It was one thing to read the description of how the girls died, but to hear it out loud was something different. It was almost like a walk-through of the last moments in their lives. *Brutal, savage, heartless.*

"What kind of testing was done?" I asked.

"Full toxicology. Both girls came back negative for alcohol, illicit drugs, or marijuana at the time they died. They were fully sober, not under the influence of any drugs."

"Any fingerprints, blood, or other sources of DNA recovered?"

"We didn't recover any fingerprints from the scene. However, the original team collected the dresses that both of the girls wore and the undergarments. They also found some additional fluids near the scene."

"Additional fluids?" Hirsch asked.

Kiki continued. "It was recovered just outside the house. It appears to be vomit — human. All we can say about it right now is what the person ate before they vomited."

"What did they eat?" Hirsch asked.

"French fries."

Not exactly unique.

Kiki's eyes widened, and she turned off the projector. "Now, Brown and I are going to go over what we think we can do with the evidence." She turned off the projector and walked over to the evidence displayed on the conference table.

Hirsch and I followed.

Gloved up, Brown lifted the top off the banker's box and laid out the evidence bags containing all the things collected at the scene.

The crumpled dresses were covered in dark brown blood. Jewelry, presumably from the girls, and fingernail clippings. "Where are the fluids you found at the scene?" I asked.

Kiki said, "Those are in the lab. They're stored frozen to preserve them. We also have blood samples that were removed from both of the girls and soil from the walls inside of the house."

"Any shoe impressions?" Hirsch asked.

"There weren't any retrievable shoe prints. Whoever did this, took the time to smear the path in and out of the crime scene erasing any tread patterns," Brown explained.

Clever.

Looking down at all the items, Brown pointed at the girls' clothes. "Kiki and I were talking. We both agree it would be good to retest all the garments for DNA. We might find if there were other contributors besides Emmy and Tinsley. Second, we want to test the vomit for DNA, as well as retest the rape kit for semen or any other biological fluids that might lead us to a perpetrator."

"Are there drawings or mockups of what the weapons would look like?"

Brown said, "Yes, I have them in my notes. Like Kiki said, it's most likely a tire iron and a four-inch knife."

I glanced over at Hirsch and back at the evidence bags. "What about the fingernails?"

Kiki said, "We'll definitely test the fingernail clippings again to see if we can get any DNA from underneath them. Tinsley had bruising on her arms — likely defensive wounds."

In my mind, I was cataloguing the possible forensic evidence to come back on the case. Blood, vomit, fingernails. Considering our witnesses weren't being very cooperative, having some physical evidence sure would be a help to the case. Looking at Brown and Kiki, I wanted to ask a question I would probably ask Dr. Scribner, the medical examiner, later, too. "If you had to guess the motive of the killer or killers, what would you say it was?"

Brown shrugged. "Despite the inverted pentagram carved on both of the girls, I don't buy that it was a satanic ritual."

Hirsch asked, "Why not?"

"Because it seemed like Tinsley was the target. How these attacks were done, it was as if the carving was an afterthought, not the main purpose. They found no candles at the scene and other than the writing on the wall, 'Satan lives' and the inverted pentagram, nothing else indicates it was a satanic ritual. Although to be honest, I'm really not an expert, but based on the crime scenes I've investigated, looks like Tinsley was the target. And maybe Emmy just happened to be there, and they needed her out of the picture."

Kiki said, "I agree with Brown. I've never seen crime scene photos of a satanic ritual, but it seemed like an afterthought."

Hirsch said, "Unless it was the perp's first time doing a ritual?"

Both Brown and Kiki nodded. "That's true. Usually, newbies are more hesitant. You ought to check records for similar crimes in the area. If this was their first kill, they may have killed again."

Vincent was already running down other similar crimes in the area — anything that had a satanic or occult connection.

Brown said, "Has Dr. Scribner given her take on the original ME's report?"

"Not yet. I figure after we get some forensics back, we'll sit down with her and review the original findings to see if they're solid or if they missed something."

Brown said, "Good idea."

After we chatted a bit with Kiki and CSI Brown about additional theories and our forensics pals left, Hirsch walked over to the murder board and said, "I sure would like to find those murder weapons."

"Me too. Are you ready to head over to Skye's house for the interview?"

It would be our first interview with one of the mean girls. Did she know why the others wouldn't talk to us? If she did, would she tell us?

12

MARTINA

Following Hirsch's directions, I exited the freeway and headed toward Skye Peters' parents' home. According to our conversation on the phone, Skye was living there and had been since high school. She didn't seem eager to speak with us; she seemed more sad than anything. When she spoke the girls' names, her voice shook, and by the end of the conversation, she was in tears. She clearly had taken her friends' deaths very hard.

Winding down Skye's street, my mouth dropped open. "Hirsch, is that the house?"

"I can't see the address from here. Get closer."

I continued driving slowly toward the house, surrounded by police cars and an ambulance. Hirsch read off the address from his notes. It matched the numbers on the curb in front of the house. After parking, Hirsch and I jogged toward the home. A few police officers were outside. They approached us and said, "I'm sorry, you can't be here now. There's been an incident."

Hirsch pulled out his badge. "Detective Hirsch with the CoCo County Sheriff's Department. We had an appointment with somebody who lives in this house."

"Who?" the officer asked.

"Skye Peters."

The officer shook his head. "Her mother just called us — possible suicide."

Hirsch and I exchanged glances. "Is she alive?"

"Paramedics are in there now. But from the sounds of the 9-1-1 call, I don't think so." Before the officer could finish his thought, the paramedics were rolling out a gurney with a zipped-up body bag on top. Behind them was an older woman with a younger woman, holding on to one another as they stared off as if in disbelief.

"Can we talk to the family?" Hirsch asked the officer.

"If they'll talk."

"Hirsch, let's go talk to them."

Hirsch tipped his head to the officer and said, "Thanks."

We trudged across the lawn to avoid the paramedics with the gurney carrying Skye Peters' deceased body and approached the women. "Are you Mrs. Peters?" I asked.

"Yes."

"Hi, I'm Martina Monroe, and this is my partner, Detective Hirsch. We had an appointment with your daughter, Skye, today."

She nodded slowly. "You're investigating Tinsley and Emmy's murder."

"That's right."

She shook her head sadly before asking the officer next to her, "Do you still need us?"

"No, ma'am. Again, I'm sorry for your loss."

She turned to face me. "Are you a mother?"

I said, "I am."

"Boy or girl?"

"I have a ten-year-old daughter."

"You know, they never stop being your baby."

Oh, I knew. "I'm sorry for your loss."

Hirsch repeated the sentiment.

Mrs. Peters said, "This is my daughter, Paula."

To the daughter, I said, "I'm sorry for your loss."

She simply nodded without a word. Mrs. Peters said, "If you'd like, I can tell you what I know."

I said, "As long as you're up for it."

Mrs. Peters said, "Come inside. I can't be out here anymore."

Without another word, Mrs. Peters and her daughter retreated into the home. Hirsch and I gave the officers a shrug and followed the women inside. Mrs. Peters moved slowly, as if on autopilot. "Please have a seat."

We settled on the sofa. She and her daughter sat next to each other. Mrs. Peters still had her arm around Paula. She unwrapped herself and clasped her hands in her lap. "Skye was never the same after Tinsley and Emmy's deaths."

"How so?" I asked.

"She'd always been a happy girl. Bright. Smart. But after the deaths, it was like her light dimmed. She'd once been so ambitious. When she started having nightmares, we took her to a psychiatrist. They put her on medication for depression and anxiety. She was never the same after that. She decided not to go to college. Instead, she stayed home with us and worked at a coffee shop in town. The last ten years have been a real struggle for Skye."

"Was this her first attempt at suicide?" I asked.

"No. Her first attempt was the anniversary of the girls' death. It was like Skye had been thrown into the abyss and was always fighting just to make it through the day. I didn't know how to help her. I couldn't help her. I tried everything. It wasn't enough," she said before looking away.

Hirsch and I sat quietly as the grieving mother wept, and her daughter wrapped her arms around her. Paula said, "It's not your fault, Mom. You did everything you could. It was all just too much for her."

Mrs. Peters wiped her eyes and looked up at us. "She told me she felt guilty. She said they should've made sure the girls made it to their car. That guilt ate her up until there was nothing left. Not to take away from Tinsley and Emmy's grieving parents, but I felt like when we lost them, we lost Skye, too."

Death affected everyone differently. Survivor's guilt could be brutal. I knew that firsthand.

"Did she mention we were coming to talk to her today?" Why had Skye agreed to meet with us if she was planning to end her life?

"She did. She said it was time."

"Time for what?" I asked.

"She didn't elaborate. It's so funny too..." Mrs. Peters trailed off.

"What is?" Hirsch asked.

"She hadn't talked to Odie, Lorelei, or Haisley since high school, but Odie called earlier today, and I thought Skye would be so happy. She and Odie were so close in high school and growing up. But after the call, Skye simply retreated to her room and didn't come out again. Have you spoken with Odie yet?"

"We have an appointment with her tomorrow."

Mrs. Peters nodded. "Maybe Odie will be able to help with the investigation. She and Tinsley were neighbors and friends since they were small."

Hirsch said, "Sounds like the girls were close."

"Oh, yes, they were. Thick as thieves. All of them were smart, pretty, and popular. They had a lot in common. It was such a tragedy," she said before staring off into the distance.

"Is there anything else you can tell us that might help with our investigation?" I asked.

Both women shook their heads sadly.

"We appreciate you talking with us today. It means a lot. Again, I'm sorry for your loss."

With that, we left our business cards and said our goodbyes. The paramedics were gone, as were most of the police cars. One of the two officers who had been inside the house with the Peters' said, "Hey."

"How are they doing in there?" the older officer asked.

"She's a grieving mother. She's devastated, but somehow, it seems like she isn't terribly surprised."

"That's what she told us. Her daughter had made several attempts before. But she could also just be in shock."

Hirsch said, "True."

"What did you talk to them about?" the younger officer asked.

"We had an appointment to talk with Skye about the Twin Satan Murders."

"Was she a witness?"

"Yes, Skye was one of four girls last to see Tinsley and Emmy alive."

"Oh, shoot. How is the investigation going?"

I said, "We haven't had too many cooperating witnesses yet."

The officer smirked and said, "Yeah, and one of them just turned up dead."

My heart nearly stopped. He was right. Half of the witnesses wouldn't cooperate, and one had taken her own life. Had the investigation triggered her depression and ideation of death? Or was it something more than that?

13
___

HIRSCH

With a dwindling pool of witnesses willing to talk to us, I was happy to hear from the law firm receptionist that Odie Johnson was alive and well and in her office. The investigation couldn't take any more hits.

My experience told me somebody knew what happened to Emmy and Tinsley, and we needed to find them and get them talking. Would that person be Odie? We also needed to find the murder weapons. Surely, there was a reason the killer did not leave them at the scene. Likely, it was because they would point toward the perpetrators of the crime. It was common for assailants to cut themselves while slashing a victim. Blood is sticky and slippery, making it easy for a person's hand to slip and then cut themselves on the knife, leaving DNA at the crime scene. A lot of killers are pumped full of adrenaline and don't realize they've cut themselves until it's too late, like when they have a new pair of silver handcuffs around their wrists.

Odie Johnson was one of four witnesses to have last seen the girls alive, and the last one of those willing to talk to us. I hoped she could provide insight into what happened that night. In agreement with Brown and Kiki, I believed Tinsley was likely the target based on the brutality inflicted upon her. If she was, in fact, the target, maybe the killing had nothing to do with ritual sacrifice. Or had the killer or killers targeted her for the satanic ritual?

These murders were too incomprehensible to not be solved. There were certainly people out there capable of these types of acts, but there weren't a lot. Vincent and team were in the process of pulling files for similar crimes that occurred in the area near the time of Emmy and Tinsley's murders. We had to find the ones who were capable of the deed and figure out which of those could have gotten to the girls.

A woman with long, flowing, blonde hair and red, pouty lips, wearing a power suit, approached us. "Detective Hirsch?"

"That's right. And you're Odessa Johnson."

With a flirty smile, she said, "Yes, call me Odie." Turning to Martina, she said, "And you must be Martina Monroe?"

Martina nodded apprehensively and shook Odie's hand.

Odie said, "Follow me. We can talk in my office."

We followed behind the stylish and curvy woman. She was beautiful in an icy sort of way. She didn't give off warm fuzzies like Kim. Odie was shrewd, and you could tell she was tough. You could argue she was perfectly suited for her profession as a corporate lawyer.

Despite the high-rise building and fancy lobby, Odie Johnson's office was rather small. She was only a few years out of law school which probably explained the lack of the corner office or floor-to-ceiling windows overlooking San Francisco. We sat and handed her our business cards.

"So, you're reopening Tinsley and Emmy's case?" Odie asked casually.

"Yes, the sheriff himself asked us to solve the crime. According to the records, you and three of your friends were the last to see Tinsley and Emmy. Can you tell us more about that night?"

She nodded earnestly. "It's so tragic. It's hard to even think about, but I remember it like it was yesterday. We were downtown, just hanging out like we always did, and I spotted Tinsley and Emmy. I waved them over to my car and asked if they wanted to hang out. Tinsley wanted to, but I could tell Emmy was hesitant. I guess they already had plans to go watch a movie or something. I don't know, but she finally gave in to Tinsley, and they hopped in the car, and we went for a drive down to one of our old stomping grounds from when we were kids."

Martina looked slightly puzzled. "And where was that?"

Odie said, "The playground at our elementary school. It was where we hung out. Most of us met in pre-k so we liked to hang out at the school — after hours, of course. Anyhow, we were at the playground that night just goofing off and being silly teenagers."

Martina jumped in quickly. "What cut the night short? Your original statement said you dropped Tinsley and Emmy off around ten?"

"Yeah, so we hung out and talked. And yes, there may have been some alcohol being passed around, but Emmy wanted to go. I guess they had rented some movies, and they had bought some junk food specially for the occasion. So, I said okay. We said our goodbyes, and then I dropped them off in the parking lot." Her cheerful demeanor softened. "And we never saw them again," she said wistfully.

"What did you do after you dropped off Emmy and Tinsley in the parking lot?" Martina asked.

"We went back to my house. Tinsley had given us the idea of watching a movie. Since my parents were out of town, we went home, watched a movie, and broke into my parents' liquor cabinet. After a while, we all passed out in my living room."

"All four of you were together the rest of the night?" I asked.

"That's right."

"Do you still keep in contact with Skye, Lorelei, and Haisley?"

"I talk to Lorelei sometimes, and Haisley, but Skye took Tinsley and Emmy's death really hard. I mean, we were all devastated. After all, if it could happen to them, it could happen to us, too, you know what I mean?"

Like you didn't care about them, but you cared about yourself? I glanced over at Martina, who seemed fascinated by Odie and was intently watching her body language.

"You knew Tinsley for a long time. Can you tell us about your relationship?" Martina asked.

"Sure. Like I said, we lived next door to each other. Our parents still live next door to each other. We used to play when we were little. We even shared a nanny for a while, and then we went to elementary school together and junior high and high school."

That was their resume, not their relationship. "Would you say the two of you were good friends?" I asked.

"Yes, of course. We were close. We hung out a lot. She was practically like a sister to me."

"What about Emmy?" Martina asked.

"She was more Tinsley's friend. They met in ballet. Emmy was really into sports and that kind of thing. Not my cup of tea. We weren't close."

"How long have you been working here at the law firm?" I asked.

"Two years. I was lucky they hired me right out of law school."

I said, "Your parents must be very proud of you."

Odessa stiffened. "Yes."

"Back to the last night you saw Emmy and Tinsley. Do you

remember anything out of the ordinary? Did you see any strange cars or people who didn't really fit in with the neighborhood?"

Odie's eyes grew large, and her mouth dropped open. "Oh, my gosh, yes. I thought it was in the police report? But yeah, like, right after we dropped off Tinsley and Emmy, I was turning the corner out of the parking lot, and I saw these strange guys in a dark car that was all banged up on the side. The men had dark skin, probably African American. They didn't look like anyone I knew from our neighborhood. I assumed they were from Oakland and had gotten lost or something. Oakland is just through the tunnel, not five minutes away. Anyway, they seemed kinda sketchy and out of place."

Interesting observation. I didn't recall reading that detail in the witness statements. "Do you have any idea what happened to Tinsley and Emmy?"

"I don't know for sure, but what I think could have happened is that those guys from Oakland saw them and just took them and did terrible things to them. Who else could have done it? Everyone knows everyone around here. I can't imagine it was someone from our town. Later, I felt so guilty leaving them in the parking lot, but the car wasn't that far away. I assumed they would be fine."

As broken up as Odie sounded, I wasn't picking up that she was exactly devastated by the loss of her friends. "We've re-interviewed some witnesses, and it sounds like before Tinsley died, you had a bit of a falling out with her."

"Oh, that was a momentary blip. We totally made up."

"And what was the falling out over?" Martina asked.

We both knew the answer. We were testing Odie. "Well, I'd been dating Jesse, and I had caught Tinsley and him flirting on multiple occasions. Eventually, I dumped Jesse and told Tinsley it wasn't cool that she flirted with my boyfriend. After all, Jesse was just some basic guy. I didn't think she'd actually date him. But she did, and I was hurt by it. After a while, we made up, and I was cool with them dating. It wasn't that big of a deal."

Interesting. "You weren't upset that Tinsley and Jesse were dating?"

"At first, you know, but I got over it pretty quick. I mean, guys like Jesse are a dime a dozen. I moved on after him."

"When did you make up with Tinsley?"

"A couple of weeks later. We realized our feud was stupid. We'd been friends our whole lives and didn't want to stop being friends because of some stupid guy. I mean, please. It wasn't worth our lifelong friendship, you know?"

I nodded. "I do." Although I wasn't sure I did. Trying to understand the inner workings of a teenage girl's mind was outside my depth.

"Anything else you can tell us about that night that might help us find out what happened to Tinsley and Emmy?" Martina asked.

"Nothing other than the sketchy guys I told you about."

"Well, we really appreciate you speaking with us today."

"Oh, yeah, sure. Of course. My heart still breaks over Tinsley and Emmy. They were such beautiful girls with beautiful souls."

Martina and I exchanged glances. We weren't sure if she'd heard about Skye's death yet. "When was the last time you spoke with Skye?" I asked.

Odie raised her perfectly teased brows. "I just talked to her yesterday. Actually, when you called me to make an appointment to talk about the case, I thought I'd call her and see how she's doing. It's been years."

"And you spoke with her?" I asked.

"I did."

"What did you talk about?"

"How she was doing and what I've been up to. Like I said, she took the deaths so hard, and I wanted to make sure she was okay — since the investigation was sure to bring up a lot of old feelings."

"How did she seem to you?" Martina asked.

"She seemed okay. Good, actually, as if she'd turned over a new leaf or something. I was thrilled to hear it."

"Really?" Martina asked with skepticism.

"Yeah."

Martina said, "Skye took her own life yesterday."

Odie gasped. "You're kidding?"

I said, "No. I'm sorry for your loss."

She slipped her hand over her mouth and shook her head. Odie swiveled around and plucked tissues from the box atop her desk. She dabbed at the corners of her eyes. "That's so terrible. I hope her mother is okay. You know, her father passed just last year. That poor family. I'm glad I could talk to her one last time."

"Indeed. Thank you for your time today."

She kept her head down, seeming sad, as we let ourselves out and headed back down to the parking garage. "What did you think of her?"

Martina said, "She didn't seem all that broken up to me, but then again, everybody grieves differently."

That was true. "You think she knows more than she told us?"

"Without a doubt."

It was exactly what I had been thinking.

14

MARTINA

Seated in a conference room at the station, Tinsley and Emmy's parents joined Detective Hirsch and me. We'd already passed the polite chitchat about the weather and whether anybody needed a beverage or bathroom break. It was time to get down to business. Hirsch and I were both fairly certain somebody from the community knew what had happened to the girls. They just weren't talking to us. I said, "Mr. and Mrs. Olson, Mr. and Mrs. Reed, thank you for coming down to speak with us today."

"No problem. Have there been any new developments?" Mrs. Reed asked.

I shook my head. "Not necessarily specific to the case, but I'm not sure if you've heard, Skye Peters took her own life two days ago."

The families whispered amongst themselves before returning their attention to us. "Do you believe Skye's death is related to the case?" Mrs. Olson asked.

Hirsch said, "We find the timing rather peculiar, considering we had an appointment with Skye to discuss what she remembered about the night the girls were killed. But when we arrived at the home, she had just overdosed on some prescription pills, not twenty minutes before we arrived. They were wheeling her out of the house in a body bag when we pulled up."

I added, "When we spoke to Skye on the phone, she seemed to want to talk to us — to tell her story once and for all, as she put it. And although the timing itself may not be significant, the fact that we haven't been able to get three of the witnesses to talk to us makes it a little strange. We're running out of witnesses. Lorelei and Haisley both refuse to give interviews. Arlo has also chosen not to speak to us other than to proclaim his innocence and say he had an alibi with the other boys that night."

Emmy's father shook his head. "They have to know something, right? I always knew they weren't telling the truth."

Mrs. Olson frowned at her husband. "Bob."

"It's true. And this whole business that they saw nothing, and they know nothing, and that it was probably some strangers that came and did this is absurd. Those stupid boys with their dark clothes and their candles and their Satan. They did this to Emmy and Tinsley."

I didn't agree with Mr. Olson's assessment completely. But I believed they all knew more than they were letting on. I said, "The reason we invited you down here today was to ask you more about the relationship between Tinsley and Emmy and their friend group, Odie, Skye, Haisley, Lorelei, and the boys, Arlo, Warren, and Jesse. From the three who would talk to us, which are Jesse, Warren, and Odie, they seemed like a tight group. They all knew each other, hung out with each other. Most since they were small children. What can you tell us about the group?"

Tinsley's mother, Mary, said, "Odie lived next door to us. We're friends with her parents. It's unimaginable to think that any of them had anything to do with this, but they were teenagers, and teenagers do stupid things. It's possible they saw something or knew something and just didn't realize how important it is. To your original question, they were close. It would seem like you always knew where the others were because they were always together. If we didn't know where Tinsley was, we'd call over to Emmy's, and if she wasn't with Emmy, she was probably with Odie, Lorelei, Skye, and Haisley or when she started dating Jesse, with him. I don't know. Maybe they're scared to say what they know?"

Sipping on my coffee, I contemplated the explanation. Maybe. Was there a huge missing piece of the puzzle that we hadn't found yet? "We heard there was a bit of a falling out between Odie and Tinsley because of Jesse."

Tinsley's mother said, "She didn't talk to us about it, but we were surprised when she started dating Jesse since we knew he'd been dating Odie. I remember asking Tinsley about it, and Tinsley just said that Odie didn't care. And that she and Odie had made up about it."

Hirsch asked, "Were you concerned before Tinsley and Emmy's murders about the group? Or the boys who wore all black?"

Tinsley's mother said, "We didn't take it seriously. Underneath the clothes and the makeup and the trips to the Church of Satan in San Jose, they were just the same kids they'd always been. And they all had plans to attend college in the fall. When Jesse was accepted into UCLA, we figured it was a phase. As you know, all three boys are quite successful today, and, for the record, Bob, I don't think they had anything to do with this."

Bob Olson turned red. "You don't know that for sure. You don't know!"

"We've known Jesse since he was a baby. Sure, he was a hormonal teenage boy and a little rebellious, but he had a good heart and would've never done that to Tinsley and Emmy or anyone. He's a doctor now, for crying out loud."

I hadn't realized the parents weren't in agreement about what they thought had happened to their children. Clearly, Emmy's father blamed the boys. Maybe that's why they were the prime suspects, considering there wasn't any physical evidence and not a motive either, other than a slight interest in satanism.

Bob said, "I don't care. I think those boys are trouble."

Mrs. Reed shook her head. "It's nothing more than satanic panic. Can we focus on finding the real killers, please?"

Hirsch said, "Let's try to keep this calm and productive. It won't help the investigation if we have fighting between the families."

Both sides quieted down.

I said, "The reason we wanted to know more about the friend group was because we really need them to talk to us. From what you've said and from what other witnesses have said, they were a close group. That is why I have found it so surprising that half of them wouldn't talk to us about Tinsley and Emmy. You mentioned that you're friends with all the families and the parents."

Mrs. Reed said in a stern tone, "Consider it done."

Puzzled by her declaration, I asked, "What is done?"

"I'll speak to the parents and make sure their children talk to you. They need to give you all the information they have about our girls. It's unacceptable that they won't cooperate. At least Odie, Jesse, and Warren had the sense to talk. I can't understand why the others wouldn't. I'll make a few calls. We have been friends for years, and I know they won't want it to get out that their families won't help the investigation."

"We appreciate that." I began to understand the full power the Reeds and Olsons held over the community. The fact that they could pressure the parents to make sure their adult children agreed to interviews with us was quite something. It also aligned with the sheriff's desire to close the case so that he would have the Reeds and Olsons supporting his campaign. They clearly had a lot of sway in the community.

The only remaining question was, would that influence work to get Lorelei, Haisley, and Arlo to talk? An even bigger question was, why had they refused to talk before?

15

TINSLEY

OUR EYES MET, AND WE RUSHED TOWARD ONE ANOTHER. Emmy grabbed my hand and pulled me behind the gym. "So, what happened?"

"He told me he and Odie broke up and that he wants to go out with me," I said, with butterflies still fluttering around in my stomach.

"So, you really, really like him?" Emmy asked.

"I do. He's, like, I don't know... It's one of those things where I never really saw him that way. But then, this year, it's like, wow, Jesse is so hot."

Emmy nodded. "Are you going to go out with him?"

"I want to. I mean, I will. He asked me to go to the movies this Friday night."

"How are you going to break it to Odie?"

"I don't know. I don't think she'll care that much, right?"

Emmy's eyes bugged out. "Are you kidding? She's going to go ballistic."

"No, I think she'll be fine. She's just dramatic. At first, maybe she'll be miffed and be all 'I can't believe you're dating my ex,' but it will blow over. I'm not worried about it."

Emmy said, "If you say so."

"I say so. Odie will get over it. Plus, Jesse said it has been over between them for a while."

"What does that even mean?" Emmy asked.

"He said that he liked her at first, but then she just wasn't what he wanted. He said they barely even hang out anymore."

"And you believe him?"

"Of course I believe him." Believe him? I wanted to believe him. After all, he just broke up with Odie so he could date me. That had to mean he liked me a lot, right? Maybe he and I were actually meant to be? Although the timing wasn't great. School was almost out, and he was going off to UCLA, and I had another year before I was finished up with high school. I guessed that was the problem with dating older boys. If we got serious, we could do long distance. With love, you couldn't let anything get in your way, right? I was sure Odie would get over it. Odie wasn't exactly hard up for a date. She was smart and gorgeous and could have any guy she wanted. Unless she still wanted Jesse.

Odie had always acted like she was in complete control of her boyfriends — like she got off on it — and said they were lucky to be with her. But I couldn't ignore that Odie had talked about attending UCLA shortly after Jesse received his acceptance. Maybe she really did like him?

Something ominous stirred inside of me.

Maybe dating Jesse wasn't the best idea? Shirking off the thoughts, I told myself it would be fine. Odie would understand. We had been friends forever, and what they said was true, right? All's fair in love and war.

_____

16

HIRSCH

After Martina and I shuffled the Reeds and Olsons out of the station, we headed back to the Cold Case Squad Room and planted ourselves in front of the murder board. Martina gazed at it and said, "Do you recall reading or hearing anyone say that the boys attended the Church of Satan?"

"Nope."

"Do you think Mr. Olson was making it up or just assuming?"

I had a feeling he hadn't made it up. "There was something definitive about his statement, as if maybe he knew it, but the others dismissed it."

"We should talk to Jesse and Warren again."

Agreed. "I'd like to hear why they didn't tell us that piece of information. They all said they wore black clothes and lit candles every once in a while and thought it was interesting but didn't say they attended church. Seems like quite the omission. Do you know anything about the Church of Satan in San Jose?"

Martina shrugged. "No. I didn't even know it existed."

We both quieted down at the sound of the door opening.

Vincent stepped through and stopped. "Sorry, do you need the room?"

I said, "No, it's fine. You can come in. Actually, do you know anything about the Church of Satan in San Jose?"

"No, but I can find out." Vincent sat down and flipped open the lid of his laptop and got to work.

I said, "While he's doing that, I'll give our friend Jesse a call."

"I'll call Warren," Martina offered.

Positioning myself at the other end of the Cold Case Squad Room, I dialed Jesse's number.

Thankfully, he answered right away. "Hello."

"Hi, Jesse, this is Detective Hirsch. Do you have a minute?"

"Sure."

"I just got some information that I was surprised to hear. Is it true you're a member of the Church of Satan?" I asked while watching Martina across the room, speaking into her phone.

He said, "Warren, Arlo, and I went a few times. One time, we thought it would be cool if we signed up. We did and got the shiny membership card. Honestly, we weren't even a first degree."

Why hadn't he mentioned it before? What else were they hiding? "What does that mean you weren't even a first degree?"

"The Church of Satan has a hierarchy. Just being registered doesn't make you active or have a role like a warlock or priest or anything like that. Like I said, we just went a few times."

"Is there a reason you didn't tell us about that when we asked you about your past?"

"Not really. I mean, the Church of Satan isn't really what you think it is."

"No?"

"Look, it's been a long time, and I don't remember exactly all of their theories and practices, but basically, they're just anti-Christian, anti-conformist, anti-...you know, being part of the herd. They were certainly not into human sacrifice or animal sacrifice or any type of sacrifice."

"Anything else you want to tell us about this Church of Satan or your Satan worshiping back in the day?" I asked, a little more than annoyed.

"It wasn't Satan worship. Look it up. They have a website — it's how we found it. I was a teenager, a rebel, and, you know, the Church of Satan just spoke to me. I remember one sin in the Church of Satan is stupidity, followed by pretentiousness. It was everything me and the guys were against since everything in our lives was just that — pretentious, fancy cars, houses, vacations, country clubs. Like I told you before, it was a teenage rebellion."

"And this church has nothing to do with worshiping Satan?" I asked, not quite believing him.

"Not at all. There isn't any worship involved. It's more like following the principles of this guy who wrote a book about it. I think his name was Anton LaVey. He wrote a book called the *Satanic Bible*. If I remember correctly, the church was started back in the 1960s. It's a little fuzzy now since it's been ten years, but the top qualities of the church were pride, liberty, and individualism. For a bunch of rebellious teenagers, it was a good fit."

Was that true? Vincent's research would tell us soon enough. "Anything else you want to tell me about this?"

"That's really it. None of us were into any kind of violent things. It's not who we are...or were."

"Thanks for your time, Jesse."

"No problem."

He knew he should've told us about it, especially considering he was saying this relatively innocent organization didn't take part in any kind of violence or condone any of it. It was strange they hadn't mentioned it before. Martina was still on the phone, presumably with Warren. I walked over and sat next to

Vincent. Leaning over, I spied his screen had the Church of Satan's website up. "What does it say?"

"It's interesting," Vincent said.

Not what I had expected.

Vincent continued, "It says they don't actually worship Satan. And Wikipedia says basically Anton LaVey formed the entire Church of Satan after he released his book, *The Satanic Bible*. He started the church in San Francisco in 1966. LaVey stood as the church's high priest until his death in 1997. There's a new priest who moved his headquarters to New York. The theology doesn't believe in any kind of worship or belief in a supernatural Satan. Rather, they describe themselves as skeptical atheists and use the word Satan as a symbol because the Hebrew root of the word is opposer or one who questions. It's interesting, but to be honest, Hirsch, I kind of agree with a lot of what they're saying."

"You do?" I asked.

Vincent nodded. "Yeah. To them, 'Satan' really just represents pride, liberty, and individualism and qualities that are often defined as 'evil' by those who worship a Christian God. And even here, in their theory and practices, their statements basically say 'Satan' represents indulgence instead of abstinence. Viral existence instead of spiritual pipe dreams. Undefiled wisdom instead of hypocritical self-deceit. Vengeance instead of turning the other cheek. Responsibility to the responsible instead of concern for psychic vampires. I don't quite get that one. Satan represents man as just another animal, sometimes better, more often worse than those who walk on all fours."

I harrumphed. "Basically, you're saying the Church of Satan believes that dogs are better than humans?"

"Kind of. And the best part is the top nine sins. Stupidity, pretentiousness, solipsism, self-deceit, herd conformity, lack of perspective, forgetfulness of past orthodoxies, counterproductive pride... you get the picture. It's accepting of all people as long as they're not stupid and pretentious and that kind of thing."

"Any possibility it's a front for something more violent or dark?"

"I haven't found anything that indicates that. It's kind of amusing. It almost seems like it's a joke, but it's not."

"Perfect for a bunch of teenagers who want to rebel from their wealthy life?"

Vincent leaned back in his chair. "Yeah, kinda."

Martina walked toward us. "Well, that was interesting."

"How so?" I asked.

"Warren said he registered as a member of the Church of Satan. But he said it was basically just like a bunch of atheists, and they only went twice. They don't worship Satan or anything like that."

"Did Warren say why he never mentioned it to us?" I asked.

"He said he didn't want us to have the wrong idea about them. Because it really was just about rebelling against their life."

"Jesse said the same thing."

Vincent said, "And I was just telling Hirsch the Church of Satan is basically a bunch of atheists who don't believe in herd mentality. Basically, a group of people who question the status quo. They don't believe in a spiritual deity like a Christian God or a physical manifestation of Satan. Therefore, no animal or human sacrifices are included in their doctrine."

I was an atheist, but I knew Martina wasn't. She believed in God and the church, so I wondered what she thought about all this Satan stuff. Did she believe the murders of Tinsley and Emmy were the result of some Satan worshipers sacrificing the girls to appease Satan?

"What do you think, Martina?" I asked.

"Interesting. Honestly, I didn't even know they existed."

Vincent said, "The Church of Satan is all over California, especially in the Bay Area. It started in San Francisco."

"Really?" Martina asked.

Vincent said, "Yep."

"That explains why the boys were targeted. Unless you investigated the Church of Satan yourself, you would assume they were what you see on the TV — bloodthirsty, murdering evil-doers killing people in the name of Satan."

"It still doesn't make sense that they didn't tell us. If they withheld that, what else are they withholding?"

Martina said, "I agree. Strange behaviors from the witnesses in this case. It definitely makes me think they know more than they have told us so far."

"Yep. Vincent, has your team found other ritualistic murders from the same area and time frame yet?"

"We got a few hits from Oakland. I'm having my team compile copies of the different case files. Also, once we get those together, we'll probably want to meet with OPD to go over the case to determine if there're any similarities. For a couple of them, the officers who conducted the original investigations are still on the force."

I said, "Excellent. Let us know as soon as we get those files ready."

"Great, more ritualistic murders for us to look at," Martina said with a wince.

"Seriously."

I wasn't looking forward to reviewing any more gruesome crime scene photos either, but if it moved us closer to finding who killed Tinsley and Emmy, it would be worth it.

17

MARTINA

Refreshed and relaxed, I strolled into the lobby of the CoCo County Sheriff's Department feeling ready to get back to the case. Weekends off were nice. It allowed me to spend more time with Zoey and Barney, our spirited ball of fluff. Mom wasn't around as much since she and Ted — or as we in the office called him, Sarge — had been in a relationship. It was as if everyone was in a relationship but me. I didn't mind, but what used to be like a singles club had turned into two couples and me and Zoey. At this point, my other half was Zoey, and I guessed I was okay with that. Smiling, I said, "Good morning, Gladys."

"Good morning, Martina. I have a message for you."

Dread filled my insides. My experiences with receiving messages at the receptionist's desk had been ominous. Gladys leaned over and pulled up some papers and then handed them to me. "This one here was for you and Hirsch, but this one says that a Haisley Charles wanted to make an appointment to talk to you about the Tinsley and Emmy case."

"Did she say when she wanted to meet?" I asked.

"She said she was very busy but to have you call her back and set up a time."

"Thank you, Gladys."

"Anytime, dear."

Well, wasn't that something? Tinsley Reed's parents had managed to get at least one witness to agree to talk to us. It was progress. Inside the Squad Room, the team was bustling. I pulled up next to Hirsch. "Hey."

"Good morning," he said in a singsong voice.

Somebody had a good weekend. "Good weekend?"

"It was good," he said with a satisfied smile.

"I'm not sure if I should ask for details."

"Maybe not," Hirsch teased, and then said, "What do you have there?"

After explaining the note, I said, "One down, two more to go." We really needed to speak with Lorelei and Arlo. If we could get the truth out of these people, maybe we would find out what happened to the girls.

Vincent and two of his crew approached, carrying boxes. He said, "We have the case files from Oakland."

They set the boxes down on the table. Hirsch said, "Thank you. We'll do a quick briefing, and then we'll start digging into those murder files from Oakland."

I said, "Then we'll call Haisley and see what time we can meet her."

Seated, I reveled at the team who filtered into the room. As they took seats, there were smiles as they chatted amongst themselves. It was Monday morning, and the team looked like they got the rest they needed.

As much as it was a carefree weekend, it wasn't like I hadn't thought about the case. This was one I couldn't turn off in my brain. At the park with Zoey and Barney, I kept thinking that something like that could happen to Zoey. Murdered, for no good reason, mutilated and brutalized. It was unconscionable to think about that happening to my girl.

The case hadn't exactly been an easy read. I wasn't convinced that Arlo, Warren, and Jesse were perpetrators, but I couldn't completely rule them out either. They definitely knew more than they were letting on. Why wouldn't they cooperate? Were they too concerned about their thriving careers and lives to help us find Tinsley and Emmy's killer or killers? Had they not realized they were living lives the girls didn't get to have? It made me so angry. And then there was Odie. She seemed as fake as her hair color. What was she hiding? Maybe it was not caring that someone killed her friends?

Hirsch began the meeting by describing everything Hirsch and I had discovered along with what Vincent had found on the Church of Satan and his interview of the witnesses, Connor Deven and Sarah Runion, the two who saw Tinsley and Emmy getting into Odie's car. At the end of the meeting, Vincent gave an update on the cases that he had found that had been labeled as ritualistic murders in the surrounding area around the time of the double murder.

I said, "Vincent, it looks like there are quite a few boxes there. If anybody has time to help us go through them to map out similarities with our case, we'd appreciate it."

Vincent said, "I can help."

I said, "Perfect."

Wolf and Ross said they could also help.

Jayda said, "I've got a long list of items to finish up on my old case but could help tonight."

Hirsch said, "We should be okay with the five of us. No need to come back tonight."

We knew the detectives couldn't just stop their other cases cold — some had more strings to tie up than others. When you're close to solving a case, it is really hard to let go. Like this case. Even if we didn't hit the two-month deadline that the sheriff gave us, I don't think we could give up the case. But I believed if we worked together, we could close all the cases, not only for the families of the victims but also for the morale of the team.

Meeting adjourned, Hirsch, Vincent, Wolf, Ross, and I broke off to work on the case files, setting up another murder board to outline the similar cases. Vincent started us off. "The team pulled everything that was labeled a satanic ritual, but I have to warn you, most of these likely aren't. And based on what my team found, there really aren't many satanic ritualistic murders recorded in history. The media sensationalizes anything that has a reference to the occult, but most of the murders I found that were originally labeled satanic rituals were literally just because the perpetrators of the crimes had said that Satan had told them to do it, not because there was a ritualistic element to their crimes. And even some of the better-known cases, like the Night Stalker aka Richard Ramirez from the mid-80s, who said he committed his crimes in the name of Satan. He murdered, raped, humiliated, and maimed but there was no ritual per se. Sometimes, he made his victims swear to Satan, but it wasn't like he had carved inverted pentagrams or upside-down crosses on them. He basically killed and raped at random with no specific victimology. The other big case I found in comparison was a cult leader out in Mexico. In the 1980s, the Mexican drug trafficker said he did human sacrifices in the name of Satan to protect himself from human law enforcement. Basically, he brutally murdered people so that the law wouldn't come after him for his drug dealing. Anyway, all that was in Mexico, and they buried all the bodies on his property. But again, there were no upside-down crosses, no inverted pentagrams, and nothing that you may have seen in the movies about Satan worshipers and their rituals."

"If that's true, what is the likelihood that Emmy and Tinsley's murders were actually a satanic ritual?" Was it just somebody who wanted to kill them and covered it up by making it look like a ritual to pin it on somebody else, like the boys? Were they trying to frame Jesse, Arlo, and Warren? They weren't actually involved in Satan worship, but not everyone realized that.

Wolf said, "Not very likely."

Hirsch said, "Understood, but that doesn't mean the girls' murders aren't connected to others committed around the same time. What's the first one?"

Vincent pinned up a crime scene photo. I instinctively flinched and averted my eyes. Vincent bent down and whispered to me, "That is the appropriate response."

"What's the story with this one?" Hirsch asked.

Vincent said, "The victim is an eighteen-year-old sex worker found with her wrists and ankles restrained with rope. He stabbed her in the torso 47 times."

"And the perpetrator of the crime?" I asked, praying they had caught him.

Vincent said, "When they arrested him, he said Satan made him do it. After he was sentenced, put in prison, and under medical care, they found he had been using PCP and had likely hallucinated any kind of satanic figures he may have seen that supposedly told him to commit the crime. Once he was off the drugs, he recanted and said he didn't believe in Satan."

Not a satanic ritual after all. Vincent had warned us. "Where is he now?"

Vincent said, "Dead. Died in prison."

Hirsch said, "Dare I ask for the next one?"

Detective Wolf pinned up a nearly equally gruesome crime scene photo. The only thing that made it a sliver less grisly was because the head was missing. There were no eyes or a protruding tongue. I said, "Let's have it, Wolf."

"Similar story. This one happened about a month before Tinsley and Emmy's murder. A hiker in the Oakland Hills ran into the wrong person at the wrong time. The head was never found, but the tattoo on her left shoulder and fingerprints confirmed it was a local schoolteacher out for a jog."

"Exercise will kill you." Hirsch smirked.

I glared at Hirsch. He said, "Sorry. Exercise is good for us. Just trying to lighten the mood a bit."

Wolf continued, "The perpetrator was never caught."

None of these had much in common with our crime scene. Ours was almost neat, like it was staged. These others were most likely a frenzied attack. "Why was it labeled as a satanic ritual killing?"

Wolf nodded and pulled another photograph from the box as he pinned it to the wall. "Next to the body was an upside down cross."

"The necklace?" I asked.

"Yep, it's a necklace. It's a crucifix that was reported to have belonged to the victim. The perpetrator yanked it off her neck and turned it upside down, whether or not it was intentional, no way to know. The original team flagged it as a satanic ritual — maybe hoping to tie it to the previous one."

It felt like we were getting nowhere fast. "What else have we got?" I asked.

Vincent said, "There is one more that was interesting."

Ross said, "That's one word for it. I'd call it horrifying."

Vincent said, "Yes, horrifying, but a lot of the wounds are similar to Tinsley's."

Ross pulled out the crime scene photo and placed it up on the board. "According to the autopsy report, blunt force trauma to the head, throat slashed with multiple stab wounds, and sexually assaulted. However, there are no carvings of an inverted cross or a pentagram — nothing like that."

"Why was it labeled a satanic ritual?" Hirsch asked.

Ross smirked. "The perp said it was a human sacrifice to his Lord Satan."

"And where is this piece of work now?" I asked.

Ross answered, "San Quentin."

"He's still alive?" Hirsch asked.

Ross said, "He sure is. Apparently, he's a model prisoner, according to the latest report."

Vincent had been right. It was interesting and similar to Tinsley's wounds. "What forensics do we have on this one, Ross?" I asked.

"Fingerprints and blood."

"Any semen present?" I asked.

Ross said, "No, the perp wore a condom."

Hirsch said, "Okay, that's one possible connection."

"When was the crime committed?" I asked.

"Three months before Tinsley and Emmy's murders."

"When was the perp arrested?" Hirsch asked.

Ross said, "A month after Tinsley and Emmy's murder."

I said, "Dang. Hirsch, I think we need to head over to San Quentin."

"I think you're right. Vincent, can your team investigate that one further and find out what you can from OPD? Ross and Wolf, you can take the other two cases to see if there is any connection to Tinsley and Emmy."

The team nodded. Vincent said, "You got it, boss. We could pull other cases, too, but these three were the only ones even remotely similar."

Hirsch said, "I trust your judgement. We'll stick to these three cases. Good work, team."

I glanced at my Timex. "It takes about two hours to get to San Quentin. You want to drive?"

"Sure, why not?"

He was in a good mood even after that horror show. Kim really had done wonders on him and his disposition.

18

MARTINA

AFTER A LONG DRIVE, WE SAT ACROSS FROM A HARDENED criminal. He had dark, bushy hair and black, soulless eyes. His neck was decorated with tattoos of an eagle and a cross. It didn't even make sense.

Hirsch said, "Thanks for meeting with us today, Mr. Ranger."

"No worries. I had some time on my hands."

Hirsch continued, "We came here today because we have a murder case that happened ten years ago that we want to ask you about."

"Well, if you read my file, you know murder's my game."

"Yes, we read your file. We saw you pled guilty to the murder of twenty-year-old Violet Wexler. You bludgeoned her in the head, stabbed her multiple times in the chest, sexually assaulted her, and then finally slashed her throat."

James Ranger smirked. "That's right."

"Why did you do it?" Hirsch asked.

"Because I wanted to."

"Satan didn't make you do it?" I asked.

He laughed as if I'd said the funniest thing he'd ever heard and then halted. "Darlin', I am the devil."

I glanced over at Hirsch as if asking, "Is this guy for real?"

"Why did you tell the police it was Satan who made you do the crime?" Hirsch asked.

"Sounded good, I guess."

"But you're not a Satan worshiper. You didn't sacrifice Miss Wexler to appease your God?"

He shook his head. "I worship no God, no Satan — there's nothing out there."

Not a Satan worshiper, just a soulless creep who deserved to be in prison for the rest of his life. Thankfully, that was exactly the plan. "Was Miss Wexler your only victim?" Hirsch asked.

"There may have been more."

"You care to elaborate?" I asked.

"I thought you'd never ask."

His calm demeanor was chilling. He had no remorse and clearly got off on his crimes. A true narcissist and sociopath. He didn't see other humans as valuable.

Hirsch said, "Do tell."

"There were a couple of cuties I made my acquaintance with."

"Which cuties are you referring to?" I asked.

"Those two rich girls, a couple of blondes. My favorite. That's why you're here, right?"

My heart rate climbed. Was he confessing to murdering Tinsley and Emmy?

Hirsch said, "You killed those two girls?"

"Yes, sir."

"How did you do it?" I asked.

"Similar to Violet. Knocked them unconscious, gave them some love — you know what I mean. Then I slashed them up to make sure they didn't tell anybody."

"Why are you telling us this now as opposed to ten years

ago?" I asked.

"I've got nothing left to lose. I'm here for life with no chance of parole."

"Why not come forward at any point after your conviction? It might have bought you a cup of noodles or something," Hirsch said skeptically.

"You two are the first visitors I've had in years, so I figured why not give you a little present?"

Something about his confession didn't sit right. "You said you gave love to both of them. Can you elaborate?" I asked.

"Kinky, aren't you?" He gave a creepy smile before continuing, "I did the one, and then I did the other."

He was lying, or he had sexually assaulted and killed both of them, and the autopsy report was wrong. We needed to get to Dr. Scribner and have her reevaluate the autopsy results and see if she had come to a different conclusion than the original medical examiner.

"Are you willing to give your DNA?" Hirsch asked.

"Sure. But I want something from you, too."

Big surprise. "What do you want?" I asked.

"Some funding to my commissary account."

Hirsch said, "You give us your DNA, you'll get one hundred dollars in your commissary."

"Deal." And then James Ranger grinned, showing a grizzly jack-o'-lantern smile with missing and yellowed teeth.

I pulled the DNA collection kit from my backpack and swabbed the inside of James Ranger's cheek before sticking it into the vial of liquid. After being that close to Ranger, I felt like I needed a hot shower.

Hirsch said, "If we get a DNA match from evidence collected at the scene of the girls' murders and confirm you're the murderer, you'll get your money."

"Hey! You said if I give my DNA, I get the money," Ranger

protested.

"We'll give you half now, half later, cool?" Hirsch asked.

He simmered down. "Fine."

Ranger had a darkness within that touched all spaces around him, including the interview room. It was suffocating. "Hirsch, are you ready to go?"

"Yes, ma'am." He stood up and said to Ranger, "We'll be in touch."

We exited the interview room and hurried out of the facility as fast as we could. Which wasn't quick, considering all the different checkpoints. Once outside, the ocean breeze brushed my skin, and I could catch my breath.

"Do you think we found our killer?" Hirsch asked.

"We'll see if the DNA matches, but you caught the discrepancy, right?"

"I did. Why don't you call Dr. Scribner on our drive back to the office and see if she can start reviewing the original autopsy results?"

"All right, I'll call her and Haisley Charles. Who knows, maybe we'll get lucky, and Dr. Scribner will either corroborate this monster's story, or maybe she has a different theory."

As I stared up at the clear-blue sky with a smattering of white fluffy clouds, I wondered how something so magical and bright, filled with God's love, could be in the same vicinity as that monster's dark force that snuffed out too many lives too soon. My pastor said you couldn't have good without evil. If that was true, I supposed that explained it. We couldn't have the sun in the sky and happy, healthy babies without the presence of darkness like James Ranger and other people who did heinous acts to the innocent. Contemplating the theory, I wondered if that made sense anymore. How could anyone justify child killers? This case would not only test my investigative skills but possibly my faith, too.

19

TINSLEY

STANDING ON MY TIPPY TOES, I WRAPPED MY ARMS AROUND Jesse's shoulders and inhaled his spicy scent. With his hands snugly around my waist, he pulled me closer and kissed me tenderly. Butterflies fluttered in my stomach, and electricity flowed through my veins. It was the best kiss I had ever experienced. My mom once told me that the best boyfriends, or in her case husband, started out as a friendship. She had said that was because we would have things in common and could appreciate each other as individuals, not just have a hormonal response to their touch. At the time, I didn't understand, but Jesse made it clear. He and I had been friends for years, and here we were together. I mean, it was our first date, so we weren't formally together since we hadn't talked about what our relationship was yet. But it was a magical date. He picked me up from my house and took me out to eat Italian food and to see the latest action flick. Standing in the parking lot of the movie theater, I beamed at Jesse after having shared our first kiss and said, "What do you say we go somewhere more private?"

"That's exactly what I was thinking. That's what I like about you, Tinsley. You're smart and beautiful."

Grinning like an idiot, I said, "I like you, too."

We walked around to the passenger side, and Jesse opened the door. "After you."

I said, "Why, thank you." But before I could climb into the car, I caught a movement from behind Jesse. Was somebody watching us? No, that would be too weird, right?

"What's wrong?" Jesse asked.

"Oh, nothing." Shaking off the idea, I climbed into the car. He shut the door behind me, and I stared out the window at the figure I thought I had seen before. My jaw dropped as I recognized her. Odie. Had she been watching us? Was she not okay with me dating Jesse? Not that we had discussed it, and as far as I knew, she didn't know. Well, the cat was out of the bag.

Maybe it wasn't a bad thing she knew, so I could prepare for how to best handle the situation. Odie was known for letting her emotions get the best of her and was someone who liked to get her way, no matter who was hurt in the process. But then again, maybe it was just a coincidence. There weren't a lot of places to hang out in our town. It was probably just a coincidence.

Inside the car, Jesse faced me from the driver's seat. "Thank you for coming out with me tonight. I'm having a great time."

My cheeks burned. "Me too."

He leaned over for another kiss before facing forward and starting the car. His smile matched my own. Talk about the best first date. As we drove, I didn't want to ruin the mood, but I said, "Did you tell Odie we were going out tonight?"

"No, why?"

"I saw her back in the parking lot. It looked like she was watching us."

Jesse's smile faded. "I think she's been following me."

"Really?" I was surprised Odie would take the time to do so. She had never seemed to put a priority on her boyfriends or those she dated, so why would she be following Jesse?

He said, "Yeah. I caught her outside my house a couple of times. When I confronted her, she told me she just happened to be in the neighborhood. It started after I broke up with her."

"Did she take the breakup badly?" It would surprise me if she had. Odie said it was his loss, and she acted like it wasn't a big deal. She didn't seem broken up by it at all and told us she had plans to go out with a new guy right away. She had even ended the conversation with, "Jesse who?" followed by a cackle of laughter.

He shook his head. "She went ballistic and cried. The whole nine yards. You know how dramatic Odie is."

Sadness washed over me. "Oh."

"Are you surprised?" he asked.

"I know she's dramatic, but I'm surprised she cared you broke up with her."

"She was probably just mad that I'm the one who broke up with her and so she didn't get the opportunity to break up with me."

That made more sense. Odie didn't like what she couldn't have. For the rest of the evening, I pushed Odie out of my mind as Jesse and I got to know each other better — back at his parents' house. It was definitely a night to remember.

20

HIRSCH

After I wrote James Ranger on the whiteboard, I looked over at Martina. "What do you think?"

Martina said, "I'm skeptical. He said he sexually assaulted both girls, but only Tinsley was sexually assaulted. He confessed too easily, too. But then again, we have no other suspects. Not real ones anyway." She pointed to Arlo, Warren, and Jesse's names on the board. "I don't think it was them. They know something, but I haven't figured out what yet."

"The interviews with Arlo and Lorelei are set for tomorrow, right?"

"Yes, sir. Tinsley's mom certainly has a lot of influence in that community. I haven't been able to get ahold of Haisley, but I'll try her later tonight or tomorrow morning." Martina hesitated and looked at her watch. "It's getting pretty late."

"It is. Did you get ahold of Dr. Scribner yet?"

Martina shook her head. "She hasn't called me back. I hope she'll be able to review the autopsy for James Ranger's victim, Ms. Wexler, and then compare it to the autopsies of Tinsley and Emmy and tell us if the same killer could have committed them both. Forensics have James Ranger's DNA and will compare it to Tinsley's rape kit. They said they would mark it as a rush."

"Any word from Kiki or Brown yet?"

"No. I'll follow up with them, too." Martina glanced at the whiteboard and the bulletin board.

The case had a lot of witnesses and persons of interest. And those were just the people we knew about. The rest of the team were looking into other criminals in the area who committed similar crimes that hadn't been flagged as a satanic ritual. Wolf called on our drive back from San Quentin and said that they had found one person who could be a potential suspect. Despite James Ranger's confession, we weren't closing the door on new suspects. Not only because we needed to verify Ranger's story, but it was also possible he had an accomplice. We had always assumed the girls were killed by more than one person, but it wasn't a sure thing.

Vincent, Wolf, and Ross strolled into the Cold Case Squad Room. Vincent said, "It's the dynamic duo. What did you find out from our prisoner in San Quentin?"

"Our guy confessed."

Vincent's eyes widened. "You're kidding."

Martina said, "Nope."

Wolf smirked. "Well, that's interesting. Our guy also confessed to killing the girls."

I shook my head in disappointment. "Really?"

It was like the air had been sucked out of the room. Two sets of investigators had two suspects confess to the same killings.

"What did your guy say?" Martina asked.

Wolf approached and wrote the name Victor Ruiz. "Victor Ruiz murdered a young woman and sexually assaulted her. No blunt force trauma to the head, but he cut her throat. He said he was on drugs for both killings and that he was remorseful."

"Did he say how he did it? Did he have an accomplice?" I asked.

"He said he acted alone and that he met the girls in the parking lot. He used the knife to scare them into his car and then drove them out to the old stone house and killed them."

"Did he admit to sexually assaulting them?"

Wolf nodded. "He said he raped both of them."

"Did you get his DNA?" Martina asked.

Vincent said, "We did."

Was Victor Ruiz a liar? "Have you dropped off the DNA sample at the lab?"

Wolf said, "We did. Kiki said that she would put a rush alongside the sample that you two submitted."

I glanced over at Martina, who looked as frustrated as I felt. I said, "Two confessions. That has to be a record, right?"

With her hand on her hip, Martina said, "I don't like this one bit. I think these prisoners are just looking for a few extra bucks in their commissary and five minutes of fame."

"Yeah?" Ross asked.

I said, "Well, only one girl was sexually assaulted, or at least that's what the original autopsy report said. We're waiting for Dr. Scribner to get back to us to see if she can take a second look at the autopsy files."

Martina's cell phone buzzed on the table. She walked over and picked it up. She answered. "Hi, Dr. Scribner." Martina nodded and explained the request.

Everyone in the room was quiet, waiting to hear when Dr. Scribner could provide expertise despite her ever-growing case load. Martina said, "Thank you. I appreciate it," and hung up the phone. "She can't meet with us until Wednesday, but she said to send over the autopsy reports from the other crime scenes and she'll try to look at them when she gets home. Apparently, she's got a couple of fresh homicides she has to prioritize."

I said, "I don't blame her. As much as this case is important, a few extra days won't make it any colder."

Unfortunately, the truth was cold cases were typically the lowest priority. As much as Dr. Scribner and the rest of the forensics teams bent over backwards to help us, fresh crimes always got priority over the cold cases. If there was one downside to working cold cases, that was it. But there were a lot of upsides to it, like a mostly Monday through Friday schedule with the occasional weekend. That type of work-life balance mattered little to me before, but now that I had Kim in my life, I wanted to make sure she knew she was a priority. When I had been married before, I hadn't always — more like not at all — prioritized my wife. Back then, I didn't think I could be married to another person and the job, but I needed to because I didn't want to lose Kim. She brought so much to my life. Balance. Love. Joy. Life was too short to give up all that. *Boy, have I gotten soft.*

Martina had been right. The job wasn't enough, and I knew I never wanted to lose Kim and had been thinking about our future together. Who was I kidding? I had been thinking about Kim and my future since we first met. Things had moved fast between us, and I was thinking of asking her to move in with me. Not only that, I was hoping to make a big promise to her — assuming she wanted the same things I did.

Martina knocked me out of my thoughts. "Whatcha thinkin' about, boss?" she said with a wink.

She only referred to me as boss when she was teasing me. I said, "It's getting late," and turned to the others. "Martina and I have our interviews set for tomorrow. Wolf and Ross, what are your plans for Victor Ruiz?"

Ross said, "We'll talk to the original detectives and get their feel on the guy and ask if he could have been in the area at the time of Tinsley and Emmy's deaths."

"Good. Let us know how it goes with the OPD. Maybe we should do the same for James Ranger or if you want to ask OPD about him while you're there."

Ross said, "No problem. We'll set up time with OPD tomorrow to get a better picture of these guys."

I said, "We really appreciate it. Martina and I finally have interviews with Arlo and Lorelei, two of the three who refused to talk to us until Tinsley's parents put a call into theirs."

Wolf said, "They're definitely from a different world than I grew up in."

"What do you mean? You didn't grow up with a silver spoon in your mouth?" Martina asked.

"Hardly. We were lucky to have a spoon, let alone a silver one," Wolf joked.

Feeling slightly uncomfortable, since I had grown up privileged, I said, "Right, well, you guys have a good night. We'll write up what we found out today, and you should do the same."

The team shuffled to their corners to write up the reports. Martina stepped closer to me. "Something on your mind?"

Sometimes, I wished Martina couldn't read me quite as well as she did. At times, it was useful, but at other times it was a little unnerving. I ushered her over to the corner and leaned against the wall. Opening my mouth to speak, I stopped. The thoughts floating around in my head were much harder to say out loud than I had expected.

Martina cocked her head. "Is everything okay?"

"Yeah, everything's great. I was just thinking about Kim and me."

"Oh?"

Biting back the fear, I said, "I want to propose."

Martina's eyes widened. "Propose marriage?"

I nodded. "I want to ask her to marry me and for her to move in with me."

A wide grin spread across Martina's face. "That's great, Hirsch. I'm so happy for you. Have you bought her a ring?"

Martina never ceased to surprise me. She had shown me over the past year she had good relationship advice, having helped me navigate some of the trickier new relationship woes with Kim. "Not yet. I was hoping maybe you would come with me to choose one?" It would be nice to have a woman's input on picking out the diamond, and Martina was my only female friend.

Light danced in Martina's amber-colored eyes. "Of course, I will. Oh, Hirsch, I'm so happy for you. Kim is very lucky."

"Thank you. I was hoping to propose this weekend or next."

"Well, Mom's home with Zoey, and paperwork can wait. We could go tonight and grab a bite to eat and then look at rings."

I nodded. "I'd like that."

"All right. Let me call Mom and Zoey, and then we can head out."

"Thanks, Martina. I mean it."

She playfully punched my arm. "That's what partners are for."

Part of me couldn't believe I wanted to be married again. I thought, after my first marriage ended two years ago, that I would never want to get married again. But I looked at the world differently back then. Since I had been seeing Kim, I realized marriage wasn't the issue. It was that I had married the wrong person. Plus, I thought the job was everything, and it was still consuming most of the time, but it wasn't enough. Not anymore. Martina had shown me that in full, vivid color, how much a family could help balance out what was otherwise a pretty dark job. Martina said Kim was the lucky one, but I knew better. Smiling to myself, I thought, *I'm damn lucky to have met Kim.*

21

MARTINA

ARLO HAD AGREED TO MEET WITH US IN THE EARLY morning hours before he had to be in court. Standing in the lobby, he had a young, pretty boy look to him with styled hair and a tailored suit with a fanciful pocket square. I could tell he tried to exude power and confidence, but considering his parents had probably forced him to speak with us, it made me think he was merely a young man and not some tough guy he wanted the rest of the world to see. "Arlo, thank you for coming down to the station to meet with us today."

"Sure. Anything to help the sheriff's department."

Right. Ever since Mommy and Daddy pressured you into it. As we walked down the hallway toward the interview room, I asked, "In your profession, do you work with law enforcement much?"

"No. Not yet, anyhow. Right now, I'm just working on a few corporate cases. Mostly employee relations kind of stuff."

"Do you like it?" I asked.

"It's a good start. But between you and me, I wouldn't mind more interesting work. I had, at one point, considered criminal law. Defend the innocent, that kind of thing."

It wasn't lost on me that Arlo's demeanor had completely changed from when we had seen him in his law office the week before. He had acted cocky, and the only thing he would tell us was that he was innocent while refusing to say anything else about the case. Whatever Tinsley's mom had said to Arlo's parents must've been something fierce. We reached the interview room, and we sat around a small table. I said, "Arlo, this is just an interview. We aren't questioning you as if you're a suspect."

Hirsch said, "That's right, you're not under arrest. We're really just trying to corroborate your original statement and find out if there's anything you may remember that you didn't remember back then."

Arlo sat stiffly in his chair, his hands in his lap. "You say this is an informal meeting?"

"That's correct."

"But you could use it against me in a court of law?"

"If there's anything you'd like to tell us off the record, we'll honor that," Hirsch said, rather convincingly.

Not that it wasn't true. If he said it was off the record, it was off the record. One thing I had learned while working alongside Hirsch was that if you made a promise to a witness, it was best to honor it. It evoked trust so the witness would give you more information.

Hirsch set his notepad down on the table and said, "All right, let's get started."

Interrupting Hirsch, I said, "Actually, off the record, I'd like to ask Arlo why he didn't want to speak to us in the first place."

Arlo said, "I didn't want anything I said to be misconstrued. And to be honest, it caught me off guard. Off the record or on the record, I swear I had nothing to do with Tinsley and Emmy's murders. Neither did Jesse nor Warren. Like I said, we were together that night, and it wasn't together killing them. Jesse was devastated when he found out about Tinsley. He really liked her and was even considering a long-distance relationship for when he went off to college, which I thought was nuts, but he was really into her. He would've never done that to her."

I glanced at Hirsch and back to Arlo. "Do you know who would hurt Tinsley and Emmy?"

Arlo looked down at the ground, then back at me. "Anything I say is just my opinion."

Hirsch said, "We would definitely like to hear your opinion."

"I'm not saying anybody did anything to them, but there's some people who kinda had it out for Tinsley."

"Like who?"

"Well, when Jesse and Tinsley started dating, Odie was not happy about it." He stopped and then said, "This is off the record."

Hirsch said, "Noted."

I said, "Please continue."

"She was pretty upset by it. She even started rumors about Tinsley basically trying to ruin her character and destroy their friend group. She was so angry that she thought Tinsley had stolen Jesse from her."

"Did that surprise you?" I asked.

"Kind of. Honestly, Odie isn't the nicest person, and she really wasn't nice to her boyfriends either. That she would care at all about the breakup was surprising, but I just figured it was a matter of pride. Jesse chose Tinsley over her. That's all I could think of."

"What rumors did Odie start about Tinsley?"

"That she slept around — and that she had an affair with a teacher — Mr. Dempsey. All completely false. Tinsley was one of the nicer girls, if you know what I mean."

"On the record, where were you the night the girls were killed?" Hirsch asked.

"I was at a basketball game in Davis with Jesse and Warren."

"Did you go straight home after the game?"

"No, we went for pizza in downtown Davis."

"What time did you get home?"

"Late. Maybe one or two in the morning."

Maybe one or two? If it was one, they could have been the killers. "Was the event planned ahead of time?" I asked.

"No, not really. Tinsley said she had plans with Emmy, so Jesse was free. He suggested we go to a game. We bought the tickets that night. You know, back then, I was surprised they didn't believe us about having an alibi. But now, as a lawyer, I think it's outrageous. It's easily verified. We had ticket stubs. They probably had cameras at the venue. We have an airtight alibi, but they still put our faces on the news and said we were criminals, murderers, Satanists."

Airtight was subjective, and it didn't sound like an airtight alibi to me. They could have come back from the game early and still had time to kill the girls. Although Arlo seemed genuine and believable. It was such a contrast to our previous meeting. Was that because Arlo could have more than one personality? Had he been capable of killing the girls?

"Back to the Satanist thing. Were you a registered member of the Church of Satan?" Hirsch asked.

Arlo shut his eyes, as if defeated. He reopened them and said, "Warren, Jesse, and I went to the Church of Satan in San Jose. We registered. We thought we were such rebels. It really wasn't that interesting. And they don't even worship Satan. It was kinda more like an antiestablishment type of place, which, for the three of us, was the opposite of where we came from. The BMWs we drove. The mansions. We had a lot of expectations put on us. Senior year had been intense as we waited for college letters in the mail. We needed an outlet. Jesse found the Church of Satan on a whim. We went there thinking we were going to see some sick stuff, but then we found out it had nothing to do with worshiping Satan. It was a bunch of atheists who didn't believe in conformity or being stupid. It was kinda what we were into. But the name of the church got people frightened. They really ought to consider rebranding."

"Did you ever think whoever killed the girls had tried to frame the three of you?" I asked.

Arlo cocked his head. "Honestly, no. I mean, I certainly thought we were being set up when we were arrested. But the charges were dropped almost immediately. I thought maybe the cops were looking for a few scapegoats, and we fit the bill. But as far as the actual murderers setting us up, it makes little sense."

Hirsch said, "What makes little sense?"

"Like I said before, we weren't really into that satanic ritual kind of stuff."

"Maybe the killers didn't know you very well and didn't understand that. Heard you were members of the Church of Satan and didn't bother to check what the organization was actually about."

Arlo shrugged. "I suppose."

"Would it surprise you if we told you there's someone who has confessed to the murders?"

Arlo's eyes widened. "Who?"

"A man currently incarcerated for similar crimes."

"A man incarcerated?" Arlo asked.

My eyes fixated on Arlo. "You seem surprised."

"Well, yeah. I mean, it's just surprising that someone would finally confess. When did this happen?"

He was backpedaling.

"You know what I think?" I asked.

"What's that?"

"I don't think you're telling us everything."

"I'm cooperating as much as I can."

As much as he can? That was gray language if there ever was any.

"You're sure you don't know who killed Tinsley and Emmy?"

Arlo shook his head. "Obviously, it was this criminal who confessed."

Sure. Hirsch said, "You need to keep that information between us for now, since we're still corroborating their story."

"Sure, yeah." Arlo became a bit twitchy and shifted in his chair.

"Is there anything else you can tell us about that time that might help us solve this case?" I asked.

"That's all I can say. It's all I know."

Hirsch said, "One more thing."

"Yeah?"

"We've been asking all the witnesses to submit a DNA sample. Is that something you'd be willing to do?"

He nodded. "Yes, of course. Like I said, I did not kill Tinsley and Emmy."

Considering we had already collected the two incarcerated murderers' DNA samples for comparison against the evidence, we might as well collect it from the original suspects. I said, "I'll be right back," exited the conference room, went back into the Cold Case Squad Room, and pulled the DNA kit from my backpack.

Vincent sat the desk, typing on his computer. "How is it going in there?"

"He's talking, but I have a feeling he's hiding something. But he agreed to a DNA sample."

"That is something."

I guess. "Any word on their alibis yet?"

"I'm still working on verifying if they were at the game. It let out around ten. If they were there and came straight home, it puts them near the crime scene around midnight. But the original statement says they went to get pizza afterwards, which makes their timeline more variable and difficult to verify."

Indeed.

"Anything else you need?"

"Can you try calling Haisley again? I've been trying to get ahold of her to set up an interview."

"Will do."

After thanking him, I hurried back to the conference room with Hirsch and Arlo. I said, "Hey. Did I miss anything?"

Hirsch said, "Nope."

After I instructed Arlo on how to get the buccal swab sample from inside his cheek, he performed the task without hesitation, as if he was confident there wouldn't be a match. Was he innocent? We thanked Arlo, and he got up to leave.

As he reached for the door handle, he turned around and said, "I really do hope you find who killed Tinsley and Emmy. They didn't deserve what happened to them."

It was exactly what the other witnesses had said. Were their statements scripted? Or were they sincere? The DNA and the verification of Arlo's alibi would confirm whether he was innocent. Until then, I was keeping a watchful eye on everybody on our list. The way I saw it, at this point, we couldn't rule anybody out.

22

MARTINA

STANDING IN FRONT OF THE TATES' MANSION, I WONDERED what it would have been like to grow up in their neighborhood. My childhood home was a trailer on Stone Island. It was so small that you could fit about twenty of them inside Lorelei Tate's parents' home. "Not too shabby."

Hirsch said, "It's a little big for my taste."

Recalling that Hirsch grew up in Marin, I teased, "Reminds you of your childhood home?"

Hirsch stiffened a little. "No, it wasn't this big, but I grew up comfortable."

That was something only rich people said. *Comfortable.* They were too polite to say they were wealthy. It was funny how two people who grew up so differently had found themselves so intertwined in each other's lives, like Hirsch and me. I said, "Well, let's go talk to Lorelei."

"I'm definitely interested in hearing what she says."

What would Lorelei tell us about the feud between Odie and Tinsley? The fact the witnesses brought it up ten years later had me wondering if it was more than a teenage girl fight. Or had there been truth to the rumor that Tinsley had an affair with a teacher?

We reached the grand entrance, knocked, and waited quietly for someone to let us in. Through the door, I could hear the faint cries of a baby. The cries grew louder before the door opened. On the other side of the threshold, a young woman with strawberry blonde hair held a wiggling baby, who was no more than six months old. Hirsch said, "Are you Lorelei Tate?"

"Yes."

"I'm Detective Hirsch. This is my partner, Martina Monroe. May we come in?"

"Of course. Sorry, the baby is a little fussy this morning."

We entered the home, and I closed the door behind us since Lorelei had her hands full. Lorelei bounced the baby as she offered us a beverage. Hirsch said, "No, I'm fine, thank you."

"I'm fine as well." I could only imagine Lorelei handling the baby and preparing beverages for us.

She said, "We can talk out in the pool house, where I've been staying."

We nodded and followed her to the back yard that featured a sparkling blue pool with picture perfect landscaping and tall redwood trees.

To the left was a small structure that matched the main house with its white stucco and red tile roof. I wondered why Lorelei's family had placed her in the back yard when they had plenty of room in the main house.

Inside, the pool house was actually quite spacious and larger than the double wide I grew up in. There was a kitchen and a living room and a hallway that presumably led to a bedroom or two. Lorelei said, "You can have a seat on the couch."

We took the hint, and Lorelei sat across from us on the loveseat.

"How old is the baby?" I asked.

"She'll be six months next week."

"What's her name?"

"Emily," she said, rather sadly.

Emily sounded a lot like Emmy. Coincidence?

Hirsch asked, "What do you do for a living, Lorelei?"

"I'm a graduate student. I'm living here while I attend UC Berkeley, but it's hard to go to school and juggle the baby, so I decided to take time off."

"What are you studying?" I asked.

"Psychology. I took the semester off, but I'll go back next semester part-time. I had a nanny last semester, but it was too hard to be away from Emily. My parents offered to let me stay here as long as I like. We stay out here because Emily isn't the greatest sleeper."

Lorelei didn't strike me as a particularly happy young woman. Was it because of her circumstances, or was it because she was being interviewed about her friends' murders?

"Are you married?" Hirsch asked.

"No. I got pregnant by my now ex-boyfriend. He sees Emily sometimes, but I have sole custody." She continued to bounce little Emily on her lap, which seemed to make the baby happy.

Hirsch said, "She's adorable."

I turned to look at him. The baby was cute, but it seemed out of character for him. Was he thinking about babies in addition to marriage?

Lorelei said, "Thanks."

I said, "Lorelei, why didn't you want to talk to us about Tinsley and Emmy before?"

The baby fussed. "I'm sorry. I need to make a bottle for Emily."

"Please, go ahead."

Lorelei appeared nervous. She had to have known before we started talking that the baby would need to be fed. Peering at

Hirsch, I saw him watching Lorelei in the kitchen with the baby. No, he wasn't looking at Lorelei, he was fixated on the baby. Would Hirsch and Kim have a baby?

We had picked out an engagement ring the night before, and it was sent off to be sized down. Sneaky Hirsch had swiped one of Kim's rings to get an accurate size. He was going to propose in a week or two, and I couldn't wait to celebrate. Kim was sure to say yes. She was head over heels for Hirsch, and Hirsch was for her. I wondered if they had discussed having children and, if so, when? Hirsch wasn't getting any younger. He was now in his early forties. Kim was younger, but not a lot. A year from now, would it be Hirsch bouncing a baby and fixing a bottle? What a sight that would be.

Lorelei returned with Emily reclined in her arms, the baby already happily sucking on the bottle. Lorelei looked at me. "Do you have children?"

I nodded. "My daughter is ten years old now, but I remember the days of her not liking to sleep through the night and the constant attention she needed." Had that phase subsided? Maybe not. Was it because Zoey was an only child that she liked to be the center of attention?

Lorelei gave a weak smile. "I can only imagine Emily at ten years old. I assume it's easier than this stage."

I nodded. "It gets easier." I thought, *In some ways, but harder in others*, but kept that to myself.

"I'm sorry for the interruption. You were asking me about Tinsley and Emmy?"

Hirsch said, "We were asking why you didn't want to provide an interview the first time we requested it."

She glanced down at the ground. "My parents' lawyers advised me not to speak with you."

"Why's that?" I asked.

Lorelei fidgeted. "They said sometimes words can get

twisted."

Twisted? "And you're okay speaking with us now, without a lawyer?"

"I have nothing to hide."

Okay. "You were friends with Tinsley and Emmy?" I asked.

"Emmy was nice, but we weren't very close. Tinsley and I had been friends for a long time."

"We've heard from a few people now that before their murders, Tinsley and Odie had a bit of a falling out and the group broke up."

Lorelei shook her head. "It was stupid. Odie had been dating Jesse. Jesse broke up with Odie and started dating Tinsley. Odie didn't like that. Not one bit. Sure, she started some rumors about Tinsley. It wasn't cool, but it was typical, you know?"

I said, "No, I don't know."

"Being a teenager. The peer pressure to go along with the crowd. It was hard not to go along with Odie. She was quite a force. She still is."

"Was there any truth to the rumors?" I asked.

"Not that I knew of. You'd have to ask Odie."

"Are you still in contact with Odie, Haisley, and Sk..." I stopped myself.

Lorelei shut her eyes, and she breathed heavily as a single teardrop escaped. She wiped it away and said, "I am. Was. Skye passed a few days ago."

I said, "I'm sorry for your loss."

"I can't believe she's gone, you know? I know she was having a hard time. She'd been having a hard time, and that was understandable. After Tinsley and Emmy died, she kind of shut down and never recovered."

"What about Odie and Haisley? Do you speak with them regularly?" Hirsch asked.

"I talk to Haisley more than Odie. Odie is a lawyer now and

a very busy one. Since I had my baby, our lives are so different. You know, being a mother makes you see things differently."

There was a heaviness to Lorelei's sadness. The baby finished the bottle, and Lorelei pulled it from her and set it down on the end table. She lifted the baby up to her shoulder and patted her back. Emily pulled down the upper part of Lorelei's shirt, exposing a scar on her collarbone. After the baby belched, Lorelei whispered to her, "Good girl," before caressing the back of her head. "I'm just going to set her down."

We nodded. Lorelei returned with a weariness to her. "Where were we?"

"Can you tell us what happened the night Tinsley and Emmy were killed?"

She nodded. "We'd been out having dinner and a few drinks in the car. Sorry, 'we' meaning Odie, Skye, Haisley, and me. We spotted Emmy and Tinsley near the theater. That's when we asked them to hang out with us."

"And they did?" Hirsch asked.

"Emmy didn't seem to want to, but Tinsley did. Odie and Tinsley had recently made up which all of us were relieved about because it was really hard not all being together anymore. I think it was a sort of peace offering from Odie. Anyway, so they agreed. We all squished into Odie's car and went to the playground at our elementary school. We drank and smoked a little weed. Tinsley and Emmy abstained because they were going back to Tinsley's house to watch a movie. They didn't really do that kind of stuff, anyway. We hung out for a while and then dropped them off at the parking lot, and then we went back to Odie's house." Lorelei didn't meet our gaze. Rather, she looked around the pool house as if she was avoiding our eyes.

Was she lying?

"Did you see anyone suspicious or unfamiliar that night?" I asked, wondering if Lorelei had seen the same suspicious men

Odie had described after dropping off Tinsley and Emmy in the parking lot.

"No. Not that I can remember."

"No strange cars?" I asked.

Lorelei shook her head. "I don't remember that, but I did have a lot to drink that night."

Was Odie the only one who had seen the suspicious characters in the banged-up car?

"What did you do at Odie's house?" I asked.

"Watched movies and gossiped before passing out. We'd had a lot to drink."

"Sounds fun. I remember those days back in high school. My best friend and I would have epic movie nights where we'd get high and eat junk food."

Lorelei gave a weak smile and nodded.

It reminded me of the type of response I would give to somebody if they had mentioned a similar story. It was difficult to be reminded of the people we had lost. I said, "I noticed you have a little scar on your collarbone. What is it from?"

Lorelei touched her collarbone. "Oh, that. When I was in junior high, we were goofing off on the playground, and I got caught on the sharp edge of a climbing structure."

I was not a medical examiner, but I'd expect an injury like that to be more jagged. "Anything else you can tell us about Tinsley and Emmy that might help us with our investigation?"

She shook her head.

Something was off with Lorelei's answers. She didn't strike me as a killer, but like our conversation with Arlo, I didn't think she was telling us everything. "We appreciate your time today. If there's anything else you want to tell us, you can call anytime."

She met my eyes, paused, and said, "I'll let you out."

My gut said Lorelei wanted to tell us more but couldn't. What was she afraid of, or more likely, who was she afraid of?

23

HIRSCH

As we drove to Haisley Charles's place of work, I wondered if she would withhold information like the other members of the friend group had. Haisley had been the most difficult to get a hold of, but when we finally caught her, she told us her time was limited, and that was her reason for not wanting to talk to us before. Did I buy it? *No.* Haisley worked as a receptionist at a dentist's office. What else was keeping her so busy? She had only agreed to meet with us during her thirty-minute lunch break — it was all she could spare. We rolled up in front of the office building, and I stopped the car. "Hey, Martina, do you want to make any bets on if we'll get good information out of Haisley?"

"Unfortunately, I think we'd be betting on the same side. So far, none of the witnesses gave us anything to go on. Although the fact they all seemed to omit details makes me think they know more. We just need to figure out how to make one of them talk. Whatever is keeping them from telling us what they know must be something pretty powerful."

It was true. But what? What were they all afraid of? Pulling into a parking stall, I said, "What about the rumored affair with the teacher?"

"Likely just a rumor, but we definitely need to follow up. Who knows, maybe that has been the missing puzzle piece all along."

Maybe.

We exited the car and headed toward the front of the medical office building. The office Haisley worked at was on the first floor, so we strolled right in to find an empty reception desk. A woman in scrubs hurried from the back of the office. "Hello. Do you have an appointment?"

"We're here to see Haisley Charles."

The woman gave us a puzzled look. "I'm afraid she's not here."

"Has she been here at all today?" I asked.

"No. She didn't show up for work, so I've been scrambling to cover the front desk."

"Did she call in sick?" I asked.

"No, we've been trying to get ahold of her all morning with no luck. Just goes to voicemail."

"Has Haisley been a no-show, no-call before?"

"No. And frankly, I'm a little worried."

"How long has she worked here?"

"Four years. If you don't mind me asking, what business do you have with Haisley?"

"I'm Detective Hirsch with the CoCo County Sheriff's Department. Haisley is a witness in a crime. We had an appointment to meet with her on her lunch break."

"Oh, dear."

Indeed. "I'll leave my card with you. If she comes in or if you hear anything, would you call me?"

"Yes, of course."

Back outside, I said, "Let's try calling her."

Martina pulled her phone and dialed. Phone up to her ear, she shook her head. "Voicemail."

"Do we have Haisley's address?"

"I've got it."

"Let's head over to her house and see if we can find her there. Maybe she's sick or just playing hooky."

"So sick she can't call in to the office? For the first time in four years?" Martina sounded incredulous.

"Maybe she has a drinking or drug problem and is hungover?"

"Maybe."

I was skeptical, too.

Outside Haisley's front door, we knocked and waited. There were no sounds coming from the apartment. I repeated this a few more times before giving up.

Martina said, "Let's go to the manager's office. They'll be able to tell us which carport belongs to Haisley, and we can see if her car is here, and they should have a key to the apartment."

"Good idea."

As we trudged down the stairs, I had a bad feeling about this one. Both Martina and I believed the answers to the murders were probably within the friend group. One of them was dead, and we were having a heck of a time finding this one. It was too strange to be a coincidence. Was Haisley trying to hide from us?

Inside the manager's office, a man wearing a suit and a smile greeted us. He said, "Hi, there. How may I help you? Are you looking to rent an apartment?"

A salesperson. "No. My name is Detective Hirsch, and this is my partner, Martina Monroe. We need some information about one of your residents." I pulled out my badge and showed it to him. "The resident is Haisley Charles in apartment 74. We need to know which carport belongs to her."

"Is there a problem?"

"We had an appointment with Ms. Charles, and we're having a hard time locating her. She didn't show up for work, and she's not answering her door."

"Oh. Okay. I can get you the carport number. I also have a key if you need to get inside her apartment."

"Thank you. We can start with the carport."

"Sure." The man sat down and tapped away on his keyboard. "C-14."

"Thank you very much."

Following the numbers above each of the carports, we found C-14. Empty. I pulled out my cell phone and called Vincent.

"Hey, boss, what's up?"

"I need you to get the DMV records for Haisley Charles."

"Driver's license and car registration?"

"Car registration. Car, make, model and license plate. We had the appointment with Haisley this morning, but she's MIA. She didn't show up for work, and she doesn't appear to be home."

"I'll get right on it."

With my phone tucked back in my pocket, I said to Martina, "We should call her family and friends to see if they've heard from her."

She nodded.

"Do you get the feeling she could be in danger?" I asked.

"Yes. Let's get the key to her apartment from the manager."

In order to enter the apartment legally, there needed to be a credible concern for Haisley's safety.

Back to the manager, I said, "I'm sorry, I didn't catch your name."

"I'm Sam."

"Sam, could you please escort us to Ms. Charles' apartment? We're afraid that she might be in danger since she didn't show up for work and her car is missing."

"Right away." He walked over to a closet and pulled out a set of keys. "Follow me." We followed Sam back to Haisley's apartment. He unlocked the door and said, "Go ahead."

The apartment was quiet. The kitchen on the left was fairly clean, with only a few dishes in the sink. The living room was in a similar state, clean and no sign of a struggle. Dining room, bathroom, and hall — all clear. The bedroom was not as neat as the living room. The bed had been made haphazardly, but clearly, someone had slept in it at some point. A few dresses lay on the bed, as if Haisley were picking out what to wear that day. No signs of any trouble.

Martina stood next to me. "Doesn't look like a struggle happened here."

"No."

"You think she's ducking us?"

"I don't know. Maybe. But she was obviously going somewhere based on the dresses laid out. If not to work, where?"

Martina shrugged.

Was she running from us, or had she been taken? If she was running, why was she running? If she had been taken, why had she been taken? What did Haisley know that would have led to her vanishing?

24

TINSLEY

With a heavy heart, I trudged down the hallway at school, wondering what I could do to make it up to Odie. She'd been so angry that I had gone out with Jesse. I had never, ever seen her like that before. She screamed I was a fraud and that I betrayed her by putting a man ahead of our friendship. But it wasn't true, was it?

After she and Jesse broke up, Odie swore she didn't care about him. Obviously, that wasn't true. I'd never seen her so outraged. In front of Skye, Lorelei, and Haisley, she proclaimed I was a horrible excuse for a human being and that she would never speak to me again. Before she stormed off, she took the other three girls with her, essentially banishing me from our group. Was Jesse worth losing Odie and the others?

I wanted to be with Jesse, but I didn't want to lose my friendship with Odie. It would be too high of a price to pay. She was practically a sister to me and to think that I made her so upset made me sick. Jesse and I would need to cool it for a bit until I could figure this out and get my friends back.

I looked up as Emmy rushed down the hall toward me. Her

cheeks were flushed, and her hair was in a state of disarray. "Oh, my God! I have to tell you something."

"What is it? Are you okay?"

Emmy shook her head furiously. "There's a rumor going around that you're having a secret affair with Mr. Dempsey."

"What? Who told you that?"

"I heard it from, like, five people. That's what everyone's whispering about."

So caught up in my Odie drama, I hadn't noticed. "It doesn't make sense. I don't play tennis or take Spanish. I don't think I've ever even spoken to Mr. Dempsey."

"I know it's crazy, but that's what's going around."

People couldn't really believe that, could they? I mean, sure, there was gossip and whispers about Mr. Dempsey because he was young and attractive compared to all the other teachers and coaches we had at school. But I barely knew the guy.

Emmy continued, "That's not all. Apparently, even the faculty knows about it, and they called Mr. Dempsey in to meet with the principal."

This was serious — not just gossip amongst teenagers. "Someone even told the faculty? Who did this?"

Emmy cocked her head. "Who do you think, Tinsley? It had to be Odie. She's the only one who's mean enough to do something like that, and she's furious with you."

How could I get through to Odie and get her to retract what she was saying? My gosh. Poor Mr. Dempsey. He could be fired or arrested! What would happen to me if they thought it was true? "Maybe I can convince Skye, Lorelei, and Haisley to help us get Odie to confess that she made up the whole thing."

"Good luck with those three."

Emmy was always so down on them, but they could be genuine when they wanted to be. "Come on, they're not that bad."

"They just sat there silently as Odie berated you. Do you really think they're your friends?"

Emmy didn't understand what it was like. I considered them all like sorority sisters. We had known each other for so long. Underneath the makeup and the boys and the gossip about other people, deep down, I believed they were good people. Odie was just mad, and I had to make it right. "Do you want to come with me to talk to the girls and see if they can help me convince Odie to retract? Assuming it was Odie who did this."

Emmy rolled her eyes. "Pass, but good luck."

"Well, thanks for telling me." I hurried to the back of the gym where I knew they usually hung out. I couldn't believe this was happening. It was one thing to punish me, but some stranger — some poor fool just trying to do his job. It wasn't cool, not at all. I approached the back of the gym and, as expected, there were Skye, Lorelei, Haisley, and Odie.

Odie stepped forward. "You're not welcome here."

I said, "Odie, this has gone way too far. It's one thing to be mad at me, but to make up rumors about Mr. Dempsey is too extreme. He could be fired. What were you thinking?"

Odie flipped her hair. "I don't know what you're talking about."

Said without a smidgeon of sincerity. "Odie, I know it was you. You need to tell the principal that you made up the whole thing. If you don't, Mr. Dempsey could get fired."

"So what if he gets fired? I've heard plenty of rumors about him. He's probably diddled multiple students. And he's just some tennis coach. It's not like he's important."

Odie's superiority complex was a bit much sometimes. She had to see this was wrong, right? Sure, I'd heard a few rumors, too, but most were jokes at parties where too much alcohol had been consumed. Considering how easy it was to spread a completely untrue rumor about me, I had a hard time believing any of the gossip was true.

I looked at the other three. "Help me out here. Some poor guy could lose his job. You think she should confess it was all made up, right?"

All three looked away. Emmy was right. Maybe they weren't really my friends. Or were they just afraid Odie would lash out at them instead of me? More likely.

"Come on, Lorelei, you know this is wrong." Lorelei glanced up briefly.

Lorelei had a good heart and rarely said anything bad about anybody unless Odie backed her into a corner. She shrugged. "Odie, she kinda has a point. If he gets fired or goes to jail, it could ruin him. I hear he's married."

Odie simply shook her head and stormed off.

I didn't know where she was going, and I didn't ask. I just hoped it was to the principal's office to confess. Odie had a way of twisting things around so it wouldn't come back to her. This was one of those times to use that power for good and get this poor coach out of the hot seat. "Thanks, Lorelei."

"It's not right."

I nodded and waved as I walked back toward the classrooms. This was a crazy situation, but in some ways, it gave me hope that maybe Odie was open to talking, and we could be friends again. Sure, she could do horrible things like make up rumors about me and a teacher, but deep, deep down, I knew there was some good in there. Now I had to figure out a way to win her back *and* keep Jesse.

25

MARTINA

Hirsch put away his phone and said, "All right. Vincent and team are contacting all known friends and family of Haisley Charles to see if they know where she's at."

"Have a bad feeling?"

"I do."

"Let's head over to her parents' house."

"Good idea. It's not too far from here."

Inside Hirsch's car, I said, "I don't like how this is going."

He shook his head. "I don't either. It feels like somebody's eliminating our witnesses, and that is a pretty bad sign."

"I agree. What are the odds that two of the four women last to have seen Tinsley and Emmy alive are now missing or dead?"

Not very high odds. The more I thought about it, the more clear it became that, despite being paraded in front of the news cameras and labeled murderers, Arlo, Jesse, and Warren's lives seemed unaffected by the girl's deaths. On the other hand, except for Odie, the women's life paths had been altered by the event. Skye had skipped college and ended up dying by suicide. Haisley had also passed on going to college, held a low-paying job, and was missing. Both had come from incredibly wealthy families, and from what I understood, the parents had pushed their kids to go to college no matter what. It was odd both Skye and Haisley would have diverted from their expected paths.

If I had to speculate, I'd say that radical behavior was consistent with survivors suffering from post-traumatic stress disorder. Lorelei had attended University and seemed to do okay, but it was hard to tell with her. Being a new mom, she was likely exhausted but had seemed shaken by our interview. The only one of the women who seemed to have followed the upper-class path to the letter was Odie. She was also the least rattled by the interviews. Perhaps she had simply dealt with the trauma differently. Although, you can't tell everything from somebody's words or their body language. Some people were skilled at hiding their true feelings and could control their movements to reflect a more confident and positive attitude. Odie was a smart lawyer. It wasn't beyond the realm of possibility that she had been trained to do just that.

Waiting in front of the Charles mansion, it occurred to me why Tinsley and Emmy's deaths may have had such a profound effect on their friends. Looking around the neighborhood with its multimillion dollar homes and beautiful landscaping, it would be easy to assume it was a clean and safe place where bad things didn't happen. It must've been a real shock to their systems that something so heinous and tragic happened to two of their own.

At the front door, Hirsch knocked three times. A woman wearing slacks and a silk blouse with a set of pearls opened the door. "Hello, may I help you?"

"Are you Mrs. Charles?" Hirsch asked.

"Yes, I'm Mrs. Charles. Is this about Haisley?"

"Yes, it is. My name is Detective Hirsch, and this is my partner, Martina Monroe. We'd like to speak with you."

"Yes, please come in. Your associate from the sheriff's department just contacted me and said that you can't find Haisley, and you're worried she might be missing."

I said, "As of right now, we haven't been able to find her. We were at her apartment and spoke with her employer. She didn't show up for work, and her car wasn't at the apartment. Inside her apartment, we didn't see any sign of struggle, but we're concerned."

Mrs. Charles invited us to sit before offering us beverages, which we declined. She said, "I've been calling her. She hasn't answered. She usually answers."

"Has this ever happened before?" I asked.

"You mean where she just disappears and doesn't show up for work?"

"Yes."

"No, not that I can remember. Haisley moved out a few months ago. She said she was finally ready to be out on her own. We were proud of her."

Hirsch asked, "Is there anywhere you think she may have gone? Maybe somewhere she found calming?"

"Not really. She likes to hike, but she wouldn't skip out on work to go on a hike."

"I'm sure by now you've heard about Skye?" I said.

She folded her hands into her lap and said, "Yes, we've heard. It's terribly tragic. Both Haisley and Skye took the murders very hard. Skye struggled for a long time. I guess she never stopped struggling." Mrs. Charles paused. "Do you think Haisley has done the same thing?"

She didn't know if her daughter could be suicidal? "Do you think Haisley would want to harm herself?"

Mrs. Charles stared straight ahead, as if trying to think of a place or time in which her daughter would have wanted to end her own life. Maybe she was thinking about Haisley's behavior, searching for any clues that she may be suicidal.

Mrs. Charles said, "I know she was shaken by the reopening of the case. All the girls were. Even the parents. It was such a devastating blow to the community. They found those two beautiful girls dead, killed in such a brutal way. Yes, I think it definitely affected Haisley. Maybe you're right. Maybe she's off somewhere trying to find peace."

"Did Haisley attend grief counseling after the deaths?" I asked.

"Yes, there were grief counselors at the school. Haisley went once or twice. Everybody was devastated by the loss, but I think because the girls were close, it hit Haisley harder. All of them were really shaken by what happened, which is understandable. You know what it's like as a teenager. Your friends are like your family."

"What's the longest time you've gone without communication from Haisley?" I asked.

"Like I said, she'd been living at home until a few months ago. Since she moved out, we still talk every day. I don't think it's ever been more than a day." Mrs. Charles raised her hand to her cheek. She asked, "Has anybody spoken to Odie? Maybe she knows where Haisley is."

"My staff is reaching out to all known friends and acquaintances of Haisley to see if they know where she's at. But maybe you could provide us a list we can cross-references to ensure nobody is missed."

"Well, as far as I know, the only ones she spoke to regularly was Lorelei and occasionally Odie." This caused Mrs. Charles to think once again. "She was devastated by Skye's death. We asked her to come home after and to stay as long as she needed, but she told me she wanted to be by herself."

"Do you have any reason to believe she may harm herself? Or that maybe somebody else may want to cause her harm?"

Mrs. Charles stiffened. "I can't think of anybody who would

want to harm her, but she was awfully depressed and refused to speak about Skye's death with me. I was worried about her, but she still called me every day. Unless..."

"Unless what?" I asked.

"My family has considerable means. There has always been a concern about a kidnap and ransom scheme. It's the reason I have Haisley call me every day."

"Have you received any strange phone calls in the past week? Or a ransom note?" Hirsch asked.

With concern in her eyes, she said, "No."

Hirsch said, "If you believe Haisley may be in danger, we can file an official missing person's report." He paused and pulled out his cellphone. "I'm sorry. I need to take this." And he got up and took the call in the hallway.

Mrs. Charles stared out again and then returned her focus to me. "Are you a mother?"

"Yes. I have a ten-year-old daughter."

"I remember that age. They're so sweet, and you're still their hero. The later years aren't quite the same. Teenagers are challenging."

"Was Haisley challenging?" I asked, having the feeling she was trying to tell me something.

"She didn't get into trouble or anything, but there was a lot of friend drama. And then, after Tinsley and Emmy, I thought I had really lost her. She spent most of her time in her room after that. She nearly killed us when she declared she didn't want to go to college. But ultimately, we just wanted her to be happy. That's what we want for our children — for them to be happy. I'm afraid we didn't achieve that."

"You don't think Haisley is happy?"

"No, I don't think so. We were hopeful when she finally wanted to live on her own. We thought she was moving on from the tragedy."

"Are you afraid she's in trouble?"

"My mother's intuition is saying yes."

"In that case, let's file an official missing person's report."

"Okay."

Hirsch returned with a long face.

I said, "Mrs. Charles wants to file a missing person's report."

He stared at Mrs. Charles. "We should have you come down to the station. The Lafayette Police Department found Haisley's car."

"But no Haisley?" I asked.

Hirsch eyed Mrs. Charles. "No. But there is evidence of a struggle."

My heart sank.

Mrs. Charles gasped. "We have to find her."

I said, "We will." I hoped it wasn't too late.

26

HIRSCH

THIS CASE WAS A WHIRLWIND, WITH TWISTS, TURNS, AND people keeping secrets, disappearing, and dying. Martina's and my assessment from the very beginning was correct. We had needed all hands on deck. It was time for us to reconvene and go over every detail. There had to be something key we had been missing. The DNA testing wasn't back for our two confessing convicts, Victor Ruiz and James Ranger. Were they the missing link? Was one of them, despite the inconsistencies in their stories, responsible for the deaths of Emmy and Tinsley?

The team was assembled inside the Cold Case Squad Room, ready for an emergency meeting to review the details we had collected on acquaintances, witnesses, and anybody inside Emmy and Tinsley's social circle. We needed to know everything. No stone unturned.

"Hey, squad. Thanks for hustling down. I've called you here for an update. Martina and I have been trying to interview the seven key witnesses in the case. So far, we both get the feeling they're not telling us everything. Not only that, but of the four last to see the girls alive, one is missing with suspected foul play involved, and one is deceased, which leaves only two remaining.

I'm concerned that we may keep losing witnesses if we can't figure this out and fast."

"Which one's missing?" Wolf asked.

"Haisley Charles. We had an interview scheduled with her today, but when we showed up at her work, the office said she hadn't shown up and they couldn't get ahold of her. We went over to her apartment. No sign of her or her car. Vincent has been calling friends and family. We met with her mother, who said it wasn't like Haisley to disappear and not call her back."

Vincent said, "So far, nobody has heard from her, but we got a call from Lafayette PD that they found her car abandoned in Lafayette. There was a substance that look like dried blood at the scene, showing Haisley may have been taken."

Martina added, "It seems like at every point in the investigation, there is someone trying to stop us from finding the truth. At first, half the witnesses didn't want to cooperate, and now half are just gone. What we would like to do is to have each of you write up on the whiteboard everything you've learned from the interviews that may stand out. Anything about the girls, the friend group, and then we'll review together to determine if we can find a pattern — something new or something we missed."

Wolf said, "Good plan. Has the DNA come back on the two convicts?"

"No. Hopefully, any day now. We have a meeting with Dr. Scribner to review the autopsy results from the crime scenes from our incarcerated felons, as well as our crime scene, to see if the same perpetrator could have committed them both."

Wolf said, "Cool."

I said, "If there's no other questions, let's get started." The teams broke off, and I turned to Martina. "Let's go over to the original murder board and look at it again. There must be something we're missing."

As we headed over, Martina said, "I can't shake the feeling

the witnesses are holding something back. We need to find something to pressure them to tell us what they know."

Martina deflated, and I wondered if she was thinking what I had been thinking. I said, "I see why this case turned cold."

"No kidding. Nobody wants to talk, and some are going to extreme measures to stay quiet, like taking their own life. They're afraid of something or someone, but what could be worse than ending your own life?"

It was a good question. What would cause someone to take their own life? "Depression. Feelings of hopelessness. Shame?"

Martina nodded. "Shame."

"It fits." Were they more afraid to talk than they were before? Shame for keeping quiet all these years?

Martina said, "We need to re-interview everyone. Let's start with Arlo, Jesse, and Warren. I want to talk to them together and separate. Let's get them down here at the station."

"Good plan. Let's walk around and see what the rest of the team has, and then we'll make some calls."

Leading the way over, I said, "Jayda, Wolf. Let's hear what you found."

Wolf said, "We met with several acquaintances who the girls went to high school with. There were some consistencies, as you can see here. They referred to them as the mean girls. They were popular, but people were afraid of them because they came from the wealthiest families. Odie was the ringleader who liked to show off her silver Mercedes any chance she got. Odie and gang used to cruise the downtown in it."

"That's what she was driving the night they picked up Tinsley and Emmy, right?"

"Yep," Jayda said.

"Does she still have the car?" I asked.

Jayda said, "That's a good question. It didn't say in any of the reports."

Vincent crept up behind us with a silly grin. "You rang?"

"Does Odie Johnson still have her silver Mercedes?"

Vincent said, "I'll find out," before studying Wolf and Jayda's notes. "I'd say that's consistent with what Sarah Runion and Connor Deven had thought of the girls as well. Those two were the ones who saw Tinsley and Emmy getting into Odie's car. The silver Mercedes."

I looked at the bottom of the list on the board. "You asked the witnesses if they thought the friend group was capable of murder?"

Wolf nodded. "I caught a few of them off guard, but as you can see from what I've written here"—he pointed to the bottom of their notes—"they all kinda said the same thing. They didn't think they would, but they wouldn't put it past them either. A solid maybe."

"Interesting," Martina said.

"No kidding. Were they really that disliked?"

"It's not that they were disliked. Well, most people weren't big fans of Odie's, but most said they wouldn't have crossed her or her friends because the friends usually went along with whatever Odie did. There wasn't too much negative feedback on Tinsley and none on Emmy."

I stepped to the right, toward Ross and Leslie with their lists. Jayda, Wolf, and Vincent joined us. "Hey. We just went over the list with Wolf and Jayda. Not too different from yours."

"Interesting."

"It is."

I said, "Wolf and Jayda asked each of their witnesses if they thought any of the friend group were capable of murder. The consensus was maybe."

Leslie said, "That's pretty telling. You think it's possible they're all covering for each other?"

Martina nodded. "It crossed my mind. The boys gave up

their DNA pretty fast, which makes me think they either aren't responsible, or they know the evidence is well hidden. We need to find something to apply a little pressure on them. Vincent, you think your team can do that?"

"We're doing a deep dive on all their backgrounds and for the teacher, Mr. Dempsey, who Tinsley was rumored to have had an affair with. I got ahold of him, and he swears he never had an affair with a student, but I think that's exactly what a guilty person would say. He agreed to come down and submit a DNA sample, so that's something. If we find anything fishy in any of their backgrounds, I'll let you know."

I said, "Great, it'll be useful."

Leslie asked, "You don't think it's one of the two incarcerated felons?"

"We're not ruling them out yet, but if they're guilty, it means all the odd behavior from the friends is a coincidence."

Jayda said, "Or maybe they've all been threatened."

"It's possible."

If someone was threatening them to keep quiet, who? The killers? Surely, all the friends had enough means to protect themselves against a single person. What were we missing?

27

MARTINA

Dr. Scribner fussed around her office, pulling together papers and folders, presumably to show us her findings. Dr. Scribner was a busy woman as the head medical examiner for CoCo County. She was smart and competent and a lovely human being. The previous year, Hirsch hosted a barbecue at his house. The whole Cold Case Squad was there. Even Sarge and Dr. Scribner showed up. At the event, I learned that, besides being a medical examiner, she was also an accomplished artist working mostly with oils but was getting into sculpting clay as well. Dr. Scribner was an impressive woman with flair and style and brains.

She set three folders down in front of Hirsch and me and said, "Okay, here they are." She sat in her desk chair and flipped open the first autopsy photos and report from Victor Ruiz's crimes against the young woman named Violet Wexler.

My stomach twisted. It never ceased to amaze me the amount of evil there was in this world.

Dr. Scribner said, "The assailant brutalized this poor woman with multiple stabbings and an extremely violent sexual assault.

I'm not a homicide detective or a profiler, but I would say this was a frenzied attack."

Thankfully, she shut the file. She stopped and looked into my eyes. "Long day?"

I said, "The longest."

"Well, this isn't the greatest way to end the day, but hopefully, it will help your case."

Hirsch said, "I'm sure it will. Dr. Scribner, we really appreciate you putting a rush on this. We know you've got your hands full."

"No worries. Anything for my favorite investigators. Say, Hirsch, how is that girlfriend of yours?"

Hirsch blushed. "Kim is doing well."

I grinned knowingly. Things were going better than good, they were going great, and I couldn't wait for him to pop the question so we could celebrate his engagement. My mom was going to be ecstatic when she heard, considering she had been the matchmaker who brought them together.

Dr. Scribner kept her hand on the file without opening the next set of autopsy photos. "Martina, how are your mom and Zoey?"

"They're doing well. Zoey is out for summer break and is looking forward to lots of fun in the sun and summer camps. Mom is quite chipper these days."

"She and Ted are going strong?"

I said, "They are."

"That's great. You know, I'm a bit older than the two of you, and I gotta say, this is a tough job. It's dark, and it's ugly. Sometimes you have to take a beat to remember the joyous things in life. Like for you, Hirsch, Kim and your love story, and Martina, you have a spectacular daughter and a vibrant mother. When it gets tough out there, remember that."

Hirsch and I must have looked pretty awful to warrant the

pep talk and break in autopsy photos. "Thank you. Sometimes, it's good to have a reminder of that. Some cases, like this one, really get to me. Two young girls were brutally murdered, and nobody wants to help bring their killer to justice. It's horrible."

She said, "There is no limit to what humans are capable of."

"I'll say."

"Should I continue?" she asked.

We nodded.

"All right, next one. This one here is what your friend James Ranger was convicted of. There are multiple stab wounds inflicted with a four-inch blade. Ranger's victim was sexually assaulted, similar to Victor Ruiz's victim. I know the reason you wanted me to compare the autopsies was to see if there're any similarities between them. I can't be definitive about this, but if you were to ask about Tinsley and Emmy's murders compared to Victor Ruiz's or James Ranger's crimes, I'd say they're not a match."

Hirsch said, "Victor said he was high on PCP when he murdered Violet."

Dr. Scribner nodded. "That makes sense and is consistent with how the wounds were inflicted."

"Would you rule out Victor Ruiz, pending DNA?"

Dr. Scribner said, "For now, I would focus on James Ranger or another perpetrator. Ranger would've committed the murder he was convicted of before Tinsley and Emmy. Both murders show deliberation and a desire to kill. The blunt force trauma to the head shows premeditation. For example, based on what I've seen from the confirmed Ranger murder, he'd probably killed before. There's very little hesitation in his knife marks. There are no bites, there's nothing that indicates frenzy, just maybe a little rage and desire to kill. Which is more consistent with the girl's murder. If you have his DNA, add it to CODIS and see if it matches any unsolved cases. Are you still with me?"

"Yes."

"Hirsch?"

"I'm with you."

"All right." She shut the folder on James Ranger's murder victim. She opened the autopsy reports for Tinsley and Emmy, showing the diagram of their bodies with markings where wounds were inflicted. "I reviewed the original medical examiner's findings for Emmy and Tinsley. I agree with the original findings, and note my opinion is based on the autopsy photographs and toxicology results. Emmy was hit on the head with a blunt object. I would guess something long, not as long as a baseball bat but shorter, like a tire iron. That was her cause of death. The other wounds, as you can see here on the diagram," she used her finger to point to Emmy's cartoon that marked stab wounds and a carving, "were inflicted postmortem. Now, this could mean a couple of things. One, they hit her first and didn't mean to kill her or the intention was to kill her to get her out of the way. There was no evidence of a sexual assault on Emmy." She took a breath. "There weren't any defensive wounds on Emmy. It was likely a surprise attack."

"We think they were killed at the crime scene — which means they likely were lured to the location and killed by someone they knew."

Dr. Scribner said, "I'd say so."

I said, "What about Tinsley?"

"Tinsley's death was gruesome. It is the one that I would say is most comparable to James Ranger's victim. She first suffered blunt force trauma to the head. I would guess the weapon was the same one used on Emmy. Based on how hard she was hit in the head, she likely wasn't completely conscious, thankfully, after that. Next, she was sexually assaulted."

Hirsch cut in. "Forensics said the rape kit was negative for semen. They had assumed the perpetrator wore a condom."

Dr. Scribner peered over her readers. "That's where I disagree."

What? "Why?"

"Tinsley was sexually assaulted by an object, not a human. Based on the cuts and the bruising, I would say that it was the same weapon that was used to inflict the blunt force trauma on her head and Emmy's."

What kind of animal would do that to another person? Not an animal — a monster. Shaking my head in disbelief, I wiped my brow. I hadn't expected this. Crime scene photos were brutal, and I hadn't thought it could get much worse, but it had.

I said, "So, it's possible they weren't assaulted by a male."

Dr. Scribner removed her sparkly red glasses. "It could've been anybody. I would have the samples retested."

Hirsch said, "The head of the forensics lab, Kiki Dobbs, is retesting all evidence. If something was missed, her team will find it."

"That's good news. If it can be solved with forensics, Kiki will do just that. I have to say this is where the crime scene differs from that of the James Ranger murder."

Surprise, surprise. The two felons lied. Part of me knew it when they had confessed. DNA wasn't back, but I was almost certain it would clear them. Why would they confess to crimes they didn't commit? Were they narcissists wanting another five minutes of fame? There should be a crime for false confessions. Although both were already in prison for life, so there wasn't much more that could be done to them. It was unfortunate.

Dr. Scribner said, "I wish I had better news, but in my professional opinion, I highly doubt that the girls were murdered by James Ranger or Victor Ruiz. Very different MOs. Different motives."

"And you confirmed Tinsley's cause of death?"

"Yes, it's from the knife wound to the neck. It severed her

carotid artery. She died shortly after. The perp may not have planned it because there were slight hesitation marks. But once they got started, they inflicted several careful stabbings to her chest before the carving."

"Careful?"

"Yes, as if the perpetrator was perfectly calm when plunging the knife — like a surgeon."

If the perp had been careful, it reduced the possibility of finding their DNA at the scene.

Hirsch said, "We believe Tinsley was the target."

"That would be my guess. Emmy was in the wrong place at the wrong time."

From all accounts, Tinsley and Emmy didn't have any enemies. Except for maybe one.

28

HIRSCH

Two minutes after stepping into the Cold Case Squad Room, my cell phone buzzed. I said, "Detective Hirsch."

"Hi, Detective, this is Kiki from the forensics lab."

"How are you?" Did she finish the evidence testing already? We had been waiting for over a week for the results. Secretly, I hoped it would be the lucky break we desperately needed.

"I'm doing well. We finished the initial testing of the evidence. I found some interesting things. Do you have time this morning to go over the results?"

The room was filling up, and folks were about to get ready for our morning briefing session. It would be as good a time as any, considering everybody in the room was working on the case. It would be easier to have Kiki tell everyone the results at once versus having to disseminate the information over and over. "Our briefing starts in fifteen minutes. It would be great if you could join us."

"Perfect. Brown and I will be there in fifteen minutes."

"Thanks. We'll see you soon."

While I tucked my phone back into my jacket, Martina said, "Who was that?"

"Kiki. She and Brown are stopping by. They finished the initial testing."

Martina lifted a finger and cracked a smile. "Give me a second. I'll pray to God for some good news."

"You do that. The meeting starts in fifteen. I'm going to grab a coffee. You want one?"

"I'm plenty caffeinated."

Coffee in hand, I finished setting up the computer to be ready for the morning briefing. I wondered if the advancements in forensic technology over the past ten years would be useful in this investigation. A DNA match would be great. We had submitted samples from the teacher — Mr. Dempsey — Arlo, Jesse, Warren, James Ranger, and Victor Ruiz. If one of them was the killer and had left any evidence behind, which criminals often did, we would issue an arrest warrant that day.

Martina took the seat next to me. "Did you get home last night, or did you sleep in the office?"

"I went home after I confirmed with Vincent all of our appointments. As you can probably imagine, it was a little trickier to get them down to the station another time. But Arlo, Jesse, and Warren have confirmed."

She leaned in. "Good. Any updates on the engagement plans?"

"Not yet. I think I need to solve this case first. I want to celebrate after, not hurry back to the office. She actually surprised me last night and brought me some pasta and salad for dinner."

"She's definitely a keeper, Hirsch."

I couldn't suppress the smile forming on my face. "That she is." The sentiment reminded me of Dr. Scribner's comments from the night before. She was right. This job was dark. We needed to have light to balance it out. We couldn't let the darkness take over.

Everyone sat at attention around the conference table, ready for the morning briefing. Looking over at the door, I willed Brown and Kiki to arrive. I said, "Team, we're going to be joined by CSI Brown and Dr. Kiki Dobbs, the head forensic scientists at the lab. Dr. Dobbs's team finished the initial testing on the evidence recovered from the crime scene."

The door creaked open, and Kiki poked her head in. I waved her in. "Without further ado, here they are. All of you know CSI Brown."

Brown waved and even curtsied. He was a fun guy who loved his Warriors basketball team and a good joke. Kiki was more behind the scenes, so I hadn't met her before the previous week, but she seemed competent, and she had Brown's endorsement, which pretty much meant she was top-notch. I said, "And this is Dr. Kiki Dobbs."

After brief introductions from the squad, Kiki said, "Okay, first off, we retested multiple points on each of the girls' clothing for blood, fluids, dirt, and anything that was in contact with their dresses and their undergarments. Second, we tested their fingernail clippings for any skin cells that may be hiding underneath, from a struggle. Three, we tested strands of hair from both girls to look for evidence of drugs or alcohol. Last, we retested the swabs from their wounds and the rape kits."

Martina asked, "And you have all the results back?"

Kiki said, "We have most, not all, of the results back. But like I mentioned to Detective Hirsch on the phone, some results were not expected. Starting with the DNA. We recovered samples from both of the girls as well as from vomit collected at the scene. From the blood collected from the girls we found DNA from multiple contributors, including Tinsley, Emmy, and one unknown contributor found mixed in with

Tinsley's wounds. We found a fourth DNA profile from the vomit."

Two DNA contributors meant there were two suspects, as we had assumed all along.

"Did any of the DNA match any of our suspects?" I asked.

"We tested DNA against Mr. Dempsey, Arlo, Warren, Jesse, James Ranger, and Victor Ruiz. They were not a match for the DNA mixed with Tinsley's or the DNA from the vomit. It was determined both of the unknown contributors were not of male origin."

The room went silent. I said, "The DNA found at the scene was female?" We didn't think the teacher, Mr. Dempsey, or the convicts were likely, but the other results were surprising.

Kiki said, "That's correct."

I turned to Martina. "We need to get the girl group's DNA."

Martina looked pale. "Yes, and if they won't give it willingly, we'll need a court order."

Nodding, I returned my focus to Kiki. "So, most likely, the perpetrators of the crime were female?"

"Based on my experience, yes. Next, we tested the rape kits again. No male DNA. The materials found in Tinsley's kit were a mixture of her own blood and a type of petroleum, maybe from a tire iron."

I said, "As if they had assaulted her with a tire iron?" Which was consistent with Dr. Scribner's findings.

Kiki nodded. "Yes, it's the same grease, or petroleum, found on both of the women's heads where they'd been struck with a blunt object. Likely, they were hit with a tire iron or a similar object and then the perpetrator sexually assaulted Tinsley with it."

My heart rate sped up. Were teenage girls really capable of doing something so heinous?

Martina said, "If it was a female, it was likely one of the girls.

The last ones to see Emmy and Tinsley alive were, in fact, the last ones to see them alive."

"Our witnesses said they believed it was possible they were capable of murder. Especially Odie," Jayda offered.

Martina said, "Maybe Haisley went with Odie and wasn't kidnapped after all?"

Wolf said, "Or she was planning to talk, and somebody didn't want her to."

Vincent said, "Wait. If it was the girls, why would the boys cover up for them? I think we all got the feeling they were holding back."

He wasn't wrong. "That's a good question, Vincent."

Martina said, "This is really helpful, but there are still a lot of unanswered questions."

I said, "Agreed," and looked up at Kiki and Brown. "Thank you, both. We'll get DNA from the females as soon as possible. Although there are only two currently available."

Kiki said, "Let me know when you get the DNA, and we'll process it right away."

Martina said, "Thank you."

As our forensics team exited, chatter broke out among the squad. This was a decent lead. One that I didn't think any of us saw coming. At least two women were present when Tinsley and Emmy were murdered. But as interesting as the evidence was, it didn't explain why any of the girls would kill Tinsley and Emmy. We knew Odie had a falling out with Tinsley over Jesse, but what about the other girls? From all our records, there was no rift and no bad blood between Tinsley and the others. And what were the boys covering up? And why would they cover up a crime if they had nothing to do with it?

The DNA at the scene didn't exactly mean it was a slam dunk for prosecution. Heck, the girls could even say they were at the scene but were victims themselves and had been threatened to keep quiet. Or the blood transfer happened before the girls dropped off Tinsley and Emmy back in the parking lot. We didn't have the murder weapons or any other evidence pointing to the women, except that they were the last ones to see them alive. One thing I knew for sure was that we needed Odie and Lorelei's DNA, and fast, before they could disappear like Haisley had.

29

MARTINA

PROCESSING ALL THE INFORMATION FROM THE FORENSICS team, I contemplated what it could mean. I also wondered what else the team would find as they continued to test the evidence. Kiki had promised to go through everything with a fine-tooth comb, and that took time. Three words continued to run through my brain. *No male DNA.*

That didn't automatically exclude any male participation in the murders, but it made it a lot less likely. Or did it? The only thing we knew for sure was that at least two females had taken part in the murders. Was it possible that two girls could overtake the other two? It was certainly possible if it was a surprise attack, which was part of our theory all along. We had theorized Tinsley and Emmy knew their killer or killers based on the location and that there wasn't any apparent struggle, except at the actual crime scene inside the old stone house. It was why we had nearly dismissed the two convicts' confessions, not only because they were wrong about some details of the crime but because it was unlikely the girls would march to their deaths with a complete stranger.

Both convicts, Victor Ruiz and James Ranger, were scary-looking dudes, especially in the girls' white-washed neighborhood where the convicts would have stuck out like a sore thumb. Well, the speculation was over, the DNA and autopsy excluded them as suspects.

Shifting our focus to female suspects, or persons of interest, I thought back to our conversations with Odie and Lorelei. Were they killers? Were Haisley and Skye? It could explain why Skye had taken her own life. Maybe the guilt of killing her friends was too much for her? Understandable. But why not confess if that was the case?

There was no tension between Tinsley, Emmy, and the other girls. The only rift was supposedly repaired, between Tinsley and Odie.

Odie.

Odie was the one female witness who had my gut stirring. She lacked sincerity in her grief, at least from what I could see. It was why Hirsch and I planned to collect her DNA first. Her reaction could be telling. We would have to get Skye's DNA from her personal effects or autopsy samples. I didn't suspect Lorelei would put up much of a fuss over a DNA sample. She seemed to care about Tinsley and Emmy and wanted to expose the truth behind their deaths. But something still didn't sit right with me about her interview answers.

Hirsch shut his laptop.

I said, "Are you ready to go?"

"Yep, you have the kits?"

"I do." Hirsch didn't carry a backpack like I did, so I filled mine with DNA test kits.

We headed out of the station. Once within the confines of Hirsch's car, I said, "Well, that was some interesting news."

"No kidding."

On the drive, Hirsch and I discussed different theories on the case and hatched a plan of attack if we got any DNA matches from today's collections. The original investigation didn't have a single female as a suspect or person of interest. It was likely because of sexist ideas about women not being capable of murder. Women were deemed the fairer sex, protectors and nurturers, not killers. It simply wasn't true. There were more female killers than people liked to believe. Not all women brutally murdered like the crimes committed against Emmy and Tinsley, but they killed nonetheless. Poisoning. Smothering. Driving their vehicles, with their children in the backseat, off a bridge. Women had killed those who had trusted them most, and a lot of the victims had been under their care.

Standing at the law firm's reception desk, we asked to see Odie Johnson. The receptionist was cold but didn't hassle us once Hirsch showed his badge. A few minutes later, Odie emerged, standing in the lobby wearing one of her power suits with perfectly applied makeup and her hair pulled back into a loose bun with blonde tendrils framing her face. "Detective. Miss Monroe. What a surprise."

I said, "We're sorry to spring this on you, but we would like to get a sample of your DNA. We're starting the process of retesting forensics. We want to rule out anybody who saw the girls that night." Smiling, I hoped she bought it and didn't realize she was, in fact, a person of interest.

"No problem. But if you don't mind, let's go into my office. I don't need the whole law firm talking, you know?"

I said, "Of course," and looked over at Hirsch, who had the same skeptical, puzzled look on his face. Neither one of us had thought she would give it up so easily. Was she not familiar with blood transfer and DNA testing? Or was she innocent and so it wasn't an issue?

As we walked back to her office, I thought about Odie's involvement up to this point. She had always been willing to talk to us without hesitation. Cooperative. Helpful. Maybe we had been wrong about her. Even though she had once been the ringleader of a group of mean girls, it didn't mean she was a killer. In her small office, she shut the door behind us. "I'm assuming you brought a kit?"

"Yes."

She was definitely familiar with the process, which meant she didn't have concerns with us finding her DNA at the scene, or if she did, it didn't show. I handed her the swab and gave her the instructions.

Within moments, she returned it, and we had what we had come for. I said, "Thank you, Odie. You've been really cooperative. We appreciate that."

"Anything for Tinsley and Emmy. It was so tragic when they died. Any news on Haisley?" she asked sweetly.

Hirsch said, "Nothing yet, but it's not looking good. Do you have any information about her disappearance?"

She shrugged nonchalantly. "I wish I did."

She seemed cooperative but not really concerned either. Maybe she was just self-centered and didn't really care that much about other people. Again, someone being a sociopath without empathy didn't mean they were a killer. Many narcissists and sociopaths were running around, not murdering their friends. We thanked Odie for her time and exited the law firm.

Hirsch said, "That was easy."

"Yeah, she's been cooperative this whole time — more so than the others."

"Yes, but..."

"But what?"

"Too cooperative? Is she acting like she has nothing to hide but maybe really is hiding something?"

"Maybe."

We continued on, driving back to Orinda to Lorelei's parents' house where she lived in the pool house in their back yard. I didn't suspect we would get much resistance for her DNA, but you never know. I hadn't thought Odie would give it up so easily. We pulled up to the mansion and knocked on the door. A handsome woman with shoulder-length blonde hair opened the door. "May I help you?"

"I'm Detective Hirsch, and this is my partner, Ms. Martina Monroe. We're here to see Lorelei."

"Oh, you're the two investigating the murders. How is the investigation going?"

"It's going. And you are?" Hirsch asked.

"I'm so sorry. I'm Linda Tate. I'm Lorelei's mother. It was so tragic when they died. It rocked our entire town. Nothing like that's ever happened here before and to those two young sweet girls. I still remember when they were little and prancing around in tutus. It really made all of us think about our own children."

"Is Lorelei here?" I asked.

"Oh, no, I'm so sorry. She's not here. She's at our cabin in Montana. I think Skye's death and Haisley's disappearance, along with the reopening of the investigation, has been too much for her. I suggested she take a break. She flew to Montana yesterday and is spending time with my husband and her brother and sister-in-law."

"When is Lorelei planning to return?" I asked.

"Next week. Hopefully, the mountain air does her some good."

I said, "The reason we're here, Mrs. Tate, is to get a DNA sample from Lorelei. As you know, she was one of the last people to see Tinsley and Emmy before they died. We're at the point in the investigation where we're trying to rule out all witnesses. And since she was with them, we'd like to eliminate her as a suspect by testing her DNA. Do you have a hairbrush or something that may have Lorelei's DNA on it?"

Mrs. Tate hesitated. "I'm sure we do. Do you need to have a court order for that or..."

Hirsch said, "We don't have one. We're asking voluntarily. However, if Lorelei refuses, we will get a court order."

Mrs. Tate gave a nervous smile. "Oh, there's no need for that. I'll get you that hairbrush." She disappeared.

I said, "Interesting? Mom seems to be cooperative. Although hesitant."

"As most people should be when someone is asking for their child's DNA."

He had a good point. What would I do if the police knocked on my door asking for Zoey's DNA? "Do you think that's all it is?"

"We'll find out."

We stared ahead into the home since Mrs. Tate had not invited us inside. She reemerged with a hairbrush in hand. "I was afraid she may have taken it with her to Montana, but she has one here." She handed over the brush, and I dropped my backpack on the ground and pulled out an evidence bag and slid the brush inside.

I sealed it and returned it to my backpack. "Thank you, Mrs. Tate. This is very helpful."

She nodded. "I hope you find out what happened to those girls. Such a tragedy."

We thanked her for her time and headed back to the station. What would Odie and Lorelei's DNA tell us?

30

TINSLEY

Standing in the parking lot, I anxiously waited for Odie to finish her tennis match. I had come to the conclusion that we had been friends for too long for it to end like this — over a boy. I didn't want to give up Jesse, but if it meant Odie and I would stay friends, then we would have to work something out. Surely, she'd already forgotten about Jesse, right? In the past, after Odie suffered a breakup, she had moved on by the next weekend. The only difference was Odie usually did the breaking up part, not the other way around. If you asked me, I thought she was less upset about losing Jesse than about being dumped for somebody else — a friend. To be fair, if the situation were reversed, I would not have liked it either. After having had some time to think about the whole situation and trying to put myself in her shoes, I thought that what I'd done was a crummy thing to do. The excitement of being with Jesse clouded my judgement. I wanted him, but not like that. Jesse was great, but he wasn't worth losing my whole social circle over.

Odie strolled toward the parking lot from the tennis courts. Right on time.

She was still wearing her uniform and strongly resembled

Tennis Barbie. Sometimes, I pondered if that was why she had asked her parents for the SUV for her birthday. So that she would look even more like Barbie. I was half-surprised she hadn't had them paint the car pink instead of keeping the standard silver color. Odie pretty much got whatever she wanted. Maybe that's what bothered her. She wanted Jesse, but she didn't get to have him anymore.

Equipped with a dozen of her favorite cookies, I was sure I could win her back. With Odie at her SUV, I hurried over as she was opening the side door. "Odie."

Odie turned around. When she saw it was me, her smile melted.

"Hey. Can we talk?" I asked.

Odie rolled her eyes. "What do you want?"

"I want to apologize."

She put her tennis bag in the back seat and shut the door. With a fist on her hip, she said, "Apologize for what?"

She was going to make me work for it. That was fine. I was prepared. "For going out with Jesse. You were right. I should have made sure you were okay with me going out with him. I'll break up with him if you want me to. He's not worth losing you as a friend. We've been friends since we were little kids. You're my next-door neighbor. I can't imagine my life without you."

Odie looked at me skeptically.

Lifting up the white paper bag, I said, "And I brought chocolate chip cookies from Dani's bakery."

Scowling, she said, "With or without M&Ms?"

I pushed the bag closer. "With."

She looked me up and down.

"Peace offering?" I said with a smile.

She accepted the bag and leaned against her silver SUV. "Would you really break up with Jesse so that we could be friends again?"

With pleading eyes, I said, "Yes." It wasn't what I wanted to do, but it was what I was willing to do.

She opened the bag and fished out a chocolate chip and M&M cookie. She took a bite. When she finished chewing, she looked at me and tilted the bag. "You want one?"

Yes! It worked. I was so relieved things could finally go back to normal. I said, "Sure," and grabbed a cookie from the bag. I took a bite and savored the brown sugary, buttery, chocolatey candy treat. "You want to go grab a bite to eat?" I asked.

"I need to shower and get changed out of my tennis clothes."

I said, "We can swing by your house real quick, and then we can go grab a bite."

"Okay." Odie eyed me. "And for the record, I'm glad we're friends. You don't have to break up with Jesse — it's fine. I was upset that he dumped me, and I saw how he looked at you. I admit I liked him, but I'm over it. Can we agree that in the future we discuss and make sure we're both okay with who the other is dating?" Odie asked.

Odie had a soft side that didn't emerge often, but I had known it was there. "Okay, I think that's a great idea. I'm so sorry. I wish this never happened."

"It's cool. Things aren't the same without you around. And for the record, you're like a sister to me. I think that's maybe why it hurt so much."

"I think of you that way, too." I sniffled, hoping I wouldn't start crying. But it was heartwarming to know Odie felt as deeply about me as I did about her. No wonder she'd been so upset. *Now, I really feel awful.* I wrapped my arms around her and squeezed. "I love you, girl."

Odie said, "I love you, too." She stepped back and said, "Let's not allow some stupid boy to come between us again?"

"Deal."

I hurried back to my car so that we could arrive home

around the same time. Most people only saw the outside of Odie. The judgy, mean girl who looked down on, well, most people. Odie wasn't perfect. She certainly could be nicer and have more empathy toward other people, but she also had the side that I saw when we were little kids. When we were younger, whatever Odie had, she would want to share it with me. And that was pretty much how things had been until she started high school. The pursuit of boys took priority over Odie's friends most of the time, and Odie dated a lot more than I did, which left me chasing our friendship right along with the other girls — Skye, Haisley, and Lorelei.

I wondered what it would be like to be Odie — having everyone want your attention? Maybe it was a blessing and a curse? All I knew was that I wouldn't ever let anything get between us again because I knew we would be friends forever.

31

HIRSCH

"GOOD MORNING, TEAM," I SAID AS I WAS ABOUT TO START the morning briefing but realized Vincent and the research team hadn't arrived yet. "Looks like we have a few latecomers. We'll give research a few more minutes."

Martina spoke quietly. "Are you sure you don't want to just get started?"

"If they're late, they probably have a good reason."

"True."

"Do we have a timeline when the DNA testing will be done?"

"Kiki said it should be pretty fast. Maybe a day or two. It'll take longer because they have to extract the DNA from the hairbrush. But she said the team would work tirelessly until it was done."

"That's good to hear."

Vincent and his three support staff entered. Flushed, Vincent said, "Sorry I'm late." He didn't sit down. "I found something interesting."

"What is it?" I asked.

"Late last night, we were putting together all the facts on the case. Stuff that maybe didn't seem all that interesting, but we found something that was sort of interesting."

"And?"

Vincent walked over to the whiteboard we had used for active discussion. "The girls were last seen getting into Odie Johnson's silver Mercedes SUV, right?"

"Right."

"I ran the license plate to see if Odie still owned the vehicle."

"And?"

"Odie Johnson reported the car stolen the day after the murders."

"Stolen?" I asked

One researcher handed the file to Vincent. "Yeah, I got the stolen car report here. Says it was stolen from outside of Odie's house."

"Was it ever recovered?" Martina asked.

"Nope."

Martina leaned back with her arms folded across her chest. "So, if this is significant, we're saying Odie or Odie and the other three girls were involved in the murders, there was evidence of it in that silver Mercedes SUV, and Odie got rid of the car and then reported it stolen?"

Vincent said, "Maybe. It's possible."

It was certainly plausible if one of those four girls or all four of them were in on it together. I still had a hard time thinking that teenage girls, or anyone, could be capable of the murders. "Any interesting notes from the investigation into the missing car?"

Vincent said, "Just that they couldn't find it, but they probably didn't look very hard. I mean, it was a stolen fancy car from a fancy neighborhood. And it wasn't the only stolen car reported that year. Before the murders, there was a wave of car thefts in the area. Apparently, it had been a bit of a problem. They never caught the thieves."

Martina said, "So, then, Odie's stolen car could have nothing to do with the murders."

Vincent said, "True. Or Odie knew there were a lot of car thefts in the neighborhood and found it a perfect opportunity to ditch the car."

Vincent was right, and it was a great catch. "Does your team have time to re-investigate to see if there's anything more you can do to find out what happened to that Mercedes?"

"We'll look into it, boss," Vincent said before turning to his researchers and whispering something. They spoke back and forth for a minute or two before he said, "They'll go back and start working on that now. Cool?"

"Cool."

Vincent took a seat as his staff exited to return to the research cave. Originally, we only had Vincent as a dedicated researcher to the squad, but they had granted us a few extra sets of hands to help when we needed it. And with this case, we needed it, and it had already paid off. The Mercedes could be a red herring or the missing link to who killed the girls.

"All right, now that everybody's here, we'll get started with the briefing." I explained the current status of the DNA from the four witnesses. Skye's DNA was taken from her tissue samples at the morgue. Haisley hadn't been found, and therefore, we hadn't been able to get hers. Odie's and Lorelei's were being processed.

Wolf said, "Do we think it's odd that Lorelei is in Montana?"

"Her mom seemed to think she needed the time off."

"Time off from what?" Wolf asked.

"Her mom said Skye's death hit Lorelei hard, plus the investigation dredging up old memories of her murdered friends."

Jayda said, "She may have been involved. Maybe she's feeling guilty. Maybe that's why she got away."

I said, "Maybe."

Jayda said, "You could have Montana's local law enforcement go check on her. Make sure she's really there."

Martina said, "That's a great idea, Jayda."

I said, "All right, after the briefing meeting, I'll find out which Montana office is closest to the Tate family cabin and have them stop by to check on her. We need to make sure we know her location in the event she becomes a suspect."

Martina said, "I can call Mrs. Tate and ask for the exact location of the cabin. Hopefully, she'll be forthcoming with that information."

Vincent said, "If not, we can check property records."

Nodding, I said, "All right, let's finish up the meeting with different theories and our plans for the next steps."

The room had a good energy, and I could feel it in my bones that we were getting close to a break in the case. What would the DNA tell us? Would we find the silver SUV?

32

MARTINA

THE POSSIBLE CONNECTION BETWEEN THE MISSING SUV and the murders swirled in my mind. On one hand, the team had yet to find a witness who saw Emmy and Tinsley after the girl group allegedly dropped them off in the parking lot. The thought stuck in my head. Not that it was a populated space at that time of night, so it was definitely reasonable that nobody saw them. It would be interesting to see what Vincent and his team could come up with for the car. I dialed Lorelei Tate's mother. Thankfully, she was listed. "Hello."

"Hello, Mrs. Tate, my name is Martina Monroe. We met yesterday when I came by the house with my partner, Detective Hirsch."

"Yes, I remember. What can I help you with?"

"We are hoping to speak with Lorelei. Can you provide the address and phone number to where she is staying in Montana?"

"Why do you need to speak with her? If she needs to come back, I could call her."

Faint sounds of crying bled from the background. "Is that Baby Emily?" We didn't leave Zoey overnight with Jared's parents until she was a toddler. Was it normal to leave an infant for a week? Different strokes for different folks.

"It sure is. I stayed behind to take care of the baby. She can get quite fussy, and like I said, Lorelei needed a break."

Lorelei wasn't with her baby, which meant she could be anywhere. "That's awfully kind of you. No need to cut her trip short, but if you could provide the address and phone number to where Lorelei is staying, I can call her myself."

"Of course." She gave me the address of her family's cabin in Montana and the phone number to the landline.

"Thank you, Mrs. Tate."

"No problem. Please let me know if I can help with anything else."

"I will. Thank you."

Upon ending the call, I said, "No problem getting the address, but get this. Lorelei is in Montana, but the baby is home with Mrs. Tate."

"Which means she could be on the run?" Hirsch asked.

"I doubt it, but yeah."

"All right, I'll call over to the local precinct nearest to the cabin and get some eyes on her."

"Good."

Hirsch refocused on his laptop computer, presumably to search for the local precinct in Montana to do a wellness check on Lorelei. There were so many stones we had overturned and many new and old witnesses questioned, but the case felt like it had turned into a waiting game. Waiting for someone to talk. Waiting for DNA. Would the DNA results give us the answers we needed? I wasn't so sure.

For all we knew, Odie, Skye, Lorelei, and Haisley's account of the night of the murders was accurate. Nobody had corroborated the story, but nobody had contradicted it either.

It was possible that the girls had, in fact, dropped Emmy

and Tinsley off in the parking lot and the killer or killers apprehended them. It had been original investigators' theory. Additional theories were few and far between. I had an itch inside of me saying we were close to a major breakthrough. I got up from my chair and walked over to the murder board, staring at the names of witnesses, suspects, the timeline, and all the information that may or may not be connected. The simplest explanation was usually the correct one.

What was the simplest explanation?

Tinsley and Emmy knew their killer.

They were lured to their death.

Last to see them alive: Odie, Skye, Haisley, and Lorelei.

Motive?

It fit and didn't fit all at the same time. I turned around to check if Hirsch had completed his phone call to Montana law enforcement. He hadn't.

At least it was Friday — my favorite weekday. It was movie night with my girl, Zoey, and I needed to stop at the store and pick up some ice cream. It would just be the two of us tonight since Mom had a date with Sarge. *Ted.* Zoey was growing up, and I was thankful we had our ritual on Friday nights to watch movies, eat pizza, and chow ice cream.

Looking at the crime scene photos was difficult because I had a hard time not superimposing Zoey's beaming face on top of their bodies. Would Zoey meet someone in her life capable of that type of violence against her? I certainly hoped not. My phone buzzed. Speaking of my girl. "Hi, Zoey."

"Hi, Mommy. I was wondering since Grandma won't be here for pizza night, can I invite Kaylee over?"

I wasn't sure Kaylee was a substitute for my mother, but she was, in fact, my daughter's best friend and had been for several years. "Has she already asked her mom?"

"Not yet."

"It's okay with me. Kaylee's mom can call me if she has questions."

"Thank you, Mommy."

"Bye, honey." I ended the call with a smile on my face. Choosing to ignore the murder board, I walked back over to Hirsch.

He ended his call and said, "Done. They'll call us after they complete the wellness check."

"Good."

"Who was that calling you?" he asked.

"Zoey. Not murder related."

"Thankfully."

Vincent rushed into the Cold Case Squad Room. "I just got a call from Lafayette PD. They found a body. They think it's Haisley."

"Who's assigned to the case?" Hirsch asked.

Hirsch had worked in the homicide department before starting up the Cold Case Squad, so maybe he knew the detective, which could be useful.

Vincent said, "Detective Winston."

"He's good. Thanks, Vincent."

"So, you know Detective Winston?" I asked.

"I do. We worked together briefly. Let's go see if he's in the office or at the scene already."

We gathered up our things and headed over to the homicide department. Hirsch peered over the top of the workstations and said, "He must already be at the scene. I'll call him." Hirsch pulled out his cell phone. "Hey, Winston, I heard you got a body."

Pause.

Hirsch said, "It might be related to my case."

Pause.

"Is the cause of death obvious?"

Pause.

"Do you mind if Martina and I stop by?"

Pause.

Hirsch said, "Great." He ended the call. "He says we can meet him down there."

I nodded. "All right, partner. Let's make this Friday count." Fingers crossed that the latest crime scene gave us some important information, and I wasn't late for movie night.

HIRSCH

Staring down at Haisley Charles's lifeless body in a thicket, I shook my head. Two of the four women last to have seen Tinsley and Emmy alive were now dead — in a matter of ten days. One a suicide and one murdered. Either Odie and Lorelei were in danger or they were guilty and eliminating the people who could implicate them. Had Skye's suicide really been a suicide? Had someone nudged her along, or did someone threaten her, or was the reopening of the case too much for her? I turned to Detective Winston. "What do you suspect happened here?"

"We think she was likely meeting someone. At the car, that someone hit her on the head with the butt of a gun and dragged her here." He pointed to a pathway. "And then shot her in the back of the head, execution style. After that pushed her over the hill out of sight. The perp covered their tracks pretty good which is why it took so long to find the body."

"A hit?" Martina asked.

"Maybe, but there's something a little strange about this one."

"What is it?"

"If it were a professional hit, the hitman would have either hijacked her car and drove here with her or followed her here. But if she was followed, why did she come here wearing a dress and heels? It's not a highly traveled location and a place usually only locals know about. My guess is she was meeting somebody she knew, and that person caught Haisley by surprise, knocked her out, and when she was disoriented and away from the road, shot her in the back of the head."

"Has the ME arrived yet?"

"Dr. Scribner was just here. She said she can't be definitive yet, but she estimates Haisley's been dead one to two days, tops."

Martina said, "That lines up with when she went missing."

"From your case, is there anyone who may want to hurt Haisley?" Detective Winston asked.

I said, "Well, if it's related to our case, we might have a few people you should talk to. I'll text you the names. If you could let us know what kind of gun was used, we can start researching whether any of our suspects have one registered in their name." Anyone who may have killed Tinsley and Emmy could also have killed Haisley.

Martina added, "It's important for us to figure this out as soon as possible. Chances are, the other witnesses are in danger."

"Who's at the top of your list?" Detective Winston asked.

"We tested DNA for five suspects with no match for what we found at the scene. We have two outstanding DNA samples being tested now. The two left to test are Odie Johnson and Lorelei Tate. Lorelei is vacationing in Montana, and Odie works in San Francisco."

Detective Winston nodded. "Let's keep in touch. If I find something, I'll let you know. If you find something, you let me know."

I said, "Sounds good. I'll send you some notes from the case file. Or if you want, stop by the Cold Case Squad Room and see what we have so far."

"Much appreciated, Hirsch."

I waved, and Martina and I went back to the car. I said, "I think we need to talk to Odie and Lorelei. If they're not the killers, they're in danger."

"Agreed. Any word back from the sheriff's department in Montana?" Martina asked.

"He said they'd send somebody out to the property in a few hours, so we should hear soon."

Martina said, "All right. Let's go pay Odie a visit."

ONCE AGAIN, WE STOOD IN THE LOBBY OF ODIE JOHNSON'S law firm, requesting her presence. She promptly arrived in the lobby and led us back into her office. With the door shut, Odie said, "What's this about, Detective and Ms. Monroe?"

"We have some bad news."

Odie raised her brows. "Oh?"

I said, "We should sit."

The three of us sat down, and I said, "Today, the Lafayette Police Department found Haisley Charles's body. She was murdered."

Odie placed her hand on her chest and gasped. "Are you sure it's her?"

"We're sure. We were just at the scene. We're going to be working close with the homicide detective investigating the case."

Odie remained unruffled. "This is terrible. How awful. Her poor parents. I can only imagine."

"When was the last time you saw Haisley?"

"I hadn't seen her in quite some time. We talked on the

phone recently, but I hadn't seen her in months. I work long hours Monday through Friday and sometimes weekends, too. I don't socialize much at all."

Martina stepped in. "Is that so?"

"It is."

"Do you know of anybody who may have wanted to hurt Haisley?" I asked.

She shook her head. "No, she's a lovely person, truly. My gosh, first Skye and now Haisley." Odie's eyes widened. "I could be next."

"Yes, you could," Martina stated matter-of-factly.

"Should I be getting protection?" Odie asked.

Martina said, "You could."

"My gosh, I should call my parents to let them know. Maybe I should get a gun in case someone comes after me."

Martina softened. "You could hire security. The firm I work for provides protection services for people who could be in danger. Usually celebrities and public figures, but there are circumstances like yours, too. Security would shadow you, to make sure you're not in danger, and protect you in public as well as stand vigil outside your home. Any of the services can be purchased."

"I'll call my parents. I think it would be a good idea to hire your firm. Can I have a business card?"

Martina said, "No problem."

"Have you spoken to Lorelei recently?" I asked.

"I have. The reopening of the case has brought back a lot of terrible memories. The four of us were there for each other back then, so when the case reopened, we've reached out to one another again. It's hard not to think of the old gang when we're all being questioned. And then Skye's death and now Haisley, too. It seems so unfair."

Odie said the words that showed she cared about her

friends, but she hadn't shed a single tear for any of them. Maybe she was someone who only cried when she was alone or in the shower?

Martina said, "Odie, where were you the morning of June twenty-first? Two days ago."

Odie said, "Right here at work, as usual."

"Would you be able to provide proof of that from a verifiable source?" Martina asked.

"Sure. The receptionist should be able to verify it. I come in every day at eight sharp."

We would definitely discuss Odie's alibi with the receptionist before we left the office. I said, "Is there anything else you could tell us that might help us find the person who killed Haisley?"

"No, but if there's anything I can do to help, please don't hesitate. I'm always available to you."

She had been.

The buzzing in my jacket caught my attention. I pulled out my phone and saw that it was an area code for Montana. I turned to Martina, said, "I need to take this," and stood up. "Ms. Johnson, thank you for your time." In the hall, I said, "This is Hirsch."

"Detective Hirsch, this is Sheriff Regis in Big Sky, Montana."

"Thank you so much for getting back to me. Were you able to verify that Lorelei Tate's in Montana?"

"We sure did. She's holed up with her daddy and her brother and sister-in-law. I'll keep an eye on them."

"I appreciate it."

"You got it. Is she dangerous?"

"She's a material witness in a double homicide from ten years ago. We reopened the case, and it's heating up. Earlier today, one of our key witnesses was found murdered. Lorelei could be in danger. We need her back in California, but it isn't urgent at the moment. We'll let you know if it becomes so."

"I'll put a patrol around her place and let them know."

"Thank you."

"You have a good day, Detective."

"You too."

At least Lorelei was safe. I approached the receptionist and asked her to verify what time Odie came in to the office two days earlier. While I waited, Martina approached silently. The receptionist said, "Her normal time. Eight sharp. I don't think she's missed a day of work since she started here, and she comes in at the same time every day."

"Thank you."

Martina and I walked over to the elevator. "So, she has an alibi."

"She does. If Haisley was killed after eight in the morning. But we won't know that for sure until after the autopsy."

"Who was on the phone?" Martina asked.

After I explained my conversation with Sheriff Regis, I asked, "Did you get anything else from Odie while you were alone?"

"No, but did you notice she didn't ask how Haisley was killed?"

"I did notice that."

Usually, one of the first things a person would ask upon hearing of another's untimely death was how they died. The guilty don't ask because they already know.

34

TINSLEY

ARMED WITH A BOUQUET OF HOT PINK ROSES, I MARCHED over to Odie's house. Dinner had been fun, like nothing had changed between us and the whole Jesse thing was behind us. Odie had even confessed to starting the rumor about Mr. Dempsey and had put an anonymous note in the principal's office that it was all made up. It hadn't stopped me from being interviewed by the guidance counselor, but at least that was over. Odie had even said she didn't care if I continued to date Jesse and that she was completely over the whole thing. She admitted she had really liked Jesse but said she was far too young to settle down with someone like that. I left dinner knowing I still had one of my closest friends.

In the spirit of mended fences, I bought her some of her favorite flowers and cookies just because. My mother had told me it was the little things in life that made a difference to those we cared about. Like the unexpected *I love you* or opening the door for a person who is coming in behind you. Kindness. I wanted to be as kind as possible, and I thought starting with Odie would be a great idea.

When we were in junior high, we used to sneak over to each

other's houses, knocking on each other's bedroom window and climbing in. It was fun, and we felt so dangerous. Those were the good times. Before high school and boys were a thing. I quietly tiptoed up to her window and glanced inside. Her desk was empty, and the light was off. Was she asleep already? It was barely nine o'clock. Maybe Odie wasn't in her room. And then, from her bed, emerged a figure. Not Odie. I froze in place. It was a hairy, naked man. An old man. Odie's dad. *Yuck.* What would he be doing in Odie's room?

Odie's bed was underneath the window and difficult to see who was inside keeping Mr. Johnson company. He redressed and exited the room, closing the door behind him. Was Odie's mom in there, too? Was this one of those weird old people's kinks where they liked to do it in their children's bedrooms? I did not understand old people and tried to erase the image of Odie's dad from my mind.

I stepped back and pressed my cheek to the wall, hoping not to be seen. After a beat, I peered inside once again. My heart sank. My mind couldn't process what I was seeing. Why was Odie naked with her dad? Odie slipped on her pajama bottoms and a T-shirt overhead. She pulled her blonde hair out of her face and tied it back into a ponytail. Her face was flushed. She shook her head, and tears dropped to the carpet. Oh, my gosh. *No.* I had no idea.

Chills ran down my spine, and goose bumps formed on my arms. Odie had been abused by her father. When had it started? Mr. Johnson was rich, and other old people said he was good-looking, and he had a wife and a perfect family. Why would he do that? My heart broke thinking of what Odie must have gone through.

How could I help her? I stepped back quietly, not sure she would want me to find out. Her head snapped toward the window, and our eyes met. She walked over to the window and slid it open. "What are you doing here?"

"I brought you flowers and cookies. Like when we were little."

Odie started to say something, but instead, her face fell into her hands and her body rocked.

"Odie, I'm so sorry."

Eventually, she looked up from her hands. "Can we go somewhere?"

"We can go to my house, or we can go out."

She slipped on a pair of shoes and climbed out the window. I grabbed her hand and walked her away from the house. The house that was supposed to protect her and be her sanctuary. I did not know Odie had such a terrible home life. Odie squeezed my hand back, and I had to do everything I could to fight my own tears. It was so wrong that anyone would hurt their daughter like that.

We made it to my driveway, and she said, "I can't go in. I can't see anybody I know right now."

"I can grab my keys, and we can go to the diner."

She nodded.

"Give me two seconds."

When I returned with keys and goodies in hand, Odie was standing next to my car. I handed her the flowers and cookies. "These are for you."

She mumbled, "Thank you."

Buckled up, I sped off toward the diner. I didn't know what to say to her, but I wanted her to know I would do anything to help her. Odie said, "Actually, can we just go to the park? I don't want to be anywhere there are other people."

"Sure, of course." I turned around at the next light and headed toward the park where that old stone house was. It was where we went with the boys or if somebody had gotten ahold of alcohol or marijuana. I rarely touched the stuff, but I hung around people who did. Parked, we ran back to the stone house, hoping nobody else was there doing God only knows what. Once inside, we sat down cross-legged in front of one another.

Odie said, "What did you see?"

"I saw your dad. Was that the first time he did that?"

She shook her head, and more tears fell. "No. It started a long time ago." She started sobbing, and I rubbed her back, trying to comfort her.

"I'm so sorry, Odie. If there's anything I can do, I will. We could go to the police. We could tell someone and make him stop. What he's doing is so wrong."

Odie stared at me. "We can't tell anyone. It would ruin my family. It would ruin everything."

Shocked, I said, "What about you? You don't deserve this."

Odie shook her head. "I'm going off to college in the fall. I can handle a few more months."

Was she serious? I had never been in the position she was in. I couldn't imagine any part of it. But why wouldn't she want to tell someone, to make it stop? Was she ashamed? Did she think it was her fault? It wasn't. "Does your mom know?"

She shook her head again. "No, she's too oblivious to notice anything that really goes on in our house."

"I'm so sorry."

She wiped her eyes with the back of her hands. "I'm tough. I can get through this."

"Yes, you can. I really think you should tell someone. He shouldn't get away with this. What if he does it to somebody else?"

"No, I won't tell anyone. No one can ever know about this."

"Are you sure? Wouldn't you feel better if it stopped? At the very least, maybe go see a counselor so they can help you deal with this kind of stuff." I was completely out of my depth and didn't know what else to say.

Odie stood up. "No, you don't get it. No one can ever know. Tinsley, seriously, if you tell anybody, I will kill you."

Her sudden change of demeanor frightened me. "I won't tell anybody, if you don't want me to."

"I mean it. You breathe a word of this to anyone, and you're dead."

My mouth dropped open as I stared at my friend who had just threatened to kill me.

"Grow up, Tinsley. This is the real world where things aren't fair. Take me home," she commanded.

I climbed to a standing position. "Sure." I didn't know if it was her trauma lashing out at me or what. I knew Odie could be mean, but I was just trying to be a good friend. It was as if nothing I did was good enough for her.

We drove home in silence. Once I parked in front of my house, Odie got out, slammed the door behind her, and ran toward her house. Even though she'd been really mean to me, my heart broke for Odie. I only wished there was something I could do to help her.

35

MARTINA

As I expected, Hirsch was already in the room with his laptop open, tapping furiously on the keyboard. I pulled out the chair next to him and sat down, dropping my backpack on the ground next to me. "Hi, Hirsch."

With a wide smile, he said, "Hi, Martina."

"How was your weekend?" I asked with a silly grin. He had told me on Friday night he was too excited and couldn't wait anymore.

He said, "It was pretty great," as his cheeks turned crimson. "She said yes."

My heart skipped a beat. "Congratulations. I am so happy for the two of you." I wrapped my arms around Hirsch and gave him a hug. It felt like my brother was getting married. I was so happy for Hirsch and Kim. And I couldn't wait to tell my mom, who I was sure was going to go nuts when she found out. She was the one who'd introduced them and had taken every bit of credit for their successful relationship. *A wedding.* I released Hirsch and glanced around the room. It was still just us. "How did you do it?"

"Before she came over Saturday night, I lit candles everywhere, and before she could ask what was going on, I knelt down on one knee and asked if she would be my wife and partner for the rest of my life."

I shook my head, and tears threatened to escape. "That's so sweet. I know this is brand new, but have you set a date?"

"Kim loves the snow, and she would love to have a winter wonderland type wedding, but she said she also loves spring, so an outdoor wedding would be nice, too. The details are unimportant to me. I'm just glad she said yes, and I get to spend the rest of my life with her. I just want to make her happy, Martina."

That got me. Tears formed in my eyes. "You know the two of you have to come over for dinner, right?"

"Of course. Kim talked about having Zoey in the wedding."

"Really? She would love that!"

"Kim thought she might."

Boy, had Hirsch lucked out with Kim. She was amazing. She was smart and talented. She was one of those women who lit up the room. Zoey adored her. Kim had always been friendly with me, even though we were completely different, but Kim had taken on my daughter like she was her niece. I was so overwhelmed with joy; I had to take a moment to thank God for bringing the two of them together.

A few members of the team started milling into the room. I lowered my voice. "Are you going to tell the others?"

"At work?"

"We don't get a lot of good news around here. I'm sure everyone will be really happy for you."

"Okay, I'll tell them."

He acted reluctant, but the fact he couldn't wipe the smile off his face made me think he wanted to share the good news with the rest of the squad. We had become like a family, and we were gaining one more — Kim. I could not wait to call my mom and let her know.

The team settled in, and Hirsch said, "Happy Monday."

The others enthusiastically replied with a happy Monday. Hirsch continued, "Before we get down to business, I have a small personal announcement."

Oohs and aahs filled the room.

Hirsch turned a shade of dark pink. "Over the weekend, Kim and I got engaged."

The room broke out in congratulations and shouts and hollers. People got up from their seats and came up to Hirsch. He stood and received handshakes and a few hugs. All I could think was, *what an amazing group of people.* Two years ago, I never would have imagined these people would be my work crew. Not only did they work their butts off every single day to bring justice for families and bring the missing home, they also supported each other like family. We celebrated our wins. We consoled each other with our losses. It was nothing short of amazing. Detective Wolf said, "All right, drinks Friday night at McCovey's Bar. My treat in honor of Hirsch and his new bride-to-be."

Hirsch nodded. "I'll be there."

The rest of the room agreed they would make it, too. Hirsch's smile fell when he looked at me.

"I'll be there, Hirsch. It's okay."

His smile returned. Hirsch and I had never gone out after work to a bar. It made sense. I was a recovering alcoholic, and bars weren't exactly where I liked to hang out, but I'd been sober for two years. I could handle going to a bar and drinking some ginger ale to support my best friend and partner.

Hirsch said, "I'll call Kim to see if she can make it." Hirsch turned around and made a call to his future bride.

Vincent stepped up to me. "Well, well, well. Detective Hirsch is getting married."

"Amazing, isn't it? How about you and Amanda? You two looked pretty cozy."

"Hey, I'm way too young for that."

I chuckled. "Fair enough."

Sarge walked in. "What's all the commotion about?"

Vincent called out, "Hirsch is getting married."

Sarge's eyes widened and sparkled a little. Hirsch ended his call. Sarge said, "Congratulations."

"Thank you."

I said, "We're celebrating Friday night at McCovey's. You in?"

"Absolutely. Can I invite..." He paused and looked over at me.

I said, "I don't think she would miss it. We'll make sure we have someone to watch Zoey."

Vincent said, "McCovey's has a restaurant side, so Zoey could probably come."

"All right, let me call my mom."

This was very unusual for our morning briefing, but it was a momentous occasion. One of our own had found a life partner. It was a reason to celebrate.

"Hey, Martina, what's up?" Mom asked.

"Guess who just got engaged?"

"Who?"

"Hirsch and Kim." I had to pull the phone away from my ear so my mother's screams wouldn't pierce my eardrums. After explaining the celebration details, I returned to the group. "Mom and Zoey will be there."

"Excellent," Hirsch said. "What do you say we do some work today?"

The team shrugged and retook their seats. He'd turned on

the projector to start the briefing when the door creaked open.

It was Kiki, the head of the forensic science lab. All eyes were on her. "I'm so sorry to interrupt. I just got some news I thought you might want to hear, but I can come back later."

Hirsch said, "Stay. What do you have?"

Kiki stepped inside. "We finished running the DNA test samples."

I glanced over at Hirsch, and he looked like he was on the edge of his seat as well.

Kiki continued, "There was a match. The DNA found mixed with Tinsley's blood is a match to Lorelei Tate and the DNA found in the vomit is a match for Skye Peters."

It felt like the wind had been knocked out of me. I hadn't expected that. Lorelei seemed distraught, still grieving over the loss of her friends. "Are you sure?"

"Absolutely."

"And there were no matches for Odie Johnson?" I asked in disbelief.

Kiki said, "There was no DNA match for Odie Johnson."

The room was quiet. We had all assumed if any of them could have been a killer, it would have been Odie.

And Lorelei was in another state.

"How's the rest of the testing going?" Hirsch asked.

"We're still sifting through the other evidence. We're trying to see if we can retrieve any fibers off the girls' clothes and shoes that could connect the suspect to the crime."

I said, "Thank you, Kiki."

"You're very welcome. I'll keep you posted if anything else pops up."

Hirsch said, "Thank you for coming in right away."

Kiki waved and exited before I turned to Hirsch. "We need to get Lorelei back here."

"Yes. Immediately." He shut the lid on his laptop and

announced, "Okay, brief break. I need to call the U.S. Marshal's office to pick up Lorelei before she can slip away."

Sometimes, cases really don't turn out the way you thought they would. Boy, had I read Lorelei wrong.

36

HIRSCH

THE DAY HAD STARTED OUT AS A CELEBRATION AND morphed into tracking a killer. A young mother would be arrested and charged with first-degree murder. Why had Lorelei done it? How had she kept the secret all these years? Even if only Lorelei and Skye's DNA could be linked to the crime scene, I didn't think we had the entire story. I hung up the phone and turned to Martina. "The Madison County Sheriff Deputy said they're working with the U.S. Marshals to serve the warrant and start the process for extraditing Lorelei back to California."

"Any idea how long that's going to take?"

"A few days at the earliest. We should have the warrant issued today, considering we have pretty compelling evidence to arrest her."

"You don't think she did this alone, do you?"

"No, but if we can get her in custody, facing life in prison, maybe she'll give up the real story."

Martina nodded. "And maybe Kiki and Brown will find more evidence linking the crime to additional suspects. You met Lorelei. I don't think she's capable of incapacitating two other girls and brutally murdering them on her own." And I doubted Skye had participated considering she'd gotten sick at the scene.

"I agree. But the other two people who were last to see her that night are dead, except for Odie."

Martina said, "We need to get Odie down here ASAP."

If my instincts were fully functioning, we needed eyes on Odie right away. No polite phone calls warning her we were coming. "Let's go talk to her and ask her to come down to the office. I want eyes on her."

"Let's go."

I grabbed my keys. "I can drive."

"You got it, boss," Martina said with a smile.

Vincent's typical name for me was boss, but it was catching on with the rest of the team. I knew Martina in no way thought of me as her boss, but she liked to tease me all the same.

On the drive to Odie Johnson's law office, I said, "They haven't found the silver SUV yet, right?"

"Nope."

"All four girls confirmed they were together that entire night of the murders. So, this is how I think it went down. They picked up the two girls in the parking lot, took them to the woods. When they reached the old house, one of them struck Emmy and she went down. Right after, the person struck Tinsley, and she went down before they finished killing her. When the deed was done, they all went back to Odie's house and cleaned up and then ditched the car and reported it stolen the next day. It would have been easy to do with four of them."

Which meant Odie had made up the whole story about seeing two suspicious males that night in order to throw law enforcement off their trail.

Martina said, "That's the only thing that makes sense with the evidence we have. I don't know how only Lorelei's blood and Skye's vomit was at the scene, but they all committed to being together that night, which means if one of them killed Tinsley and Emmy, then they all did."

"Yep. Now all we gotta do is prove it. I sure would like to find that silver SUV."

Martina nodded, and I returned my focus entirely to the road in front of me. My adrenaline was pumping because I knew we were close to solving the case. I could feel it, but something was still niggling in my gut. "What I'm having a hard time with is why. Why would the girls kill Emmy and Tinsley? Surely, they wouldn't do this just over Tinsley dating Jesse, right?"

Martina said, "It doesn't make sense to me either. But honestly, I can't think of any reason why anybody would do what they did to those two girls. Let alone their friends. Maybe there's something else we don't know about. A secret. A secret they were willing to kill Tinsley and Emmy for. Maybe they committed another crime we haven't uncovered yet."

"Maybe one involving the boys: Arlo, Warren, and Jesse."

"It would explain why their stories seem to have holes in them."

It'd been clear to Martina and me all along that the friend group, both girls and boys, was hiding something. We just couldn't figure out what. Was that the missing link all along?

Vincent had confirmed the alibis for Arlo, Warren, and Jesse for most of the night that the girls were killed. But not all night. According to Vincent, they had gone to the basketball game, but from all accounts, they returned home between midnight and two in the morning. According to the boys, it was closer to two, but no one other than the three boys could corroborate it. Their alibi was far from rock solid. There was none of their DNA found at the scene, but that didn't mean they weren't there. Had the boys been involved?

Jesse and Warren both chose careers helping others. Was it

penance? Guilt? They didn't seem like cold-blooded killer types. Arlo, on the other hand, was a corporate lawyer and, frankly, corporate lawyers weren't always known for being humans with a heart of gold. It still didn't mean he was a killer or a criminal. The more details of the case that emerged, the more difficult time I had being able to wrap my head around it.

WE MARCHED UP TO THE RECEPTIONIST AT ODIE'S LAW firm. Instead of asking politely to see Odie, I showed the receptionist my badge and said, "We need to speak with Odie Johnson. Is she in her office?"

The receptionist's mouth dropped open. "She's not here today."

Martina and I exchanged glances.

"She call in sick?" I asked.

"She did. She said she wasn't feeling well."

Before I could turn around and leave, Martina said, "Let's check the office before we head out, just to make sure Odie isn't hiding there."

Good thinking. I said, "We're going to do a quick look for Odie."

The receptionist's eyes were wide.

"Is that okay?" I asked.

"Uh. Yeah, I guess."

It was enough for me. Martina and I rushed around the offices, checking in closets and behind doors, looking for Odie.

After the office was sufficiently searched and we'd gotten more than a few side eyes in our pursuit, we wound up back in the lobby of the law firm. Martina said, "She's not here. We should go to her house."

I said, "I'll call Vincent on the way down and get her current license plate information. I want to know where she's at. I don't like the feel of this — not one bit."

"I don't either."

Down in the parking garage, I dialed Vincent's number. "Hey, boss, what's up?"

"I need to get a license plate number and the car, make, and model for Odessa Johnson. Once you get it, submit a BOLO."

"Is she missing?"

"She didn't show up for work today — the first time in two years. We're headed to her house now."

"I'm on it."

Vincent, understanding the seriousness of the request, hung up with none of his typical banter. I glanced at Martina across the car. "Vincent's on it. Let's go find her."

On the drive back to the East Bay, Vincent returned my call. I said, "You're on speaker."

"It's done. There's a BOLO for her car."

"Thanks."

"Anything else you need?"

Martina said, "We have enough for a warrant to arrest her, right? She said she was with Lorelei all night. So, she either lied about being with Lorelei all night or lied about killing the girls. If nothing else, obstruction of justice?"

Vincent said, "We could give it a shot."

I said, "Vincent, can you work with Wolf or Jayda or whoever is available to get the warrant request written up?"

"You got it, boss."

After the call ended, Martina shook her head. "What are the odds Odie's at home sick, eating a bowl of chicken soup?"

"Not very good."

We pulled up at Odie's house. There wasn't a car in the driveway. We exited the car, popped open the trunk, and fished out our vests. I slipped mine on. "You good?"

Martina nodded.

We rushed toward the front door and knocked. And waited.

While I stood there, Martina canvased the house, peeking through windows and running around the perimeter. The home wasn't large and therefore without a lot of hiding spaces if Odie was inside. It was modest. Maybe a three-bedroom, fifteen-hundred square feet. Martina returned to the doorstep. "From what I can tell, there's nobody inside. Can you break down the door?" Martina asked.

"We'd have to have probable cause for that." And I wondered if I wasn't there, if Martina would break it down anyhow.

Martina said, "She could be in danger. Like Haisley was."

"Let's give it a minute. Could you see inside the garage?"

"There's a window on the side door to the garage. There's no car inside."

I shook my head. "She's not here."

"Well, where the heck is she?" Martina asked.

That was the million-dollar question.

Was Odie on the run, or had she been taken?

37

TINSLEY

Jesse approached, looking grim. What was wrong? I hadn't seen him outside of school in over a week. I had been so excited to tell him that Odie was okay with us dating, and that everything was fine. Well, not everything was fine. Odie was being abused in her own home, and she wouldn't let me help her. And she got really mad and weird and threatened to kill me. The whole thing was so sad and strange. "Hi, Jesse."

"We need to talk."

My stomach flip-flopped. *We need to talk.* Never words you wanted to hear from your boyfriend. Not that we were officially boyfriend girlfriend, but we were pretty much there. He grabbed me by the arm and dragged me over to the corner of the hallway where there weren't any other students. "I just heard something from someone."

"Could you be more specific?" I asked, pulling my arm back. What was up with him?

"I heard that over the weekend you had a three-way with Mark and Tim. Like, they both did you at the same time. I heard there are pictures."

My eyes popped wide open. "What?"

"Are you saying it's not true?" he asked skeptically.

"No, of course, it's not true. Who told you that?"

"I heard it from Warren."

"Who told him? It's not true. Not at all. I barely even talk to those guys."

"He said he heard it from a girl in his band class."

A girl? *Odie.* I shook my head, trying to figure out why she would do this. Was this her second attack on my character? First the rumor about Mr. Dempsey and now this. How many people had heard the story?

"Are you sure it's not true? They said there are photos."

This was unbelievable. How could he believe I would do that? "Really? Did you see them?"

"No."

"And you won't because they don't exist. I can't believe you thought I would do that."

"Everyone's saying it..."

Really? "Yeah, well, before Odie and I were friends again, she started a rumor that I was dating Mr. Dempsey. Did you think that was true, too?"

"No."

I shook my head with my heart pounding furiously. *Odie.*

"If you made up with Odie, why would she start a rumor about you?"

Why indeed? "She got mad about something. She's being dramatic." This would have been the perfect time to tell the truth about Odie, to explain why she was upset with me, but unlike Odie, I wouldn't stoop that low. Was our entire friendship a lie? This crossed a whole other line. She wanted to ruin my life when all I did was try to be a good friend.

"Is it because of me?"

"No, she said she's totally fine with us dating." Was I okay with it, considering he thought I had a random three-way over the weekend?

"Then what?"

"Just some stuff. I'll talk to her." She wouldn't get away with this — not this time.

"Are you okay?"

"I was before you thought I hooked up with a couple of jerks over the weekend."

"I'm sorry. I shouldn't have believed it. You're not like that, I know that. Forgive me?" he asked with a goofy grin.

Giving him the evil eye, I thought, *maybe*.

He clasped his hands together. "Please. Dinner at Antonio's Saturday night?"

"Fine. I'll forgive you this time. But there better not be a next time."

He leaned in for a quick peck on the lips. "Deal."

We said our goodbyes, and I rushed off to confront Odie.

When I approached the group, Odie gave me a sickly sweet smile. "Hi, Tinsley, what's up?"

"I need to talk to you alone."

"You can say whatever you want to say in front of the others. I don't have any secrets."

I stared directly into her eyes. Eyes that were once sparkly blue had turned dark. "I'd like to speak with you alone." She was egging me on to talk in front of the other girls. Why would she do that? I was really beginning to wonder if I knew Odie at all.

I had cherished our friendship so much, but she was a completely different person than I knew before. She was like a stranger. Was there a way to come back from this?

Odie rolled her eyes before shrugging. "Fine, let's go talk *alone.*" She said it as if the proposition annoyed her.

I pulled her behind the gym and said, "I know you started rumors about me."

"What rumors?" she asked, obviously playing stupid.

"That I had a three-way with Mark and Tim. It's all over school. Why would you do that?"

"Hmm. I did hear that. I just assumed it was true."

"You're such a liar. You know it's not true because you started the rumor."

"I can't believe you think I would do that. I thought we were friends again."

Was she seriously denying this? "I thought so, too."

Odie said, "I swear it wasn't me, Tinsley. I value your friendship so much. You know that."

I tried to find a trusting bone in my body, but for Odie, I was having a difficult time finding one. I said, "Just knock it off. I mean it," and I stormed off. If she didn't stop spreading rumors about me, she would be sorry. *Really sorry.*

38

MARTINA

Smiling at the tall, dark, and handsome detective, I said, "Detective Winston, thank you for meeting with us." What was that feeling I was having? Was I attracted to Detective Winston? I glanced down at his left hand and thought, *Of course*. Not that I was ready to date. Where were these ideas coming from? Was it Hirsch and Kim's engagement making me wish for something similar? Shaking off the thoughts, I focused on the case at hand.

"No problem. I figured we could probably help each other out."

Hirsch said, "Please sit down."

Vincent, Hirsch, Detective Winston, and I sat down around the table. We were meeting with Detective Winston, the homicide detective working Haisley's murder, hoping he had some new insight into who'd killed her and could help us figure out where Odie had gone.

Detective Winston said, "We retrieved the bullet that was lodged inside Ms. Charles's brain. It's from a Sig Sauer p245. We're now looking for anybody who owns that type of gun and looking for the weapon itself. Any of your suspects have a gun registered?"

Vincent gave a cocky smile. "We have one."

Hirsch and I looked at each other and then back at Vincent. "We do?"

"Knowing we were meeting with Detective Winston, I did a quick search for our prime suspects, Odie Johnson and Lorelei Tate. Anybody want to guess what I found?" Vincent asked.

Detective Winston didn't seem amused, and neither was I. "No."

"Fine, so cranky."

Hirsch said, "It's been a long day, Vincent."

"I hear you. Lorelei Tate doesn't have any weapons registered to her. However, Odessa Johnson has two handguns registered. One is a Sig Sauer p245, and the other is a Glock 26."

My gut was screaming that Odie hadn't been kidnapped — she was on the run. "So, one of our prime suspects in the murder of Tinsley and Emmy is the owner of a Sig Sauer p245 and a Glock 26. Coincidence? I don't think so."

Detective Winston pulled his arms across his chest. "Well, I'll be darned. Sounds like we have a common suspect. Any idea where Odessa Johnson is right now?"

"Nope. We put out a BOLO for her car earlier today. We went by her work and her house. No sign of her. We don't know whether she is on the run or has been taken, but it's more likely she's on the run."

"I have to agree," Detective Winston said. "Where's your other suspect?"

"We have a warrant for Lorelei Tate. She's currently in Montana. We're working with the locals to arrest her and bring her back to California. The charges are first-degree murder."

"Did you find anything else at the scene? Any physical evidence that could be tied to a suspect?"

"We took scrapings from underneath Haisley's fingernails. It looks like she might've scratched someone."

I said, "Good to hear. Did you get a time of death?"

"Dr. Scribner says between 6 and 10 AM Friday."

I said, "There goes Odie's alibi. The receptionist at her law firm confirmed she was in at 8 AM, but if Haisley could have been dead at 6 AM, Odie had plenty of time to kill her, change her clothes, and stroll into the office at her normal time."

Hirsch said, "It sounds like we have enough cause for a search warrant."

Detective Winston said, "I'd say so."

Hirsch looked over at Vincent, who said, "I'll put in the request."

Detective Winston said, "Cool. Once it's issued, let's go in and search together. The cases are obviously linked."

I said, "I hope we find her soon — she's dangerous."

Hirsch said, "Starting from when she was seventeen years old. Who knows what else she's done that she's gotten away with."

I can only imagine what else Odie has done.

Winston said, "You're sure she killed the two girls, too?"

Hirsch said, "We don't have any physical evidence tying her to the murders, but there is circumstantial evidence."

I said, "I got sociopath vibes off her. We've interviewed her a few times. She doesn't have a sincere bone in her body."

Detective Winston said, "We better find her, and fast. People like that do terrible things when they feel desperate. Your squad caught quite the case. Here I thought cold cases were kind of boring."

I laughed, and Hirsch smirked. "Hardly. You should see some of the things we've experienced in the two years since we set up shop. People are capable of terrible, terrible things, even decades after their initial crimes."

"Yeah, we see that in homicide, too. Do you have an arrest warrant for this Odessa Johnson?"

"We do," Vincent said.

I said, "We just have to find her."

Hirsch said, "The boys are coming down tomorrow. It'll be interesting to hear what they say now that we have warrants issued for Lorelei and Odie. Maybe they'll have some insight into Haisley's death."

Detective Winston said, "Boys?"

"Arlo, Warren, and Jesse. They were the original three suspects ten years ago. Like the others, we felt like they were holding back information in their interviews. We don't have evidence they took part in the murders, but we're fairly certain they know more than they told us."

Detective Winston said, "Let me know what you find. And I think we need an APB out on Odessa Johnson to get her off the streets before anybody else loses their life. Your team is working on the search warrant. My team can send out the APB."

Hirsch said, "Thanks, Winston."

It was a solid plan. The only thing that bothered me, well, one thing that bothered me was that we had no physical evidence matching Odie to the crime. How could that be? In my mind, it was most likely Odie was the mastermind and the one most capable of the heinous crime. But we never found the knife or the tire iron or the SUV. Making a knife and tire iron disappear was easy enough but a car? The other major thing that bothered me was I couldn't figure out why the girls had been killed. What motive did the killers have?

What Hirsch said made sense about Odie but not about Lorelei. Odie didn't have any empathy or genuine emotions for anybody. Had she been born that way, or had she been made? And what had triggered her to kill Tinsley and Emmy and then ten years later be willing to kill her friend Haisley in cold blood to hide her crimes? With a bullet to the back of the head? Had Odie become completely unhinged and no longer able to put up the façade of a normal and successful woman?

39

MARTINA

AFTER SEARCHING EVERY NOOK, CRAWLSPACE, AND cupboard, we didn't find any evidence at Odessa Johnson's house linking her to any of the crimes we suspected she was guilty of. Neither gun that was registered in her name was found, which meant she could very well be armed and dangerous.

There had been zero leads regarding her whereabouts since we put out the BOLO and APB the day before. Could she be hiding out with her parents? Were her parents the type to hide their daughter, even if she was accused of committing multiple homicides? It was far more common than anyone would want to admit. Would I be that type of parent if Zoey had accidentally killed someone or, God forbid, killed somebody on purpose? If she did, I was sure she'd have a good reason, like self-defense or something like that. No, I wouldn't hide her. I would tell her to keep her mouth shut and hire her the best lawyer we could afford. Knock on wood, I'd never have to worry about that. Zoey was loud and sparkly, but she'd never hurt a fly. She loved animals and people and learning new things. Had Odie Johnson once been like that, too? What about

Lorelei Tate? Lorelei was a mother herself. Did she regret what she did?

Leaning against the side of my car, I waited outside Odie's house for the team to wrap it up. Vincent and Hirsch approached empty-handed, like most of the team. The only thing officers took from the home was Odie's laptop. Nothing else seemed to be of importance.

Vincent said, "Hey."

I said, "Are you ready to head back? Warren and Jesse confirmed this morning and should be at the station in about twenty minutes."

"What about Arlo?" Hirsch asked.

Vincent shook his head. "I tried him multiple times today. He's not answering."

"Hirsch, should we pay him a visit?"

Hirsch said, "Maybe. We could send some people out to find him while we talk to the others."

Vincent excused himself to answer a phone call.

"Not a bad idea. Are you surprised we didn't find anything in Odie's house?" I asked. *I wasn't.*

"No. Odie seems organized, thoughtful, and meticulous. I didn't think she'd leave any trace behind."

So far, she hadn't, but that didn't mean she wouldn't be caught and prosecuted for her crimes.

Vincent returned, cheeks flushed. "Hey, that was the office. One of the guys just got a call from Arlo's lawyer. He said that Arlo has nothing more to say and that if we continue to contact him, they'll file harassment charges."

I shook my head. "Who are these people? Two young, innocent girls were murdered in cold blood, and they can't be bothered to answer questions?"

Vincent said, "They're probably covering their own butts."

I said, "You're right. That's exactly what it is. My gut says

Arlo is at the heart of this. I don't know how or why, but his lack of cooperation makes him look pretty suspicious in my book."

Hirsch said, "Mine too. Let's get back to the station."

***

VINCENT, HIRSCH, AND I STEPPED THROUGH THE automatic doors of the CoCo County Sheriff's Department and immediately spotted Jesse and Warren sitting in the lobby waiting for us. Neither appeared to have a lawyer with them. Vincent waved and went back to the offices as we stopped to greet Warren and Jesse.

"Thank you for coming down today."

Jesse said, "Anything to help."

I said, "We'd like to question you separately. Jesse, I'll have you come with me. Warren will go with Hirsch. Questions?"

Good. No questions. I walked past reception, waving to Gladys as I went by, guiding Jesse to Interview Room One. Opening the door, I gestured for Jesse to enter. He took the chair on one side of the table, and I took the other. "How are you doing, Jesse?"

"I'm doing all right. It's my day off, so this worked out pretty well."

"It's good to hear. I just want you to know, first, we really appreciate how cooperative you have been with the case. Unfortunately, that hasn't been the situation for some of our key witnesses. One reason we asked you down here is because we have new evidence, and we're pretty sure we know what happened to Tinsley and Emmy."

Jesse nodded, looking nervous. I said, "We issued an arrest warrant for Lorelei Tate for two counts of first-degree murder. Another arrest warrant has been issued for Odessa Johnson relating to perjury, lying to police officers, and obstruction of justice."

Jesse lowered his eyes. "They did it."

"Was that a question?" I asked.

Jesse scratched the top of his head slightly, pulling at his hair. "Not a question."

"Jesse, I need you to tell me everything you know. If you don't when you're in front of a jury, you will be cited for perjury and obstruction of justice. Just to name a few. I'm not a police officer, and I don't even really know all the charges they could hit you with. I'm a private investigator who was hired to find the truth. I need you to tell us everything, or things will go very bad for you. You've obviously spent many years of your life working toward a career that helps other people. Now, if you want to keep that life, you need to help Tinsley and Emmy's parents understand what happened."

Jesse bowed his head and nodded. He raised his head and met my eyes. "I'll tell you what I know."

"Great." I glanced up at the camera in the ceiling's corner. "I need you to tell me what happened ten years ago on the night that Tinsley Reed and Emmy Olson were killed." What Jesse was about to say was going to be big. I could feel it in my bones. Jesse had known what happened all those years ago. Why hadn't he come forward? What was he afraid of?

He finally spoke. "The night Emmy and Tinsley died, I was at a basketball game with Arlo and Warren. We returned from the game around one in the morning. We all drove in one car, and we went back to Arlo's house where Warren and I had parked our cars. Before we drove home, we went inside Arlo's house to get some drinks and snacks and play video games — that was the plan anyhow." His voice trailed, and he paused, clearly having a difficult time telling the truth after all these years.

"And is that what happened?" I asked.

"No. That was the plan. When we arrived at Arlo's house, he received a frantic phone call from Odie — Odessa Johnson. She said something terrible happened and that she needed our help."

"What did she need your help with?"

"She said that Tinsley and Emmy were dead and there was nothing we could do about it now. But she needed help to get rid of her car and all their bloody clothes."

My mouth dropped open, and my heart nearly beat out of my chest. *They had known all along.* Arlo, Warren, and Jesse. They all knew who had killed the girls and told no one. They just went about their lives and moved on to college and started careers. "What did you do next?"

"Warren and I refused to help them. We wanted to go to the police."

"But you didn't?" I asked rhetorically.

"No. Arlo said it would ruin their family. Arlo and Odie are cousins. He said if we ever told, it would ruin their family name."

What? How had we not known Arlo and Odie were related? Maybe they were hiding out together after all. "So, you just went along with it because you didn't want to ruin Arlo and Odie's family's name? After they murdered two young, innocent girls?" My voice was raised. I tried to calm myself down but struggled. How could they have been so selfish and stupid to let murderers get away with killing two innocent girls?

"Arlo threatened us. He had some dirt on us, explicit pictures of us with some, um, professional women. If he'd released the photos, it could have jeopardized our college acceptances. Looking back, it sounds so stupid. But at the time, we were eighteen years old about to go to college. Everything we had worked toward our whole lives, Arlo threatened to take it all away. I can't speak for Warren, but at the time, I just couldn't risk it all, and there was nothing I could do to save them, you know?"

"No, I don't know. You could've saved Tinsley and Emmy's family ten years of anguish over not knowing who killed their daughter! Not to mention, we think Odie killed Haisley to keep her quiet. Your silence killed Haisley!"

A knock on the door forced me to gain my composure. "Hold on. Don't go anywhere." Shaking, I opened the door. Hirsch's blue eyes were filled with questions. I slipped out of the room and shut the door behind me.

"How's it going with Jesse? Are you okay?"

I shook my head. "He just told me everything."

"You're kidding? Warren won't say a word. He's sticking to his original story."

"That's not the case with Jesse. He told me everything. Odie called Arlo in the early morning of the murders and asked for help to clean up the evidence. Arlo and Odie are cousins. According to Jesse, Arlo strong-armed them into agreeing to not call the police."

Hirsch's eyes widened.

I said, "I know. C'mon in."

Staring at Jesse, I said, "I just told Detective Hirsch what you told me. We'll pick up where we left off. After Arlo threatened your college status, what did you do next?"

Hirsch leaned up against the wall, and I stood with my arms crossed against my chest.

Jesse blanched. "I told Arlo I wouldn't help. It was one thing not to call the police, but there was no way I was covering up a murder."

Was he delusional? He had covered up a murder. Maybe he hadn't actually destroyed physical evidence, but he was a participant in the coverup of a double murder. I was so furious and angry and sick; I feared I may vomit. Hirsch put his hand on my shoulder. I glanced up at him. "I'm fine."

He nodded.

I'm not sure if he believed me. "What did you do next?"

"I went home."

"And Warren?"

"He went home, too."

"And what did Arlo do?"

"He told us he was going to help Odie and the rest of the girls."

"Can you be more specific? The names of the girls?"

"The girls were Odie Johnson, Haisley Charles, Skye Peters, and Lorelei Tate."

"All four of them were there when the girls were killed?"

"According to Odie."

Arlo told Jesse that Odie had told him the other three were there. Not exactly evidence. "What else do you know?" I asked.

"That's it."

Hirsch said, "Why haven't you come forward before?"

Jesse lowered his head once again. He glanced over at Hirsch and then at me. "Selfish reasons. I was afraid I would get into trouble — lose my medical license and the life that I built. Tinsley and Emmy didn't deserve what was done to them."

I looked inside myself, trying to find some sort of pity or empathy for Jesse, but I came up empty. He had known the true identity of the murderers for ten years and said nothing. "Why are you telling us now?" I asked.

"You've already figured it out." He paused. "You have warrants for Odie and Lorelei. Is that true?"

Hirsch said, "It is true. Do you have any idea why they killed the girls?"

He shook his head. "I have no idea. Arlo said something

about a prank gone wrong, but... how could any part of that have been a prank?"

There was no way it was a prank. "It couldn't."

"Are you still afraid you'll lose your medical license now?" Hirsch asked.

"If it happens, it happens. I was wrong all those years ago to not say anything, but I'm an adult now. Someone who literally holds people's lives in my hands. I feel like a hypocrite."

Finally, he was thinking like a mature adult. I said, "It sounds like we have reasonable cause for a warrant for Arlo."

Hirsch said, "I'll tell Vincent."

Without another word, Hirsch exited the interview room. "Thank you for telling us the truth. I can't pretend I'm not angry or sad that you kept it in all these years, but what matters is you told the truth now. I don't know what the prosecutor's going to do with your statement, but for what it's worth, I think it's a good thing what you did today. And you're probably a good doctor."

Jesse shut his eyes, and tears escaped. "Tinsley wanted to be a doctor."

What a tragedy. So many young lives ruined and traumatized. And for what? Why had they killed Tinsley and Emmy?

40

HIRSCH

I HUNG UP THE PHONE. "ARLO IS HERE WITH HIS LAWYER."

Martina smirked. "Let's go nail him to the wall."

Her colorful reference made me laugh — on the inside. I could tell her emotions were bubbling over in this case. I was sure it wasn't easy for her to look at crime scene photos of young girls. It must remind her of Zoey. Heck, they reminded me of Zoey. She was the only young girl I knew personally. I could only imagine what it would be like as a parent going through what they were going through. Knowing your baby was carved and murdered in cold blood. I was with Martina on this one. If Arlo helped covered it up, I also wanted to nail him to the wall, metaphorically speaking. I followed Martina out to reception. Sure enough, there was Arlo, in one of his shiny, expensive suits, with his lawyer who had about twenty years on Arlo but in just as shiny a suit.

"Thank you for coming down and turning yourself in," Martina said.

"My client is simply here to talk. Your arrest warrant is garbage. You and I know it," the lawyer said.

I said, "Let's go into the interview room and talk about what kind of garbage was in that warrant."

They agreed, and we led them back to interview one. Arlo remained silent. I said, "Please, Arlo, Mr..."

The lawyer said, "Spartak, but you can call me Lenny." He handed me his business card.

"Thanks, Lenny. Why don't you and your client take a seat, and Martina and I can explain the arrest warrant in more detail if you'd like?"

They sat, and I sat across from them. Martina shut the door and took her seat next to me. Lenny, the lawyer, said, "Okay, what do you have? Why is there an arrest warrant for my client?"

"Well, we have an eyewitness saying that Arlo, ten years ago, helped cover up a double homicide. By helping to destroy evidence, we believe he's lied to us throughout the investigation, which is what we call obstruction of justice."

The lawyer didn't flinch, and Arlo didn't say a word.

"Do you have a statement to make?" I asked.

"You say you have an eyewitness?" Lenny asked.

"Yes, we do. Two of them." Thankfully, after Jesse told his entire story, I went back to Warren and got him to talk. He corroborated Jesse's version of events. I thought it was knowing that the truth was coming out that he realized he might as well set himself free. I wasn't sure what the DA would do with them since they didn't actually have a hand in the cover-up. We could get them for obstruction of justice, but I had a feeling their cooperation would likely mitigate any charges. I wasn't terribly concerned about that at the moment. I was more concerned with Arlo, Odie, and Lorelei paying for what they did to those two girls. "That's right, two. And that's just the beginning. We have arrest warrants for two other people associated with the murders of Tinsley Reed and Emmy Olson."

"Who?" the lawyer asked.

"We have an arrest warrant for Lorelei Tate. As a matter of fact, she's already been arrested and is being extradited to California as we speak. I'm sure she'll be more than willing to cooperate once we have her back in the Bay Area."

That got a reaction out of Arlo. He shut his eyes and gritted his teeth. He knew his goose was cooked.

Martina said, "Arlo, I think you know, and we know, this is going to go a lot easier if you talk. Because if our corroborating statements come from the actual murderers, that puts you in a bad position. After all, with the physical evidence tying both of them to the crime, why wouldn't they roll on you to save their butts? Maybe even shave a few years off their sentences."

I glanced at Martina. We still didn't have physical evidence against Odie, but I had a feeling as soon as we got ahold of her gun, they'd be able to match ballistics to the bullet that killed Haisley Charles.

The lawyer whispered into Arlo's ear. Arlo shook his head. "I'd like to have all charges dismissed for my client."

"Not a chance. If I were you, I'd advise your client to talk now, before we have a mountain of evidence against him."

The lawyer remained steely. "We'll take a chance with the judge. When is the arraignment?"

"Unfortunately, we can't get him arraigned until tomorrow. Arlo, that means you'll be spending the night with us."

The lawyer turned to Arlo. "We can get you out tomorrow. Just hang tight."

I stared into Arlo's dark eyes. "Are you sure you don't want to talk now? Lorelei will be in our custody tomorrow. If she implicates you, it's all over."

He glared at his lawyer and then back at me. "Who else do you have a warrant for?"

"Your cousin, Odie."

Arlo shut his eyes, as if frustrated and angry at the situation.

I said, "Last chance to tell us what you know."

A knock on the door, as planned. A uniform poked his head inside the room. "Detective Hirsch, is the prisoner ready to be booked and brought to holding?"

"It will be just a minute. He doesn't want to cooperate."

Officer Snicker said, "I'll be right outside the door."

"Last chance, Arlo."

"I have no comment."

I shrugged and stood up. Martina did the same. "All right, well, you have a good night's rest in the holding cell with the other criminals."

Martina opened the door and ushered the lawyer outside. I followed behind. Turning to the officer, I said, "You can take him."

"Yes, sir."

Martina said, "You know your client is going to prison, right?"

Lenny, the lawyer, said, "I don't think so."

"Oh, I know so. He's guilty of covering up a double homicide. Do you think the people of this community will just look the other way? Do you know who the girls' parents are? Tinsley Reed's family practically runs the social circles in Orinda."

Lenny swallowed.

Martina said, "Good night, Lenny."

He shook his head and walked out of the station.

"What time is Lorelei arriving tomorrow?" Martina asked.

"They said bright and early."

"What is bright and early?"

"Could be as early as seven."

"Yikes."

I chuckled. "I'll call you as soon as I get the exact time from the Marshals."

"All right."

What a day. What would we learn from Lorelei Tate? Would she confess to everything like Jesse, or would she stonewall us like Arlo had?

41

TINSLEY

Emmy and I exited the diner, practically laughing our heads off. I was glad we had a night where it was just the two of us. It had been a strange time lately, and being with Emmy was so easy. We liked to tell people we were twins. Lots of people believed us since we had the same long blonde hair, blue eyes, fair skin, and were the same height. We were the twin ballerinas. But Emmy was more than that. She also loved sports. I didn't know how she found the time to do it all. Between schoolwork and dance practice, and Jesse, I barely had any time left. I had been looking forward to that night. We were going to splurge and get some ice cream and red vines and watch a movie. We headed out to the parking lot, and lo and behold, a silver SUV pulled up, full of girls. In the front seat sat Haisley. "Hey, Tinsley. Hey, Emmy."

"Hey."

The back window rolled down, and I could see Skye and Lorelei. I waved and glanced over to Emmy, who faked a smile. I knew she wasn't as big a fan of the group as I was. It was okay for us to have different friends and different interests. Like how Emmy was into sports, and I wasn't.

Odie called out from the driver's side. "What are you two up to?"

"We're heading back to my house to watch movies. What are you guys doing?"

"We're going to the stone house to get our party on. You want to join us?"

I had to think about this. In our last conversation, Odie had acted so strangely. This was more the normal Odie. Sweet, loving, fun. I turned to Emmy. "You want to go?"

"Not really."

Turning back to the car, I said, "We'll catch you another time."

Odie turned off the engine, jumped out of the car, and ran over to us. "Please, please, please, please come with us. And for the record, I'm sorry about before. You know I didn't mean it. And I swear I didn't start the rumors. I talked to Mark and made him confess it had been him to start it. He's such a jerk."

Was she being sincere? It was hard to tell. I said, "We already have plans. Another time."

"It's going to be so much fun, though. It's not the same without you, Tinsley. Please..."

She smiled brightly, and I thought Odie was back to her old self, and that made my insides smile. Maybe she had been having an off day. I mean, she'd been through a lot in her life, and from what I understood, it was continuing to go on. Maybe this was one of those situations where I had to be the bigger person so that she knew there were people who cared about her, so if she ever decided to get help, she would have a friend by her side. I turned to Emmy. "How about if we go for a little while, and then we can watch movies after?"

Odie said, "We're only going to go for like an hour or so."

Emmy shrugged. "Fine."

Odie said, "That's the spirit. Emmy, I'm glad you're here, too." She jogged back to the driver's seat.

Lorelei opened the back door. Emmy said, "There's not room for all of us."

Odie said from the driver's side "Squeeze in. You two are little skinny ballerinas, you can fit. It's not far."

Emmy did a slight head shake before climbing in next to Lorelei and Skye. After we were squeezed into the back seat of the SUV, Odie yelled out, "Yahoo," and sped out of the parking lot.

Haisley passed an almost-empty bottle of vodka to the back seat. "You want some?" she asked with a slight slur.

Emmy shook her head. "No, thanks."

I said, "Sorry, I have to drive later."

Lorelei said, "Yes, please!" and pressed the bottle to her lips.

From how the girls were acting, I assumed they had been drinking all night. This wasn't the beginning of their party. It was more likely closer to the end. Odie appeared sober or was at least driving normally, albeit a bit fast.

Odie parked and hopped out of the car. Haisley opened the front passenger door and stumbled out. Yep, she was good and drunk. I opened the door and stepped out onto the gravel road.

A strange feeling stirred inside of me.

Maybe this hadn't been such a good idea. Skye and Lorelei were obviously wasted, like Haisley, as they wobbled and stumbled out of the car. I had enough experience being the only sober person at the party to know this would not be fun. Maybe I should make up an excuse so we could leave.

Odie was at the back of the SUV with the hatch open. "What are you doing?" I asked.

"Oh, nothing. Just getting a few things. Go ahead to the house. I'll meet you there."

With hesitation, I turned and started walking toward Emmy. She said, "I don't like this, Tinsley."

"I'm sure it will be fine." I wasn't sure, but I also wasn't sure what to do about it.

Emmy whispered, "What if Odie gets drunk and can't drive us back safely?"

It was a legitimate concern. "It's not that far from the main road. We could probably walk somewhere to get a ride. Or we could take her keys, and I can drive back."

Emmy's face was long. "Okay."

We headed down the path and entered the small stone house where the other three girls were already inside, taking turns sipping from the bottle of vodka and a second bottle of liquor. I thought, *They are going to be so hungover tomorrow.*

Odie stepped into the doorway with an angry look on her face. She shined the flashlight inside, illuminating the interior.

Lorelei said, "Oh, yeah, that's better." She giggled.

"Are you ladies ready for some fun?" Odie asked in a weird way.

"What do you mean?" I asked.

Odie held the flashlight under her chin. "Let's tell ghost stories."

The girls cheered. We all sat in a circle on the ground. An hour or two into the whole thing I was over it and I could tell Emmy wanted to leave. I stood up. "It's getting really late. We want to get back."

Odie popped up. "Not yet."

Emmy put her hand on her hip. "Yes, Odie. Now."

Odie glared at Emmy. "No. Before we go, I think we need to teach the two of you a little lesson."

"What do you mean?" Emmy asked.

"Well, I think some of you have a hard time keeping your

mouth shut. We're going to remedy that," Odie said, with a chill in her voice.

"What is that in your hand?" Emmy asked.

I looked over at the other girls. "What's going on? I thought we were just hanging out?"

They only giggled.

Emmy had a terrified look on her face. Turning to Odie, I said, "Okay, we're done here. This isn't fun. We're leaving."

Odie stepped in front of the doorway, blocking the exit. "Nobody's going anywhere."

Despite the summer heat, a shiver ran down my spine.

I had made a terrible mistake.

42

MARTINA

HIRSCH WAS STANDING OUTSIDE THE SHERIFF'S department holding two paper coffee cups. Having drained my entire travel mug on the drive in, I was mighty thankful. Seven was very early, especially for us. I was an early riser but not that early. Hirsch handed me a cup.

"Thanks."

"No problem. Lorelei is already inside."

"I still can't believe it. I hope she'll talk to us, but I'm not holding my breath." I hoped to appeal to her, mother to mother. Surely, Lorelei would want to know the truth if something ever happened to her own daughter. Between her new status as a mother and being ten years older, she couldn't be the same girl she was ten years ago when the girls were murdered.

"Same here."

The night receptionist waved.

I said, "Good morning, Frank."

"Good morning, you two. It's awfully early."

I said, "Yes, it is."

Frank said, "You have a good day now."

We waved and walked toward the interview room where

Lorelei was being held. One of the U.S. Marshals outside the door said, "You must be Detective Hirsch, and you must be Martina Monroe."

I said, "Yes, sir."

"I'm Jake."

Smiling, I said, "It's nice to meet you."

His handshake was firm, but something about him put me at ease.

Hirsch repeated the gesture and added, "We appreciate how you expedited the transfer."

"It's our pleasure. It was about time somebody paid for what happened to those two girls. Even if it meant a sixteen-hour drive."

I said, "Indeed. You must be beat." He didn't show it. Jake must be trained for operating while lacking adequate sleep. Maybe ex-military.

Jake said, "It was a long drive. I admit I'm ready for a hot breakfast and then to get back home. We'll release the prisoner to your custody and be on our way."

I wondered if Jake was going home to a wife and kids. Boy, had Hirsch's engagement gotten into my head. It was that, or I was almost ready to be open to dating. The idea made me nervous, but I supposed that was progress.

Hirsch said, "Well, then let's get to it so you can be on your way." Hirsch turned the knob of interview one and stepped inside. I followed behind, as did the two U.S. Marshals.

Lorelei sat with her head bowed, her hair a curtain covering her face. She glanced up with bloodshot eyes and pale skin.

Jake said, "Ms. Tate, we are releasing you to the custody of the CoCo County Sheriff's Department. Please stand."

Lorelei stood up without hesitation. Jake unlocked the handcuffs and removed them from her wrists, then said, "Y'all take care."

"Thank you. Safe travels."

Jake and his partner left with smiles and nods.

Hirsch walked over to Lorelei and said, "Please put your hands in front of you on top of the table."

She complied without a word.

"Do I need to cuff you, or can I trust you'll stay put?" Hirsch asked.

She said, "You don't need to cuff me."

A knock on the door turned her attention to the entrance to the interview room. I climbed out of my seat and walked over to the door and opened it. "What's this?"

"Sorry to disturb you, ma'am, but this man says he's Lorelei Tate's lawyer."

I glanced back at Lorelei. "Did you hire an attorney?"

"I didn't. My mom probably did."

The aggressive man stepped inside and handed a card to Lorelei. "I'm Jack Purdue. I was procured by your parents. Say nothing to these two. Understand?"

Lorelei remained silent.

Hirsch said, "I'm Detective Hirsch. This is my partner, Martina Monroe. Please have a seat."

Jack Purdue sat down.

Hirsch began. "As you may realize, your client has been charged with two counts of first-degree murder."

"What evidence do you have against my client?" he asked.

"We have forensic evidence linking her to the crime scene and witness testimony stating she was involved."

Jack Purdue stiffened.

I said, "That's right. There's blood evidence matching Lorelei's DNA. Her blood was mixed with the victims' at the scene. There was no explanation for the mixture unless Lorelei was there."

The lawyer glanced at his client. "Don't say anything. We will get you out of this."

I said, "I don't think so. Lorelei will not get away with murdering two teenage girls in cold blood. First, she bashed the two girls in the head before slitting Tinsley's throat and sexually assaulting her with a foreign object. Lorelei is *never* going home."

Lorelei swallowed, and her eyes widened as if she was surprised and nervous that we knew what happened to Tinsley and Emmy.

Hirsch said, "It's really in the best interest of your client that she tells us everything that happened that night. We don't believe she acted alone. Her cooperation could go a long way with a judge."

Meeting Lorelei's terrified gaze, I said, "If you want a chance to see your daughter grow up, you'll talk."

Tears streamed down Lorelei's face. "I'll tell you everything."

"Don't do that, Lorelei."

She turned to her lawyer and said, "Their parents deserve to know what happened to them. It wasn't right, and it wasn't fair, and it should've never happened. I can't live with the guilt anymore. You can leave if you prefer."

Mr. Purdue said, "I'm not going anywhere, and you won't say another word."

My heart pounded. Would she really tell us everything?

Lorelei said, "You're fired. You can leave now."

Hirsch said, "You heard her. You've been fired. You can leave now."

"You're making a big mistake, Lorelei. If you fire me and talk, you'll never see your daughter again."

She repeated, "You're fired."

He shook his head, pushed back his chair, and exited the interview room. Lorelei fixed her gaze on us. "I'm ready."

Hirsch and I exchanged glances. I said, "Please begin."

Lorelei wiped the tears from her cheeks. "The night Tinsley and Emmy died, I was out with Odie, Skye, and Haisley. We were at Odie's house drinking vodka and tequila when we decided to go out for fries. Actually, Odie suggested it. She was the only one who hadn't been drinking. We brought the vodka and tequila with us, and we drove down to McDonald's to get fries. After we were done, we cruised down to Nation's. Odie said she wanted pie, but before we parked, she spotted Tinsley and Emmy. Odie pulled up in front of them and invited them to come out with us to the stone house."

"Did Odie know that Tinsley and Emmy would be downtown?"

Lorelei shrugged. "I don't know. Maybe she did."

Hirsch said, "Please continue."

"So, we invited them to come out with us, but they didn't agree right away. I think Odie got out of the car to convince them. It's a little fuzzy because I was pretty tipsy. I don't think Emmy wanted to go, but eventually, they agreed, and they got into the backseat. We offered them some vodka, but they didn't want any. So, then we drove down to the old stone house in the woods. You know the place. We were all pretty buzzed — drunk is probably more accurate. We gathered in the old stone house, drinks in hand. It was dark, and it was kind of weird, and then Odie came in, and she had a flashlight. She had two. She gave me one, and she used the other. For a while everything was fine. We told ghost stories and gossiped about people like we normally did. A few hours later, Tinsley and Emmy said they wanted to leave. Odie said she wanted to teach them a lesson."

"What was Odie trying to teach them?" I asked.

"I don't know. It didn't make any sense to me." Tears streamed down Lorelei's cheeks once again.

Hirsch said, "I'll be back."

Watching this young mother, I still couldn't believe she'd been involved in the heinous murders of those two girls. We didn't speak while Hirsch was out of the room, to give her time to calm herself. Hirsch returned with bottled water and a box of tissues.

Lorelei quietly said, "Thanks," before grabbing tissues and drying her eyes. She took a drink of water and set the bottle down. "So, they wanted to leave, but Odie was blocking the doorway, so they couldn't. Then they tried to leave out the back, and Odie told us to block it. Skye and Haisley did as Odie asked. They were giggling, and I guess we all thought it was a joke or something. We didn't think it was — what it turned into. Anyway, so Odie starts screaming at Tinsley that she's a liar and an awful friend and had made up stories about her and was trying to ruin her and her family."

"Do you know what stories Odie was referring to?" I asked.

Lorelei shook her head. "I didn't know what she was talking about. None of us did. And that's when it got bad. Tinsley was yelling back at Odie, and she said, 'I don't know what you're talking about. I've been nothing but a good friend to you. I would never tell your secret. What are you talking about?'" Lorelei took another drink of water. "And then Odie said 'You'll never make up another story about me again.' Odie raised her arm, and there was a tire iron in her hand, and she hit Emmy really hard in the head. We all started screaming. And before I knew it, Odie hit Tinsley really hard, and then both Tinsley and Emmy were on the ground and bleeding a lot from their heads. We were all screaming except for Odie. I rushed over to Odie and said, 'Why did you do that?' And that's when Odie pulled out a knife, and she jabbed it into my collarbone and said, 'Shut up, or I'll kill you too.'" Lorelei pulled down the front of her shirt, showing the scar on her collarbone. "That's where she cut me."

My heart sank. Odie had been the mastermind. It fit. "What happened next?" I asked.

"Tinsley didn't move, and Emmy didn't move either. I thought they were both dead. There was so much blood. And then Tinsley kinda moaned. I couldn't tell what she was trying to say. And Skye said she was still alive and that we should get help. She was pleading with Odie to get help, and Odie stared at Skye with this evil look in her eyes. Odie told her to shut up and that it was too late. She basically said if anybody talked, our lives were over and that we were all in this together." Lorelei stopped to dry her eyes once again.

If what Lorelei was saying was true, the killing of Emmy and Tinsley had tormented her and the others for the last ten years. They had lived with the guilt of not doing more to stop Odie. It was probably why Skye had taken her own life. Maybe Haisley had been ready to tell the truth, and Odie silenced her. That was my working theory anyhow. I really wished we could find Odie. Who knew what else she was capable of?

Lorelei continued, "Finally, Odie stopped screaming at us, and we were quiet. Odie knelt down next to Tinsley with the knife and cut down Tinsley's dress and then." Lorelei shook her head. "She took off Tinsley's underwear and put the tire iron inside of her. I remember I gasped in horror. I asked Odie what she was doing. Odie said we had to make it look like a man did it. I had to look away. It was so... she was still alive. After she did that, she grabbed the knife and cut Tinsley's neck. Blood spurted everywhere. Everywhere. By this point, Haisley, Skye, and I were huddled together trying not to look. Trying to be somewhere else. I think somebody threw up. And then Odie started stabbing her and then drew a symbol on her and then did the same to Emmy. I'm pretty sure Emmy was dead. She didn't move or make any noises."

Hirsch asked, "What happened next?"

"After that, we were pretty sure they both were dead. Odie said, 'We're done here,' and then she ordered us to take off our tops to use to wipe our foot prints as we left. Bloodied and topless, we all climbed back into the SUV, and Odie drove us back to her house. We pulled into the garage. Her parents weren't home. She told us to take off the rest of our clothes and to put them in the car. We all showered and put on some of Odie's clothes. After that, she called Arlo for help. Arlo took Odie's car. A couple of hours later, Odie picked up Arlo. When Odie returned, she acted like nothing ever happened."

Lorelei was a sobbing mess. I believed her story. The details were too vivid, too real, and they matched the evidence and Jesse's statement. "Do you know where Arlo dumped the car?"

"I'm not certain, but I think Odie said something about Pittsburg."

"Like the Pittsburg Marina?" I asked.

"Maybe. I've never been there or heard of it."

Not unusual considering where Lorelei had grown up. Pittsburg was quite far, on the other side of the tracks.

"Why didn't you ever tell anybody what happened?" I asked.

"Odie threatened to kill us and our families, too. She called me right after you first interviewed her and threatened me. I think she threatened Haisley and Skye, too."

Hirsch said, "She couldn't kill you if she was in prison."

Lorelei nodded sadly. "You're right, we were cowards. We're all guilty. We should've stopped her."

Stunned, Hirsch and I sat in the interview room while Lorelei sobbed. I turned to Hirsch. "This is probably enough for today."

He nodded. "I agree."

"Lorelei, we're going to take you back to holding. Are you hungry or thirsty? We can have them bring you something before you go back."

"I don't need anything."

Hirsch said, "Okay, we'll take you back."

She said nothing. She simply nodded.

I pushed back my chair and stood up. Lorelei said, "Will I be able to apologize to them?"

"To who?" I asked.

"To Tinsley and Emmy's parents. If anything ever happened to my daughter like this, I think it would kill me. I'm so sorry."

Hirsch said, "You'll get your chance. An officer will be in shortly."

We exited the room and met with the officer waiting outside. "She's ready to go back."

"Did she talk?" Officer Todd asked.

"She did."

"Is she guilty?" Officer Todd asked.

"She was there, and she didn't stop it."

"Unbelievable."

That was exactly my thought. It was almost unbelievable that four teenage girls could be responsible for the heinous murder of two of their friends. It certainly wasn't the first time it had happened, and probably wouldn't be the last, but it didn't make it any more conceivable.

43

MARTINA

HIRSCH AND I STOOD BACK AS WE WATCHED THE OFFICER escort Lorelei Tate into a holding cell. I still couldn't believe anybody could stand by and watch two innocent people have their life extinguished at the hands of a sociopath. Is that what Odie was? She had to be. The other girls had been intoxicated, which probably contributed to their fear and inability to stop Odie, but *still*. What would turn a privileged young woman into a killer? Into someone who didn't care about other people's lives. I didn't think I would ever understand, and maybe that was a good thing. I turned to Hirsch. "We've got to find Odie."

"No kidding. There have been no hits on her car or her person."

"Officers went last night over to her parents' house to check it out, right?"

"Yes, I went with them after you went home. There was no sign of her at the Johnson house, and the parents said they hadn't seen or heard from her in days, but they said that wasn't unusual."

Guilt filled me up. It had been a long day, and Hirsch had encouraged me to go home since we were finished up — or so I had thought. I should have known better that Hirsch would continue working tirelessly like he always did. "You should've told me you were going. I would have gone with you."

"Not necessary. She wasn't there. If she was, I would've called you."

"Did they say where they thought she might be?"

"No, but they weren't very helpful, either."

Figures. Would Odessa Johnson's family hide her? Did they have the power to save their daughter from a life in prison? It gave me an idea. "If Odie's parents aren't cooperating, maybe we should ask the Reeds to throw their weight around. The Reed family is the head of the social circle of the entire area. We need to update them on the investigation anyway. We should go over there and ask them to use their social clout, their money, and their power to help us find their daughter's killer."

Hirsch said, "I'll drive. You call Tinsley's parents on the way over."

We hurried out of the station and headed toward Hirsch's car. After getting off the phone, I explained, "Mrs. Reed is inviting Emmy's parents over. We can update them together."

He nodded, and I thought, *I hope this works.*

SITTING IN FRONT OF THE FOUR GRIEVING PARENTS, Hirsch and I waited as they cried and discussed among themselves the disbelief that the girl next door killed their daughters. Once calm, Mrs. Reed, Tinsley's mother, looked at us. "You have Arlo and Lorelei in custody but not Odie?"

"That's right. We searched for her yesterday. We questioned her parents and looked at her house and her place of employment. She's nowhere to be found. There is an all-points-bulletin and a be-on-the-lookout for her car. She's labeled as armed and dangerous. We also think she's responsible for Haisley Charles's murder."

Mrs. Reed gasped. "I didn't think she was capable of such a thing. And the girls and the boys all knew. This is hard to take. We've known them all since they were little."

The other parents agreed.

Mrs. Olson said, "And you don't know why Odie did this?"

"All we have is Jesse and Lorelei's testimony, which conflicted. Jesse said it was a prank gone too far, and Lorelei said Odie was angry at Tinsley for telling her secrets and trying to ruin her family."

"What secrets?" Mrs. Reed asked.

I said, "Lorelei didn't know."

Mrs. Reed exchanged glances with Mrs. Olson. "What can we do to help?"

I said, "We figure somebody has to know where Odie is. She needs to be found before she hurts someone else. We also want to make sure she pays for what she did to Tinsley and Emmy. We aren't getting much cooperation from Odie's parents or anybody else. Would you be able to use your influence to get people to talk?"

The parents turned to one another, discussing different scenarios as Hirsch and I waited patiently for them to work out a plan. This was a world I didn't understand but was seeing the less obvious benefits of being rich and powerful. If anybody could bring Odie out of hiding, it would be this group.

Mr. Reed put his hand on his wife's thigh and said, "We'll get on the phone and talk to friends and acquaintances. We'll put out the word that we need to find Odie, and anybody who doesn't help will have to pay the consequences. In addition, we'll open up a reward for her capture. One million. We'll put it on the news — national. I have a connection."

Hirsch said, "Excellent. Let's find Odie."

Less than an hour later, we stood outside the Reed home; the families pleaded in front of the cameras for anybody who had seen Odessa Johnson to call the police immediately, that she was armed and dangerous, and that anybody who could bring her in would be rewarded with one million dollars. No questions asked.

It was a brilliant idea, and at the very least, it would force Odie to take action. I hoped it worked.

After the media left, we headed back to the station. Inside the Cold Case Squad Room, Hirsch sat down with a harrumph. "What a day."

"And it's not even noon."

As if on cue, Kiki and CSI Brown entered.

"Hey, what's up?" Hirsch asked.

Kiki said, "We have concluded further testing, and we have some interesting results."

I said, "Okay, let's hear it."

Kiki said, "We've just updated Detective Winston in Homicide but thought you'd be interested to hear that the scrapings under Haisley Charles's fingernails are a DNA match for Odessa Johnson."

Thank the lord. The physical evidence in the double murder was weak for Odie, but without a shadow of a doubt, we would get her on first-degree murder charges for Haisley Charles, and she would spend the rest of her life in prison. It wasn't fair we couldn't make her pay for what she did to Tinsley and Emmy, but it was better than nothing.

Hirsch said, "That's great news."

CSI Brown said, "That's not all, folks."

"No?" I asked.

Kiki said, "My team retested the hairs found at the scene — even the blond ones assumed to belong to Emmy and Tinsley. We found two strands of hair that had been embedded in Tinsley's wounds that don't belong to Emmy or Tinsley. Embedded in such a way that it would have been placed after the wound was created."

"Did they have a root?" Hirsch asked.

Kiki smiled. "They sure did. They are a match for Odessa Johnson."

Hirsch and I both exclaimed, "We've got her!"

We just had to find her.

44

HIRSCH

Running on fumes myself, I said, "More coffee?"

Martina nodded. "I could use about a gallon at this point."

"How about we start with one cup?"

Martina shrugged. "If you insist."

With that, we headed over to the break room to get ourselves some sheriff's department issued java. After the events of the day, we had done all our paperwork and called in everything we needed to call in, but we were still waiting to hear from the dive team and were on standby for any credible tips as a result of the press conference.

They had deployed the dive team to the Pittsburg Marina to corroborate the story that Arlo dumped the SUV to help Odie cover up her crimes. If we couldn't find the car, it would be difficult to make the charges stick against Arlo. If we couldn't find it, it was hearsay and completely circumstantial.

Placing my mug under the machine, I inhaled the scent of the freshly brewed coffee, hoping for a pick me up. When the machine was done, I added a couple of packets of sugar and a shot of creamer.

Martina leaned up against the counter and sipped her coffee. She swallowed and then said, "Do you think it'll work?"

"I hope so. It was your idea."

"I couldn't think of anything else that we could do. Odie's family has the means to get her out of the country."

"They do. Fingers and toes crossed."

"Should we order dinner soon? Maybe pizza and salads from Freddie's? The folks manning the phones must be getting hungry, and I could eat."

"Not a bad idea."

My phone buzzed, and I pulled it out of my jacket pocket. I didn't recognize the number. "Detective Hirsch."

"Hi, Detective, this is Lieutenant Blackwell of the San Jose Police Department. We have eyes on Odessa Johnson."

Glancing over at Martina, I said, "Where is she?"

"She's inside a Target store on Coleman Avenue. I have my team on standby. I'm assuming you'd like to be here to take her down."

"Absolutely, but if she looks like she's running, don't wait. We'll be right there."

"Yes, sir."

Phone in hand, I said, "They found Odie in San Jose."

Martina set her coffee cup on the table. "Let's go."

We ran back to the Cold Case Squad Room, grabbed my keys, and then jogged out to the parking lot and my car.

We sped off, heading south toward San Jose. I wondered if Odie was headed for the airport or if she was planning a trip over the border into Mexico. Either way, she wasn't escaping. San Jose cops were no joke. They saw a lot of really terrible crime. There was no way Odie had a chance of fleeing.

The thirty-minute drive was excruciatingly long, but it gave us a chance to call in the latest to the team and the Reeds and Olsons.

We pulled into the Target parking lot, which was filled with a dozen SJPD black and whites. I parked the car but didn't bother to close my driver's side door and ran toward a man with a bullhorn. Badge in hand, I said, "I'm Detective Hirsch. This is Martina Monroe."

"I'm Lieutenant Blackwell. We spoke earlier. Good to see you, Detective. She hasn't come out yet."

"Who called it in?" I asked.

"One of the staff saw her picture on the news and called us. Last report was she was in the food section." That staff member may have just become a millionaire.

"How long has she been in there?" I asked.

"Thirty or thirty-five minutes."

I said, "That seems like a long time."

Martina said, "It is Target. I'm not a big shopper, but I spend at least that long each time I go. There's a lot of stuff to look at. Maybe she's loading up for a trip. Or she knows she's been spotted and is hiding inside while she comes up with a plan to escape."

Most likely she's planning an escape.

"Any law enforcement inside?" I asked.

"We have a few plainclothes on the way. We didn't want to spook her."

A woman ran up. "Lieutenant, I heard you need me on scene. What's up?"

"Andy, this is Detective Hirsch and Martina Monroe. They're after Odie Johnson for a double murder. Odie's inside. We need you inside."

She nodded. "It's nice to meet you. You have a photo?"

Lieutenant Blackwell showed the photo that had been on the news and circulated to all the surrounding police departments. He said, "She's wearing blue jeans and a black tank top. Her dark blonde hair is up in a ponytail."

Andy studied the picture and said, "The suspect in the Twin Satan Murders?"

I said, "That's right."

Andy said, "Dang."

Lieutenant Blackwell said, "Get miked up in the van and head in. Report on everything you see."

"Yes, sir." With that, Andy jogged off toward a white panel van.

My adrenaline pumped. I couldn't wait to slap cuffs on Odie Johnson. A true psychopath who should be locked away for the rest of her life. She started her crimes at the tender age of seventeen. What else had this woman done? Probably a lot of things we would never know about.

Martina said, "Did you find her car?"

Lieutenant Blackwell said, "The red BMW is right there." He pointed to a car parked five stalls down. He said, "When she comes out, she'll be surrounded."

Odie must not have seen the news to be driving her own car and be out shopping. Where had she been?

I surveyed the scene. "I think your team needs to be more hidden. She'll likely see the black and whites from inside. She could run."

"She'd be on foot, but you're right. I'll have them pull back. We can nab her as she approaches her car."

Martina asked, "What about the back entrance? Who is covering that?"

"It was my understanding there is only one entry and exit."

Martina said, "For customers, but not for staff. There are probably loading docks back there."

"I'll send someone around."

As he got on the line, I said, "We need our vests. She's armed and dangerous."

The few minutes we'd be out of play would be worth it. I would not let Zoey become an orphan.

We jogged back to my car, suited up, and returned to the scene. Thankfully, the police cars had moved out of view so they wouldn't tip off Odie when she came out of the department store.

We stood waiting next to Blackwell for a few minutes until he got a call on his radio. He said, "She's run out the back."

Martina and I looked at each other. Martina said, "She's not getting away," before sprinting toward the back of the building. I ran after her. She was fast, but so was I. We continued to the rear of the building. I could make out the sound of officers following us. Back-up was always nice to have. I pointed ahead. "There she is."

Odie ran out of the parking lot, into a residential neighborhood, and I increased my speed, sailing past Martina. She nodded in acknowledgment. I sprinted toward Odie until I was within earshot. I yelled, "Stop! Police! Hands up!"

Instead of stopping, she turned and brandished a weapon and fired. I fired back, hitting her in the leg. The gun flew into the street, and Odie hit the pavement. I ran to assess the scene. It had knocked her down, but it was merely a flesh wound. I flipped her over and put my knee on her back and cuffed her while I read her rights. The evidence against Odie Johnson was mounting. Attempted murder of a police officer and first-degree murder of Haisley Charles, Tinsley Reed, and Emmy Olson. I glanced up to give Martina a thumbs up, and my heart nearly stopped.

I left Odessa and rushed over to Martina, who was now lying on the ground with blood pooling beneath her. "Martina."

I heard the rush of boots, and I looked up. "The suspect's on the ground. The gun is in the street. She's cuffed. We need a bus ASAP. Someone call NOW!"

Martina's eyes fluttered open. "Hirsch."

Studying Martina, I saw that she'd been hit in the shoulder, and there was a slug in her vest. That was probably what knocked her down. I glanced back into Martina's eyes. "You're okay, Martina. Stay with me. Help is on the way."

An officer approached, and I said, "I need something to stop the bleeding." One cop handed me what looked like a T-shirt, and I shoved it onto Martina's shoulder, applying pressure to stop the bleeding.

Martina winced and groaned.

"Sorry, I have to stop the bleeding."

She nodded slightly.

Heart pounding, I glanced around. Good. Someone was attending to the wound on Odie. Staring down at Martina, I continued to press on the T-shirt. Sirens rang out. "Hang on. They're on their way."

45

HIRSCH

Betty and Zoey rushed toward me. Wide-eyed, Betty said, "Where is she?"

"They took her up to surgery. They need to take the bullet out."

"Mommy was shot? Is she gonna die?" Zoey asked, with tears in her eyes.

"No, she's going to be fine. The doctor has to take the bullet out so it doesn't move throughout her body and cause some bad things to happen."

This was the moment every police officer dreaded. Having your partner shot and having to meet with their family to tell them what happened. Luckily, I believed Martina would be okay. *She has to be.* The surgeon had been confident they could remove the bullet before it could continue to move into her chest cavity. I said, "Let's all have a seat. The surgeon will come out and let us know when everything's all done, okay?"

Zoey traced my arm with her fingertips. "Is that Mommy's blood?"

Dang it. I hadn't done a good enough job cleaning up. "It is, but don't worry, she has plenty more," I said, trying to lighten the mood but failing miserably.

Finally, I convinced them to sit down. Betty said, "What happened?"

"We were pursuing a suspect, a really bad person. Martina was hit twice. Once in the chest and once on the edge of her shoulder. The one in the chest was lodged into her vest, and it didn't cause any damage but probably gave her a pretty good bruise."

Thank goodness I had made her put her vest on. I never wanted to have to tell Betty and Zoey that Martina was gone.

"How long is the surgery supposed to take?" Betty asked.

"The doctor thinks one to two hours. He says it's a relatively simple procedure, but they needed to act fast."

Betty wrapped her arms around her granddaughter. The sounds of clickity clack on the linoleum filled my heart. I ran over to Kim, wrapping my arms around her. "Thank you for coming."

"Of course. Your partner was shot. Of course I'm going to be here. Hi, Betty. Hi, Zoey."

Zoey's eyes lit up a little. "Mommy's in surgery."

Kim rushed over to Zoey and embraced the little girl. Kim was going to make a wonderful mother. Because she was a wonderful person — loving and caring. Kim unwrapped herself from Zoey and sat next to her.

Sitting next to Kim, I placed my hand on top of hers. "She's going to be okay."

The women nodded, but their faces were pale and looks of worry remained.

Zoey said, "Did you get the bad guy who shot Mommy?"

I said, "We sure did."

"Good. Did the bad guy hurt somebody else, too?"

"In this case, it was a bad girl. She hurt a lot of people, but don't worry about that. She's going to go to jail for a very long time and can't hurt anyone ever again."

"Good."

My heart broke for Zoey. Being with Kim, I had realized I wanted a family, and I wanted children, but I feared my child would be in Zoey's position one day. I didn't want my child to be teary-eyed in a hospital waiting room, wondering if their father would make it. We had a dangerous job, and Martina and I were prone to working with some really bad people.

Zoey took Kim's hand. "I heard you're getting married."

Kim smiled widely. "That's right."

"Can I see your ring?"

Kim untangled our fingers and showed Zoey the diamond ring Martina and I had picked out for her. Zoey smiled. "It's so sparkly! I love it. Good job, Uncle August."

"Did you know your mom helped me pick it out?"

Zoey's jaw dropped. "No, she didn't tell me."

"It's true."

"And you know what else?" Kim asked Zoey.

"What?"

"I was hoping you'd be in the wedding as our flower girl."

Zoey's blue eyes sparkled. "Seriously?"

"Yep."

"I would love to! How about Mommy? Will she be in the wedding, too?"

I had considered it. She was my best friend and my partner. Would she be a bridesmaid or a groomsman or groomsperson? Was that a thing? "If she will agree to it. Absolutely," I added.

Zoey exclaimed, "I can't wait!"

The ladies chatted about the wedding, which was a pleasant distraction. Two hours later, the surgeon approached our group. "Detective Hirsch."

We jumped to our feet to face the surgeon, who was still wearing blue scrubs but with his mask down near his chin.

I said, "This is Martina's mother and daughter."

The surgeon nodded. "The surgery went really well. She's tough. She's going to be okay."

Betty hugged Zoey, and I hugged Kim. "When can we see her?" I asked.

"She's still out of it, but you can go in now. She should wake up pretty soon."

I said, "Thank you, doctor."

"Anytime."

Thank goodness. I *could not* lose Martina. *We* could not lose Martina.

Zoey said, "Let's go see Mommy, okay?"

"Okay." With that, the four of us headed down the hall while I thanked the universe Martina was okay.

46

MARTINA

With my good hand, I waved to Hirsch as he approached my hospital bed. Mom and Zoey had been by my side from the moment I woke from surgery until I fell asleep again and woke up this morning. It felt good to know that when things were down, I was surrounded by people who loved and cared for me. I was truly blessed.

"How'd you sleep?" Hirsch asked.

"Like I slept in a hospital bed," I said, teasing.

"How's the shoulder?" Hirsch asked.

"Sore."

"When are they letting you out?"

"A little later today."

"Good."

"What's going on with the case?" I asked, wanting to make sure that everybody who was responsible for Tinsley and Emmy's murders were brought to justice. And Haisley's killer. It all pointed to one person, and I hoped the DA had enough evidence to put her behind bars for the rest of her natural life.

Hirsch glanced over at Mom and Zoey. Mom took the cue. "Zoey, let's go get a snack at the cafeteria."

Zoey pleaded, "But it was just about to get good..."

My mom shook her head and said, "C'mon Zoey," and ushered her out of the room.

"Now what's the latest?" I asked.

"They released Odie from the hospital last night."

"What do you mean?"

"When she fired at us, I fired back. She took a hit to the thigh — through and through. She'll have a limp for a while, but she's fine and is in lockup."

I said, "Small favors. Anything else?"

"Well, as you can imagine, she's already lawyered up. Denies everything, despite all the physical evidence against her. We should get ballistics back today, but I'm fairly certain the bullet from Haisley's murder will match one of Odie's guns. We searched her vehicle in the parking lot and found her other gun, a bag full of cash, and a suitcase. Odie planned to run."

"Not fast enough."

"Nope."

"So, what's next?" I asked.

"We wait for forensics and ballistics."

"When is it coming in?"

"Soon."

Footsteps approached. "Hey, Doc."

"Good morning, Martina. I'm just here to let you know everything looks good. We can send you home."

"Great news."

The doctor said, "You take it easy. You should be at home, resting, for at least a week."

Hirsch said, "At least a week, Martina. I will hold you to that."

"This is my partner, Detective August Hirsch."

"Nice to meet you, Detective. I believe you when you say you'll make her rest."

I shook my head. "Without a doubt." I wished I could fight, but I was too tired. My injuries zapped my energy as my body healed. Hopefully, I'd be back to full strength in no time. But I had to admit, some time off sounded nice.

"Do you have questions before you're released?"

I said, "No, I think we covered it all."

"All right, then. You take care, and it was nice to meet you, Detective. Take care of your partner, here."

"I will."

"This case is just about wrapped up. You will take time off, right?" Hirsch asked.

"Yes, sir."

"You've earned it. This was a tough one. Everybody who needs to be arrested is behind bars. Our forensics team and the DA will make sure they stay there. That's their job now. Your job is to feel better and get better. I don't think that shoulder can take much more abuse."

He wasn't wrong. It was the second time I'd been shot in the shoulder and would happily avoid a third.

"You'll give me updates, right?" I asked.

"Of course."

"Thanks, Hirsch."

"Any time, but if you could not get shot anymore, I'd really appreciate it."

"I'm not sure I can make that promise, but I can try."

"Can I come back in now?" Zoey asked from the doorway.

"Yes."

"Uncle August, are all the criminals in jail now?"

"Yep. We're just waiting on forensics and the DA to put all the charges together."

Zoey cheered. "Good job. Another win for the Cold Case Squad!"

Indeed. I glanced over at Hirsch, who was staring at his

phone. He said, "I'll be right back." I couldn't help but wonder what the call was about. Was it the case? Was Odie planning to talk? Would she plead out and avoid a trial? Would we finally learn why she had killed Tinsley and Emmy?

I looked back at my little girl. "Yes, it is. And guess what?"

"What?" Zoey asked.

"I get to go home."

"Yeah! Are you going to be home for a little bit, or are you going back to work?"

"I'll be home for a few weeks."

Zoey said, "Cool."

My poor girl had always had to share me with work. This case had taken me away more than the previous ones. And I was, in fact, looking forward to being at home with Mom and Zoey. Barney too. It must be the drugs or my overall fatigue, but the idea of sleeping in late and wearing pajamas all day sounded amazing.

Hirsch returned.

"Who was that?" I asked. Not that it was any of my business. It easily could have been a personal call.

"That was the forensics lab. We got the ballistics back on the Haisley Charles murder." He glanced over at Zoey and shrugged sheepishly.

I nodded.

He said, "It's a match for Odie Johnson's Sig Sauer p245."

"Odie will go to jail for the rest of her life for killing Haisley, Tinsley, and Emmy."

Hirsch said, "Yep. After I talked to forensics, I called the DA. He's already put together all the charges for Odie. They're still working on dredging up the car out of the Pittsburg Marina, but as of now, Arlo has been released on bail. If we don't find the SUV, it's likely all charges against him will be dismissed."

"What about Lorelei?"

"She's rehired her attorney, and it looks like she's going to make a deal. They're going to verify that she had no active participation in the murder and simply didn't stop it, but we think that is the case. The DA says she'll likely plead down to manslaughter or obstruction of justice. She may not serve any time."

I nodded and let that sink in. Did Lorelei deserve to be free? If what she told us was true, I thought so. She had to live with the guilt and torment of what she had witnessed and failed to stop. I had a feeling she wouldn't spend any time in jail considering she had a physical scar, proving she was in fear for her own life when she chose not to do anything to help Tinsley and Emmy. "It sounds like all we have left to do is talk to the family."

"I'll be talking to the family. You have to go home and rest."

Suddenly very frustrated, I said, "Fine."

Hirsch said, "Martina, you just had surgery. You need to rest."

"I get it."

"And we're postponing our engagement celebration until you're better. Kim and I both agree we want you to be there to celebrate with us."

I said, "Thanks." Hirsch and Kim were so sweet.

Zoey jumped up. "When is the celebration, Uncle August?"

"We'll do it in two weeks. Does that work for you, Zoey?" Hirsch asked.

"Yes, I think so. Grandma, you'll be there too, right?"

Mom said, "Of course I'll be there. After all, I am responsible for these impending nuptials."

Hirsch smiled. "Yes, you are, and I will be forever indebted to you."

"Good," Mom said with a smile.

"Okay, now you get out of here so I can get dressed and get out of this hospital room."

Hirsch said, "All right. I'll call you later."

I nodded, and Hirsch squeezed my hand before he exited.

Had I cursed myself by saying I hadn't been attacked or stuck in the hospital in so long? Perhaps. Had it been worth it to make sure Odessa Johnson never hurt another person ever again? *Absolutely.*

47

MARTINA - THREE MONTHS LATER

HIRSCH LAUGHED AS I RELAYED THE CONVERSATION I'D HAD with Zoey and Kim about what I would wear to his wedding. Hirsch had asked me to be his groomsperson and stand next to him and his brother when he tied the knot. I had assumed I would wear a suit to match the best man, Hirsch's brother, but Zoey had other ideas. The bridesmaids and the flower girl, Zoey, would wear pink, and after some back-and-forth, I had agreed to wear a black dress to match the suits to be worn by the groom's party. But according to Zoey, it had to have a little sparkle. Kim had loved the idea.

Hirsch grinned. "Zoey has great negotiation skills."

"That she does. How's the wedding planning going?"

"It's pretty good. Kim basically picks everything out. I'm just looking forward to the day I get to call her my wife. The other details don't matter as much."

That's how I had felt when I married Jared. We were young and in love, and the details didn't matter. I knew he was the person I wanted to spend my whole life with, and I thought that's how it's supposed to be. A wedding itself is just one day. One afternoon where you spend a lot of money to celebrate with your friends and family. But that's not marriage. Marriage is being there for one another, supporting one another, respecting one another, and being a true partner in all senses of the word. I had that with Jared, and I honestly wasn't sure if I would ever find it again. But watching Hirsch and Kim, it gave me hope that one day, I might. Hirsch's phone buzzed. He answered. "Detective Hirsch." His eyes widened, and his head bobbed up and down. "We'll be right there."

"What is it?"

"The jury's back with the verdict."

Without hesitation, we grabbed our things and rushed out of the station.

It had been a long time coming. Odie had refused to admit guilt or discuss the crimes she had been charged with, forever holding onto the secret of why she had murdered Tinsley, Emmy, and, ten years later, Haisley.

The trial had lasted two weeks, and I was eager to hear her fate as determined by a jury of her peers. Odie had been charged with two counts of attempted murder, one for trying to kill me and one for trying to kill Hirsch. Three counts of first-degree murder for Tinsley Reed, Emmy Olson, and Haisley Charles. Last but not least, she was being charged with two felony counts for desecration of a human corpse in relation to Emmy Olson and Tinsley Reed.

The witnesses' testimony, along with the forensic evidence linking Odessa Johnson to all crime scenes including DNA under Haisley Charles's fingernails, the ballistics match to the gun that killed Haisley Charles, hairs at the scene of Tinsley and Emmy's murder, and the discovery of her SUV in the Pittsburg Marina should be enough to find her guilty. However, I had learned over the years that despite how guilty the accused may appear in the courtroom, it didn't mean they would actually be found guilty. Not surprisingly, Odessa Johnson had an excellent group of attorneys known for winning unwinnable cases. There was a bit of niggling in my gut that maybe this horrible monster would get off on all her crimes. I had prayed every day of the trial and on the way to the courthouse that morning that it wouldn't be the case.

Lorelei Tate ended up taking a plea. Besides testifying against Odie, she was charged with a misdemeanor accessory after the fact and given probation. The fact that she never told the authorities what she had witnessed that terrible night made her guilty. But the district attorney, Greggs, and Hirsch and I agreed we thought Lorelei had served her sentence and would continue to live with the guilt of not helping Tinsley or Emmy. Her testimony against Odie, in detail, of what she had done to the two girls horrified the jury and unfortunately, the families who had been in attendance. Lorelei was free and continuing on with graduate school as she raised her daughter, Emily, who we later found out had been named after Emmy. I believed Lorelei feared for her life in the moments before Odie killed the girls. And although I hoped others wouldn't act as Lorelei had by keeping the secret for ten years, I believed justice was served.

Arlo, on the other hand, was somebody with darkness in his heart. After they found the SUV disposed of in the marina and Lorelei corroborated that he took the vehicle from Odie to dispose of it and hide the evidence of the crimes, Arlo was charged with accessory after the fact and tampering with evidence. He could have faced a felony conviction as well as served time, but he pleaded to the misdemeanor charge of tampering with evidence, agreed to testify against Odie, and received probation. In most circumstances, I would say that wasn't enough. However, the fact that he was also disbarred and could never practice law again made it seem a bit more justified.

Despite eyewitness testimony and mountains of evidence, Odie maintained her innocence. A true sociopath who perhaps believed her own lies. I prayed to God as we drove to the court-house that the jury would come back with guilty verdicts on all counts. Because Odie was guilty. I could feel it in my bones and in my gut and in my being.

As Hirsch pulled up to the courthouse, the news cameras were assembling out front. Once we had solved the case and had everybody in custody, Sheriff Lafontaine wasted no time shouting it from the rooftops and to every media outlet. Hirsch and I had both been thanked personally by Tinsley and Emmy's parents, swearing they would do anything they could to repay what we had done for them. Of course, we told them that was nonsense. This was our job. It was what we did.

Hirsch and I had never shied away from the tougher cases. In fact, I had been accused, on more than one occasion, of running toward them. Just because the case was tough didn't mean it didn't need to be solved or shouldn't be investigated by the best team available — the CoCo County Cold Case Squad.

Parked, Hirsch and I hurried toward the courtroom, trying to avoid detection by the press. Since our last high-profile case, we had been assured we wouldn't be paraded in front of the news cameras anymore because it was dangerous, but some of the news crew still recognized us from the early days of the Cold Case Squad. It was why I wore a ball cap, as did Hirsch.

We made it to the courtroom and found seats in the back. Not surprisingly, the courtroom was packed, waiting for the trial of the decade to conclude. Waiting for the judge to arrive and for the jury to come in to read the verdict, Odie and her lawyers sat stoically on the defendant's side. Hirsch turned and whis-pered to me, "Let's say a quick hello to Greggs."

We had worked with District Attorney Greggs on multiple cases now. He was strong, and he was fair, and I was glad he had been the lead prosecutor on Odie Johnson's trial. We strolled up, and Greggs smiled. "How are my two favorite investigators?"

Hirsch said, "Doing fairly well, thank you very much."

I turned and glanced over at Odie, who glared in our direction. I thought, *That's right. We put you there and, you're going to go to jail for the rest of your life.* I hoped.

Hirsch and I both shook Gregg's hand, and I said, "You did a great job. Let's hope the jury agrees."

"Me too."

We headed back to our seats and waited. The noisy room was full of people chattering about the potential verdict, silenced when the judge entered, followed by the twelve members of the jury. After the judge made his opening comments, he turned to the jury to read the verdict. The jury foreman stood up and said, "We, the jury, find Odessa Marie Johnson on the charge of first-degree murder of Tinsley Reed, guilty..."

The rest of the verdicts were difficult to hear from the hoots and hollers and screams and chatter within the courtroom. The judge banged his gavel and warned the courtroom to be quiet while the jury finished. The jury foreman continued, "On the charge of first-degree murder of Emmy Olson, guilty. On the charge of first-degree murder of Haisley Charles, guilty. On the charges of desecration of a human corpse in the case of Emmy Olson, guilty. On the charges of desecration of a human corpse in the case of Tinsley Reed, guilty. On the charge of attempted murder of Detective August Hirsch, guilty. On the charge of attempted murder of Martina Monroe, guilty."

Upon the final reading, the courtroom erupted into chatter and cheers. It was clear everyone other than Odessa Johnson felt the verdicts were just. But most importantly, the families of Tinsley Reed, Emmy Olson, and Haisley Charles received the justice they deserved for their daughters, who had died at the hands of the killer that was Odessa Marie Johnson. I leaned into Hirsch. "We should get out of here before the media finds us."

"Good idea."

We snuck out the back, slipped on our black hats, and hurried down the steps of the courthouse. The news vans, reporters, and camera crew were assembled and ready, but thankfully, they paid us no mind. Safely inside Hirsch's car, he said, "Let's call the team and have them meet us at Freddie's for a celebratory lunch."

"I'm on it." And with that, Hirsch and I celebrated another win for the Cold Case Squad.

THANK YOU!

Thank you for reading *Secrets She Kept*. I hope you enjoyed reading it as much as I loved writing it. If you did, I would greatly appreciate if you could post a short review.

Reviews are crucial for any author and can make a huge difference in visibility of current and future works. Reviews allow us to continue doing what we love, *writing stories*. Not to mention, I would be forever grateful!

Thank you!

ALSO BY H.K. CHRISTIE

The Martina Monroe Series is a nail-biting crime thriller series starring PI Martina Monroe and her unofficial partner Detective August Hirsch of the Cold Case Squad. If you like high-stakes games, jaw-dropping twists, and suspense that will keep you on the edge of your seat, then you'll love the Martina Monroe crime thriller series.

The Neighbor Two Doors Down is a a dark and witty psychological thriller. If you like unpredictable twists, page-turning suspense, and unreliable narrators, then you'll love *The Neighbor Two Doors Down*.

The Selena Bailey Series (1 - 5) is a suspenseful series featuring a young Selena Bailey and her turbulent path to becoming a top notch kick-ass private investigator as led by her mentor, Martina Monroe.

A Permanent Mark A heartless killer. Weeks without answers. Can she move on when a murderer walks free? If you like riveting suspense and gripping mysteries then you'll love *A Permanent Mark -* starring a grown up Selena Bailey.

For a full catalog, or to purchase signed paperbacks and audiobooks direct from H.K. Christie go to: **www.authorhkchristie.com**

At **www.authorhkchristie.com** you can also sign up for the H.K. Christie reader club where you'll be the first to hear about upcoming novels, new releases, giveaways, promotions, and a **free e-copy of the prequel to the Martina Monroe Thriller Series, *Crashing Down*!**

ABOUT THE AUTHOR

H. K. Christie watched horror films far too early in life. Inspired by the likes of Stephen King, Dean Koontz, true crime podcasts, and a vivid imagination she now writes suspenseful thrillers.

She found her passion for writing when she embarked on a one-woman habit breaking experiment. Although she didn't break her habit she did discover a love of writing and has been at it ever since.

When not working on her latest novel, H.K. Christie can be found eating & drinking with friends, walking around the lakes, or playing with her favorite furry pal.

She is a native and current resident of the San Francisco Bay Area.

To learn more about H.K. Christie and her books, or to purchase signed paperbacks and audiobooks direct from the author, or simply to say, "hello", go to **www. authorhkchristie.com**.

At **www.authorhkchristie.com** you can also sign up for the H.K. Christie reader club where you'll be the first to hear about upcoming novels, new releases, giveaways, promotions, and a free e-copy of the prequel to the Martina Monroe Thriller Series, *Crashing Down*!

ACKNOWLEDGMENTS

Part of the inspiration for *Secrets She Kept* came from the real case of twelve-year-old Shanda Renée Sharer who was brutally tortured and murdered by three teenage girls in 1992. The details of the case are *chilling*. I was so rocked when I heard the story on a true crime podcast, that when it came on a true crime documentary series I was watching I had to turn it off. My deepest condolences to the family and friends of Shanda. May she rest in peace.

In addition, I was inspired by the story of the West Memphis Three, whom are mentioned in the story. I thought it would be interesting to contrast what would happen to three boys accused of murder that had the money and means for a defense versus without, like in the case of the West Memphis Three. Thankfully, by the time of this publication all three men of the West Memphis Three, whom I believe are innocent - as do most people - have been released from prison after eighteen years.

Note in *Secrets She Kept*, the names, characters, businesses, places, events and incidents are either the products of the my imagination or used in a fictitious manner. Any resemblance to actual persons, living or dead, or actual events is purely coincidental with the exception of the reference to the West Memphis Three mentioned above.

I extend my deepest gratitude to my Advanced Reader Team. My ARC Team is invaluable in taking the first look at my stories and spreading awareness of my stories through their reviews and kind words.

To my editor Paula Lester, a huge thank you for your careful edits and helpful comments. And many thanks to my proof reader, Becky Stewart. And my wonderful readers Sharon A. and Jane D. for your keen typo-spotting skills! To my cover designer, Odile, thank you for your guidance and talent.

Last but not least, I'd like to thank all of my readers. It's because of you I'm able to continue doing what I love - writing stories.

Made in the USA
Middletown, DE
02 October 2023

40013102R00163